ASTRIDE
THE
TWO
CULTURES

ARTHUR KOESTLER
AT 70

ASTRIDE THE TWO CULTURES

ARTHUR KOESTLER AT 70

Edited by HAROLD HARRIS

RANDOM HOUSE · NEW YORK

Grateful acknowledgment is made to Harcourt Brace Jovanovich,
Inc., for permission to reprint excerpts from *The Collected
Essays, Journalism and Letters of George Orwell* in the
T. R. Fyvel essay "Arthur Koestler and George Orwell."

Library of Congress Cataloging in Publication Data
Main entry under title:
Astride the two cultures.
Bibliography: p.
CONTENTS: Harris, H. Introduction.—Webberley, R.
An attempt at an overview.—Graubard, M. The sleep-
walkers. [etc.]
1. Koestler, Arthur, 1905-   —Addresses, essays,
lectures. I. Koestler, Arthur, 1905-   II. Harris,
Harold Arthur.
PR6021.04Z57   828'.9'1209   75-29459
ISBN 0-394-40063-1
Manufactured in the United States of America.

Contents

Just as one could not feel the pull of a magnet with one's skin, so one could not hope to grasp in cognate terms the nature of ultimate reality. It was a text written in invisible ink; and though one could not read it, the knowledge that it existed was sufficient to alter the texture of one's existence.

THE INVISIBLE WRITING (Danube Edition, page 432)

This oceanic feeling of wonder is the common source of religious mysticism, of pure science and art for art's sake; it is their common denominator and emotional bond.

THE ACT OF CREATION (1964, page 258)

The creativity and pathology of the human mind are, after all, two sides of the same medal coined in the evolutionary mint. The first is responsible for the splendour of our cathedrals, the second for the gargoyles that decorate them to remind us that the world is full of monsters, devils and succubi: they reflect the streak of insanity which runs through the history of our species, and which indicates that somewhere along the line of its ascent to prominence something has gone wrong.

Preface to THE GHOST IN THE MACHINE (1967)

Chronology

1905	Arthur Koestler born in Budapest, September 5th.
1922–6	Studied science and psychology at the University of Vienna.
1927–30	Foreign correspondent for the Ullstein chain of newspapers in the Middle East and later in Paris.
1930–2	Foreign editor *B. Z. am Mittag* and Science Editor *Vossische Zeitung*, Berlin.
1931	Member of the Graf Zeppelin polar expedition.
1932–8	Member of the Communist Party.
1935	Married Dorothy Asher (div. 1950).
1936–7	War correspondent of London *News Chronicle* in Spain. Captured by Nationalists, imprisoned and sentenced to death. Exchanged after international protests.
1939–40	Interned in French detention camp.
1940–1	Joined French Foreign Legion. Escaped to Britain.
1941–2	Served in British Pioneer Corps. Later worked for Ministry of Information, London, and as a night ambulance driver.
1945	Special correspondent in Palestine for *The Times*, London.
1948	Special correspondent in Palestine for the *Manchester Guardian* and *New York Herald Tribune*, and *Le Figaro*, Paris.
1948	Became British subject.
1950	Visiting Chubb Fellow, Yale University, Connecticut. Married Mamaine Paget (div. 1953).
1957	Fellow of the Royal Society of Literature.
1964–5	Fellow, Center for Advanced Study in the Behavioral Sciences, Stanford University, California.
1965	Married Cynthia Jefferies.

1968   Recipient, Sonning Prize, University of Copenhagen. LL.D., Queen's University, Kingston, Ontario. Organized the Alpbach Symposium, 'Beyond Reductionism: New Perspectives in the Life Sciences.'

1972   C.B.E. (Commander, Order of the British Empire.)

1974   C.Lit. (Companion of Literature of the Royal Society of Literature.)

Bibliography

The year of first publication is given in each case. Books marked★ are available in the Danube Edition of the Collected Works. From *Scum of the Earth* (1941) onwards, Koestler has written all his books in English.

1933 *Von Weissen Nächten und Roten Tagen* (Ukrainian State Publishers for National Minorities).

1937 *Menschenopfer Unerhört* (Paris)
SPANISH TESTAMENT (Available in Danube edition abridged as DIALOGUE WITH DEATH★)

1939 THE GLADIATORS★

1941 DARKNESS AT NOON★
SCUM OF THE EARTH★

1943 ARRIVAL AND DEPARTURE★

1945 THE YOGI AND THE COMMISSAR and other essays★
TWILIGHT BAR: An Escapade in Four Acts (play)

1946 THIEVES IN THE NIGHT: Chronicle of an Experiment★

1949 INSIGHT AND OUTLOOK: An Inquiry into the Common Foundations of Science, Art, and Social Ethics.
PROMISE AND FULFILMENT: Palestine 1917–1949.

1951 THE AGE OF LONGING★

1952 ARROW IN THE BLUE★

1954 THE INVISIBLE WRITING★

1955 THE TRAIL OF THE DINOSAUR and other essays★

1956 REFLECTIONS ON HANGING★

1959 THE SLEEPWALKERS: A History of Man's Changing Vision of the Universe★

Introduction

Harold Harris

Almost the first piece of advice which a publisher's editor may pass to a tyro author is, 'Never begin by saying what you are *not* doing.' When the subject of a book is as various, as many-sided, and as iconoclastic as Arthur Koestler, the temptation to break even such an elementary rule is overwhelming. This volume, then, is not an attempt to encompass Koestler within one pair of covers. Any such project would be doomed to failure, for he has crossed too many frontiers, explored too many territories, left his imprint on too many maps for this to be remotely possible. It is not even a summing-up; there is no reason to undertake such a task at this stage of his career. His seventieth birthday is a purely arbitrary date, and finds him in mid-career, perhaps even starting a new stage of it. For, at the time that the contributions to this book are arriving, he himself is at work on a new project concerning which his publishers are in complete ignorance. All he has vouchsafed is that it is a historical study. Apart from THE GLADIATORS, which is a historical novel, and THE SLEEP-WALKERS, which concerns the history of science, history is one of the few branches of literature which he has not already attempted. Seventy is, then, merely a convenient calendar date at which to salute Koestler, but not a significant one from the point of view of his accomplishments and his intentions.

This is not even a *Festschrift* in the usually accepted sense of the term. Had it been that kind of celebration, more contributors would have been included and their essays would not have been so rigorously concerned with the various facets of the recipient's own work. The brief to contributors to this volume has, for the most part, been to concentrate on some particular aspect of his writing and thinking, in the hope that the resulting volume might throw light on some of his extraordinarily varied interests, bringing into focus what he has contributed to human knowledge on many different subjects and at the same time presenting, hopefully, a picture of the man. For the contributors, though so diverse in their interests and their locations, have two things in common: they are all experts in their field and they all know Koestler well.

One drawback of this plan is that a certain amount of over-lapping has been inevitable, and for this the editor must take full responsibility; but on reflection it seemed helpful to retain, for instance, the various viewpoints on his anti-behaviourist polemics, even at the cost of some repetition, so that the reader could judge the impact of his thinking in so many different directions. For what does emerge from this collection is not merely the aston-ishing breadth and variety of Koestler's interests and activities – this, indeed, is common knowledge – but rather the unity and singleness of purpose which have informed his whole career.

It is noteworthy, and part of the pattern, that among his fiction *œuvre* there should be three novels which in the author's eye stand together as a trilogy on the subject of ends and means – THE GLADIATORS, DARKNESS AT NOON, and ARRIVAL AND DEPARTURE; and that, similarly, his scientific writings should be dominated by the towering trilogy on the mind of man – THE SLEEPWALKERS, THE ACT OF CREATION and THE GHOST IN THE MACHINE. The three novels range in focal points from ancient Rome via a Moscow death-cell to a psychiatrist's couch in wartime Portugal; the three non-fiction works from a study of Copernicus, Galileo and Kepler via a seminal study of creativity to a highly technical discussion of the evolution of the brain. Nothing could, superficially, be more diverse. But the reader of this volume (which contains separate essays on DARKNESS AT NOON, THE SLEEPWALKERS and THE ACT OF CREATION) will be struck not so much by their diversity, but by the way that Koestler has persistently and patiently pursued the same truth ever since, at the age of fourteen, he felt 'a mystic elation – one of those states of spontaneous illumination which are so frequent in childhood and become rarer and rarer as the years wear on. In the middle of this beatitude, the paradox of spatial infinity suddenly pierced my brain.'[1] It is not such a far cry from that schoolboy revelation in Budapest to the adult preoccupation with what Rubashov in DARKNESS AT NOON calls 'the grammatical fiction', the inner self which, as Goronwy Rees points out in his perceptive essay, Koestler seeks to identify and preserve in all his work – whether he is analysing the creative process or fictionalizing the slave revolt in Rome. Without 'the grammatical fiction', as Rees suggests, life becomes meaningless, and it was the denial of this truth that caused Koestler to leave the Communist Party on the one hand and to oppose the deterministic philosophy on the other.

Expressed thus, it is a gross over-simplification, but the continuity of Koestler's whole career and output is convincingly argued by Dr Webberley in his 'overview' which precedes the more detailed examination by experts of various aspects of Koestler's contribution to scientific thought. While there are articles also on his novels, on his various campaigns, and (invaluably) on his writing habits over a quarter of a century (by Cynthia Koestler, who spent the first part of this period as his secretary, and the latter part as his wife), it may be argued that there is no biographical article as such nor a separate article about him as a personality.

So far as the former is concerned, this was calculated. Koestler's own autobiography is available, and a new biography by Iain Hamilton, who contributes to this volume, is in the course of preparation. Contributors have been free to incorporate as much biographical detail as they needed in their own articles. In the same way, it is to be hoped that a picture of Koestler the man does emerge from the writers' knowledge of the man himself.

If I may now depart from the editorial third person and the formality of the surname, my own acquaintance (and subsequent friendship) with Arthur goes back to 1963 when THE ACT OF

CREATION was in the press. I had joined his publishers in the previous year and had once mentioned that I was looking forward to meeting this distinguished author, whose books I had read and so much admired ever since, as a young man, I was first won over by the Left Book Club edition of SPANISH TESTAMENT, later to appear (minus its political propaganda) as DIALOGUE WITH DEATH.

I was warned to be careful, not to interfere; Koestler was a *very* difficult author; the least unguarded comment might upset him; better stay clear. So it was entirely by chance that I first met him, and introduced myself, at some literary function – a fortunate chance, for normally he shuns large gatherings. But he professed to be glad to have the opportunity for a talk since he was beside himself with perplexity. He had received the proof of THE ACT OF CREATION and had been dismayed to find that the extracts which he had quoted from other works had all been dragooned into what was then a standard house style, irrespective of the way in which they had been set out in his typescript. It is unnecessary to go into technical details, but he felt that the rhythm of the book had been upset and that the quoted extracts were difficult to distinguish. He had been forced to spend laborious days going through the seven-hundred page proof putting the matter right, only to find himself involved at the end in a seemingly endless correspondence with a senior member of the Production Department on the virtues of consistency in book design. It was from this situation that he now, with some hesitation, asked me to extricate him.

This was not too difficult, although the type of a great part of the book had to be completely re-set. My own much valued copy is inscribed by the author, 'Hoping for twenty years of happy co-operation.'

I have told this rather simple story at perhaps too great a length in order to underline the two significant facts about Arthur which struck me forcibly at this first encounter and about which, in the ensuing twelve years, I have not found it necessary to change my mind. One is that, in spite of his reputation for being a 'difficult' author subject to tantrums, he had behaved with immense forebearance and took pains to avoid causing personal difficulties for the member of the firm who had been involved. Secondly, the terms in which he had expressed his disappointment were so diffident as to betoken what seemed to me to amount to a lack of self-confidence, which was something I myself had certainly not expected to find.

When I mentioned this to him some years later, he referred me to a passage in his autobiography. Speaking of his 'boundless timidity and insecurity' at the age of sixteen, he quotes a Comintern agent's gibe some twenty years later: 'We all have inferiority complexes of various sizes, but yours isn't a complex – it's a cathedral.'[2]

The contradiction which I detected between Arthur's reputation and the reality which I encountered was subsequently confirmed in many different aspects of his personality, especially when viewed in the context of that cathedral-like complex. He dislikes appearing on TV and radio because of his strong Hungarian accent – surely an excess of sensibility in a writer of his distinction – apparently in the strange belief that his words would carry more weight if they were delivered in the accents of an English public schoolboy. He refers in his autobiography to the embarrassment his youthful appearance caused him in early manhood, and even today one feels that he entertains fantasies of being seven feet tall instead of being a man of medium height or slightly less. More importantly, it has always seemed to me that recognition of his contribution to science has meant far more to him than the much wider international reputation he enjoys as the creator of one of the great novels of the twentieth century. And yet, of course, as Professor Barron points out in his article, there is in fact a community and not a dichotomy between art and science: a common theme in this volume, for nowhere is it better displayed than in the work of Arthur Koestler.

These paradoxes and contradictions are symptomatic of Arthur's attitude to life and to his work – especially, perhaps, to life. He sees himself as a split personality, the man of action alternating with the man of contemplation: 'The resulting tug-of-war is one of the recurring *leit-motifs* of this report. It is reflected in the antithetical titles of my books.'[3] A glance at the Bibliography will reveal the evidence for this statement: THE YOGI AND THE COMMISSAR, INSIGHT AND OUTLOOK, THE LOTUS AND THE ROBOT, THE GHOST IN THE MACHINE, ARRIVAL AND DEPARTURE, DARKNESS AT NOON (with its even more antithetical French title, *Le Zéro et L'Infini*). He adds that the underlying pattern of these titles only dawned on him long after they were published.

But if Arthur is right in his assessment of the split personality, no one who reads this book will accept his insistence that his life's story is a 'typical case-history of a central-European member of the educated middle classes'[4]. These pages contain all the evidence that is needed to show that neither in his work nor in his life nor in his outlook is Arthur typical of anything but himself and his unique gifts. It was, perhaps, this very lack of typicality that in one field after another prevented the immediate recognition of his achievements. DARKNESS AT NOON was published in 1940, but it was many years before he became accepted as one of the outstanding European novelists of the decade. When he harnessed his artist's imagination and creative insight to the discipline of the history of science, he was fiercely attacked by some historians, as Dr Graubard relates in his essay on THE SLEEPWALKERS. Even fiercer were the attacks of scientists when he returned to his early preoccupation with biology and evolution, a field in which he has made a lasting and major contribution.

Arthur was never a member of the club, and he still is not. His reputation is all the more secure for that. But – one final paradox – for all the learned detail in some of these essays, this volume is not so much a salute to his many achievements as an expression of the true affection in which he is held by his friends. The loner turns out to be the nucleus of a group – a convincing example of his own hierarchic theory of holons.

REFERENCES

1. ARROW IN THE BLUE (1952), Danube edition (1969), p. 67.
2. *ibid.*, p. 93.
3. *ibid.*, p. 131.
4. THE INVISIBLE WRITING (1954), Danube edition (1969), p. 515.

An Attempt at an Overview

Roy Webberley

Over a period of forty years, the nature of Koestler's output has changed decisively at least three times. Each break with the past has required the generation of a new readership, and each new readership has reacted with a distinctive set of critical values. It is one of the ironies of such versatility that distorted pictures of Koestler have thus emerged; that few, if any, of his more influential exponents have known the whole man. A *Festschrift*, surely, is a time for an overview, when the controversies of yesterday become as germane as those of today; when some literary accounting must be done.

Koestler's novels have earned him one of the ten Companionships of the Royal Society of Literature; his political and philosophical essays have caused him to join Sir Winston Churchill and Earl Russell as a recipient of the Carl Sonning Prize for contributions to European culture. Certain individual works, such as THE ACT OF CREATION and THE GHOST IN THE MACHINE, have led to his presence at scientific symposia in many countries, not merely as participant but as editor and convenor. Most notable among the latter has been the Alpbach Symposium upon reductionist tendencies in the life-sciences, which figured among its contributors the psychologists Piaget and Bruner and the biologists Paul Weiss, Ludwig von Bertalanffy, C. H.

Waddington and W. H. Thorpe, who makes his own contribution to this volume. That such persons did not attend merely to meet Arthur Koestler should be evident; yet it is typical of the high regard in which he is held that they accepted the invitation. And yet the same hand which signed the invitation to the Alpbach Symposium had also written DARKNESS AT NOON, a novel which, under its French title of *Le Zéro et L'Infini*, was bought in entire stockloads from booksellers and burnt in the streets, in an apparently unsuccessful effort to prevent its influencing, rightly or wrongly, the French Referendum of 1946. Similarly, his novel THIEVES IN THE NIGHT, set in pre- and postwar Palestine, was said by some members of the United Nations Commission on partition to have influenced their thinking. All of his works have been banned in Communist Russia, some in Catholic Ireland, and one in India. To be judged as contentious by such varied cultures may be no proof of worth; it certainly seems to indicate a fairly high degree of impact upon those who banned him. As Koestler himself has wryly put it,[1] writers of pornography find it easy to collect such accolades; essayists have to work harder for them.

Mere fame or notoriety, mere hobnobbing with men of genius are scarcely new. What does catch the attention is the sheer breadth of Koestler's cultural impact. While his colleagues C. P. Snow and Robert Ardrey may claim to have crossed artistic and scientific frontiers, it is doubtful whether they have ranged so widely and so effectively as Koestler in his coverage of the novel, the political essay and the scientific thesis. Yet it is precisely this breadth which renders his work so difficult to assess. Studies such as that of Atkins[2] in 1956, and Jenni Calder's more recent analysis[3] treat Koestler as a novelist of taut, politicized intensity, a magnetizing talker; but that is the end of the brief they set themselves. At the other end of the intellectual spectrum, reviewers such as Medawar[4] and Miller[5] have argued as to whether Koestler is an amateur in the field of science, but have paid lip-service only to the political writing. In fact, since his formal farewell to politics in the 1950s,[6] Koestler is often discussed as if he were two writers rather than one. While it is understandable that literary and scientific realms of discourse should be thought irreconcilable, it is a pity: for what distinguishes Koestler as an interdisciplinary figure is his capacity not merely to cross a cultural chasm, but to take the same essential problem with him. To the extent that he succeeds in doing so, he achieves far more than a sociological party-trick: he shows that a *genuinely* interdisciplinary concern is possible. To the extent that we can trace a continuity in his thought, we can provide some sort of perspective against which some of the previous partial accounts may be placed.

In spite of having renounced politics over twenty years ago, Koestler is in one sense still an activist. What typifies his scientific work, at base, is a concern with consequence as much as with idea. Throughout THE ACT OF CREATION and THE GHOST IN THE MACHINE, one hears a voice no less lacking in commitment, no less fierce in its defence of freedom than that of Rubashov in DARKNESS AT NOON. In a death-cell in Seville, in the memories of friends who did not return from the Moscow trials, Koestler had seen and felt the physical consequences of theoretical allegiance. His faith in historical determinism had led him to Seville and almost to the firing squad; earlier it had led to mental acrobatics and self-deception as he journeyed through Stalinist Russia. In science, Koestler fears, causal explanations which led man to exploit nature (with consequences we now can judge) will lead to manipulative conceptions of man himself: a theory which says that man is at the end of a micro-deterministic chain or that behaviour is the sum of its quantifiable components is as fraught with consequence as one which asserts that the individual is as flotsam on the river of history. The determinist with a microscope is to be watched as closely as the determinist with a gun, though in neither case would Koestler necessarily reject the determinism out of hand. The view that man is a conditioned automaton is, he believes, 'depressingly true', but only up to a certain point. Where it ceases to be true is in the creative act.

In short, what agonized Koestler in his early novels is, in its essence, what still agonizes him in THE GHOST IN THE MACHINE and BEYOND REDUCTIONISM: the debate between freedom and determinism. While the titles of several works suggest a seemingly more varied set of dilemmas (DARKNESS AT NOON, INSIGHT AND OUTLOOK, THE YOGI AND THE COMMISSAR), it becomes apparent on reading them that there is only one paradox, one antithesis which really matters. Political and psychological freedom, creativity, the living organism are discussed *in terms* of freedom, *in terms* of determinism. When not explicit, freedom forms the conceptual substratum on which the other thoughts rest like outcrops, exposed to the weathering of debate. From the mutual tension of freedom and its opposite springs the energy of Koestler's thinking. The man who was thrice imprisoned, and has known the paranoid world of an underground movement, has an understandable concern with the topic.

However, few conceptions remain totally unmodified, and in Koestler freedom emerges as a theme with three distinct variations. Certain works, such as THE GLADIATORS, DARKNESS AT NOON and THIEVES IN THE NIGHT, are explicitly concerned with the problem of political ends and means; some, such as the first essay in THE YOGI AND THE COMMISSAR, deal with activist and quietist approaches to existence; yet others, such as THE GHOST IN THE MACHINE, are critiques of the supposed reductionist bias mentioned previously with respect to modern science. Unfortunately, one cannot draw a neat graph to show the serial development of Koestler's thought; instead, freedom grows like an embryo, assuming first one form, then another in its development, yet retaining its genetic identity. By 1945, the essentials of Koestler's philosophy are in evidence.

ENDS AND MEANS

'At the centre of all Koestler's political writing', says Jenni Calder, 'is the dilemma of the individual embroiled in the conflict between collective necessity and individual morality. The battle of ends and means is the battle that rages through Koestler's writing. It is a battle that would have no meaning without the individual consciousness.'[7] As an analysis restricted to the political writing, Mrs Calder's statement is both economical and precise: deny the validity of private consciousness, and you have denied the political problem of ends and means. Among early Behaviourists, Ends and Means retreated before their denial of 'consciousness' as an explanatory factor of behaviour, and their consequent rejection of the idea that activity could have a purpose. Among Marxists, the theory that economic forces are the determinants of private ends entails a rejection of individual responsibility: private ends are carried forward by the river of history, and the individual must abandon them and trust to the flood. The classic Freudian position, while not denying the existence of conscience or private ends, achieves a similar result by suggesting an unconscious dimension to the personality; thus the unanalysed individual is supposed to have no clear awareness of whether his ends are reality-centred or the result of childhood traumata. By thus denying consciousness, the historical significance of the individual, or the validity of private motives, one renders the debate over ends and means so complex as to remove its immediacy for those involved. In one way or another, Koestler's own discussions of the problem seek to reconcile these three deterministic creeds with the ethical self-determination of the individual. Expressed in these terms, the debate over ends and means is a debate about freedom.

In THE GLADIATORS, DARKNESS AT NOON and ARRIVAL AND DEPARTURE three revolutionary heroes are each confronted with a different form of ethical choice. Spartacus, the leader of a slave-rebellion which threatens Rome, is inspired to found a communistic 'Sun State' but brings about its collapse and, with it, the failure of the rebellion, by his decision not to execute some dissidents:

He hesitated for a fraction of a second, although he realised with acrid clarity that now and here, at this moment, the future was being determined. If he gave the order awaited by the silent bull-neck behind him – if he did, a fresh and very bloody massacre would rack the camp itself, and he, Spartacus, would most probably prevail – much hated, much feared victor and absolute leader of the revolution. That would be the very bloody and very unjust detour which alone would lead to salvation. The other, kind, human, friendly road inevitably led to rupture and hence to perdition.[8]

In Marxist terms, Spartacus's efforts to direct this fickle, reeking mob are in vain almost by definition: his isolated dilemma of ends and means is irrelevant before the forces of collective awareness and collective action. To this extent, the novel supports the Marxian dialectic. And yet it is a novel about a revolution which went wrong. The masses do not triumph. Bereft of the Spartacist vision, they stumble blindly into the arms of the Romans. Koestler seems to be saying that the point where collective, historical determinism ceases to be true is the point where private inspiration transcends the vision of the mass. There have to be sages, prophets, wise men to nourish the saps of mass enthusiasm and give them roots. In fact, there has to be a creative insight – a point which is relevant to his later works. What symbolizes the tragedy of the human condition is that Spartacus can only continue to be this inspiration so long as he is prepared to employ cruel local means to maintain the general end of peace and discipline.

Like Spartacus, Commissar Rubashov in DARKNESS AT NOON is a symbolic figure. He stands for a particular type of Communist, the old Bolshevik, who fought for and in the Revolution, and whose inspiration was Marx with a dash of honour. As a loyal Party member, Rubashov has suppressed his conscience, minimized his selfhood, become a tool of the cause. His unflinching ruthlessness, his silence under Nazi torture and his dedication to consequent logic have earned him a hero's place in the Party. Recently, however, he has been unable to smother his doubts as the principle of expediency is applied throughout Russia, and as he himself has recently become the means of betrayal to the Nazis of several German Communists, whom the Party has accused of deviationism. His arrest, interrogation and subsequent execution on a ridiculously false charge are finally accepted by Rubashov on the grounds that to plead guilty is a last act of service to the Party: by blackening the wrong and gilding the right, Rubashov will help to preserve national unity as war approaches. His expiation thus carried out, Rubashov dies with his doubts still unanswered, but with the beginnings of a fresh metaphysical insight that his sense of personal identity is at least as important as his social loyalties.

In his last moments, these later factors themselves become linked with a more cosmically oriented awareness, where 'all thoughts and all sensations, even pain and joy itself, were only the spectrum lines of the same ray of light, disintegrating in the prisma of consciousness'.[9] Commissar Rubashov has met Rubashov the yogi. The consequent logic which has compelled him to plead guilty is finally confronted with the para-rational, the mystic, with an experience which does not have to make sense. There are two motifs of freedom in DARKNESS AT NOON: freedom from the dominance of ends over means – a battle which Rubashov loses; freedom from the very rational apparatus by which ends are justified – which is not a victory for Rubashov so much as a revelation. The dilemma of ends and means has begun to yield to the dilemma of action versus contemplation, or, in the language to which it later became refined, of self-assertion versus self-transcendence. The origin of Koestler's first essay in the YOGI AND THE COMMISSAR anthology becomes apparent.

In ARRIVAL AND DEPARTURE, the struggle against destiny moves to a new battleground, where Koestler grapples with the forces of inward compulsion. Peter Slavek, a refugee from Nazi torture, arrives in Neutralia (Portugal), intending to journey on to Britain, where he can continue the war. Following an abortive love affair, he suffers a mental breakdown and loses the use of his right leg. He is finally cured by his countrywoman, Sonia, a psychoanalyst, who is able to show him that much of his revolutionary fervour stems from childhood experiences. Peter is thus caught between a force which seeks to reduce his moral imperatives to meaninglessness and a private awareness of choice, an experienced freedom, which finally survives psychoanalysis and forms the basis for his decision to go to England after all. Guilt is seen to have an ethical significance: it is when Peter discovers that self-evaluation persists after analysis that he rejects the easy option of seeking refuge in what was then a neutral America. Beyond the neurotic compulsion there is not nihilism, as Sonia would have him believe, but the freedom of a genuine self-judgement.

Whereas for Spartacus the issues are concrete and specific, in Rubashov freedom becomes more refined to its philosophical essence, and to be associated with experience of a new order in which political and moral liberty dissolve, as Koestler puts it, like salt in the ocean of cosmic experience. Consciousness becomes liberated from the confines of the self. In Peter Slavek, however, this new form of consciousness scarcely occurs; freedom is locked in battle with psychological determinism and there is no yogi-figure to play the referee. Koestler's concern with this problem has, by this time, passed to a more philosophical medium of expression in the first of two essays entitled THE YOGI AND THE COMMISSAR, which was written in 1942, the same year in which ARRIVAL AND DEPARTURE was begun.

ACTION AND CONTEMPLATION

To these two essays we must now turn, since they represent a stage in his thinking that is as crucial as it has been neglected. Between THE YOGI AND THE COMMISSAR, I and II, stretches a bridge between the socially committed notions of the thirties and the post-war concern with the life-sciences. The second essay, dated October 1944, was specifically written to close a collected edition with the same title. This book begins with a discussion of the activist and contemplative tendencies which Koestler considers to be inherent in man. Then follows a miscellaneous group of literary and political essays, succeeded by two studies of communism and totalitarianism. The closing essay, like the first, bears the title THE YOGI AND THE COMMISSAR, but is a study of free will and determinism. Thus the concrete studies of a directly political nature are flanked by two title-essays revealing a shift away from ends and means. Already, some ten years before his official farewell to politics, Koestler is beginning to turn to other matters. In making the shift, however, the same, nagging overriding concern is still there: there is a loose tooth in the jaws of determinism, and it continues to ache.

The first essay suggests that political attitudes form a spectrum, ranging from the activism and expediency of the Communist militant to the detachment of the Hindu mystic, who stand as types of extreme behaviour. The Commissar believes in the rational, externally imposed change of society by revolution and totalitarian methods, whereas the Yogi considers such activity meaningless, as 'garish colours in the veil of Maya'[10] and believes in change-from-within, by a process of visionary enrichment via a complex and difficult technique of meditation. Between the two extremes lie the more settled political attitudes, but the spectrum is not static: in certain periods of history, Koestler believes, there occurs a form of mass-migration from one end to the other, and the present century is marked by a return towards the yogi. Particularly is this true of the scientific field, he suggests, where thinkers are freeing themselves from the mechanistic conceptions of the nineteenth century. He goes on to explore the implications of his spectrum-analogy for the socialists of the thirties and forties, and concludes that many have indeed made the return towards the yogi, with varying degrees of suffering and success.

Indeed, Koestler is scathing about the 'monkey-like agility' of some of his colleagues from the Pink Decade, who 'were so quick to find the right reasons for their expatriation from the infra-red to the ultra-violet. In these matters clumsiness is respectable and glibness abject'.[11] It is an attitude which possibly explains why Koestler did not find a greater personal solace in mysticism following his break with the Party in the late thirties. More importantly, it probably explains his efforts to point out that, while the yogi's situation may be the reverse of the commissar's, he too faces a dilemma of ends and means:

Either the Means are subordinated to the End, or vice versa. Theoretically you may build up elaborate liberal or religious half-way houses; but if burdened with responsibility, and confronted with a practical decision to be taken, you have to choose one way or the other. Once you have chosen you are on the slope. If you have chosen to subordinate the Means to the End, the slope makes you slide down deeper and deeper on a moving carpet of common-sense propositions; for instance: the right of self-defence – the best defence is attack – increase of ruthlessness shortens the struggle etc. . . . . To subordinate the End to the Means leads to a slope as fatal as the inverse one. Gandhi's slope started with non-violence and made him gradually slide down to his present position of non-resistance to Japanese conquest: the Japanese might kill off a few million Indians but some day they would get tired of it and thus the moral integrity of India would be saved.[12]

Thus no longer is the self-transcendent experience to be seen, as it was in Rubashov, as a form of release from the determinism of consequent logic: if such a release occurs, it is not because the yogi-dimension provides a superior answer to problems such as social injustice. In his condemned cell in Seville, Koestler's own yogi-experience was triggered not by a *mantra* but by a proposition of Euclid: his conception of the para-rational experience is one of a freedom positively based – not of a hypangogic flight into Nirvana. It is this which distinguishes him and puts him in a different class from the followers of the Maharishi cult.

While the second essay also pursues the theme of action versus contemplation, it welds this topic and that of ends and means into the framework of a general debate on Freedom. As usual in Koestler, it is an argument by paradox. One of the key determinants of man's behaviour, Koestler claims, must be disbelief in the notion of determinism itself. Were it otherwise, the mental experience of an apparently free choice (which Koestler considers an irreducible datum of observation) would be impossible, or, at the best, unimportant, and we would all know what we would choose in any set of alternatives. Destiny versus the experience of free choice, or explanation versus volition, is an eternal duality in man's mental structure: his 'cosmic anxiety' seeks 'reassurance in explanation', a reassurance which has developed from the animism of the primitive through various levels of religious sophistication to the point where quantitative explanations supersede them. Eventually, 'destiny', which had previously operated solely through a deity from above, began to operate from below: the macrocosm yielded, during the nineteenth century to the physical and biological microcosm as a source of deterministic explanation. Yet man, whether believing himself determined or not, continued to act with the subjective experience of free choice, and in his dealings with the source of destiny merely shifted from the propitiation of deities to the exploitation of nature. The paradox of man's condition is that, while his cosmic anxiety drives him to seek increasingly complete explanations, these very explanations draw the web of determinism ever tighter about him.

Strangely enough, it is from religion that Koestler draws the answer to the paradox. It is an answer so important that it has played a central role in his philosophy ever since. And yet, typically, it is not in itself 'religious'. One escape from the tightening net of explanation is indicated by an analogy drawn from the Christian notion of a division of the universe into the two levels of divine and human volition. On the human plane, man's freedom is no longer illusory; on the superhuman plane, divinity is all-powerful and all-knowing. The two levels stand in a hierarchic relationship, in that the laws of divine logic are impenetrable by human rationality, whereas human reason is completely open to the deity. The tribal and totemistic diety was anthropomorphic in conception and behaviour, and the primitive world was largely homogeneous as a result. The Christian world is discontinuous in that separate principles govern the separate levels of divine, human and animal existence. From this notion of separate principles, Koestler distils the following characteristics of all hierarchies:

The laws of the higher level cannot be reduced to, nor predicted from, the lower level;
the phenomena of the lower level and their laws are implied in the higher level, but
the phenomena of the higher order if manifested on the lower level appear as unexplainable and miraculous.[13]

This passage bears the same relationship to Koestler's work as Darwin's study of finches bears to the forty years he spent subsequently in checking, exemplifying and corroborating. When Koestler began his novels, it is evident that his Marxism had already begun to merge into a more general concern with ends and means, which had led, via Rubashov's discussions and experience of personal identity, to the more broadly based concern with freedom and determinism that is found in ARRIVAL AND DEPARTURE. In THE YOGI AND THE COMMISSAR II, these threads are pulled together, and the fundamental notion of hierarchy emerges, and has remained at the root of Koestler's thinking ever since – it is the basic conscious motif. Into it are woven his views on the theory of knowledge; his theory of creativity; his theory of ethics and his conception of freedom. It is the starting-point for his theory of the emotions, his attacks upon Behaviourist psychology, and recent critiques of Reductionism. The vast majority of his writing since 1945 may be seen as an amplification of this single essay. For neither Koestler nor Darwin would have had much of significance to say if their ideas had remained in embryo-form; in both cases, it is their substantiation and elaboration which are important.

From the three principles outlined above, Koestler proceeds to consider aspects of scientific, micro-determinism, arguing that, following the experiments of Rutherford and Soddy in 1903 with radio-active atoms, there has been increasing evidence that explanations involving simple, linear patterns of cause-and-effect cannot give a satisfactory account of a variety of phenomena, such as tissue-development in embryos:

... we have to note that Science is reverting to the same expedient for solving its paradoxes as religious explanation once did; it renounces the idea of a homogeneous universe ruled by one comprehensive law, and replaces it by a hierarchy of 'levels of organisation'. This is not ... a regression into religious thought; it is merely an analogy *in method* to solve the paradox of freedom and determinism which remains hidden and latent so long as a type of explanation is still incomplete, but explodes in a crisis, as it becomes perfected.[14]

Because a hierarchy consists of a series of levels of organization, there will exist throughout its structure a series of part-whole relationships, in which components at one level will be subordinate to the organizational level above, and supraordinate with respect to components of which they themselves are composed. In later works, Koestler gives the name of 'holon' to entities with such dual attributes. The implications for the issue of freedom are that

the 'freedom' of a level consists in those new values and relationships which were not present among the determinants of the lower level; the 'destiny' of a level is its dependence on the laws of the next-higher level - laws which it cannot predict or reduce.[15]

The inverted commas are used because Koestler is speaking of biological systems in general, rather than of man in particular. Koestler believes that man, as a biological system, also has an hierarchic relationship with his exterior and interior environments as well as with his social institutions; that his mental functions also operate on a hierarchic basis. It follows logically that various 'levels of freedom' are implied, and that the governing principles which operate on one level are not necessarily those of another level. Accordingly, any attempt to reduce the freedoms of one level to the terms of reference of a lower level is invalid. The highest level of 'freedom' of which man is aware is his subjective experience of free choice, as defined earlier – apart from mystic, contemplative experience, in which choosing ceases to be relevant.

While THIEVES IN THE NIGHT (1946) and THE AGE OF LONGING (1949) are both evidence that Koestler's fictional concern with political issues had not ceased, it is INSIGHT AND OUTLOOK (also 1949) which reflects the main course of his thinking. By the time he wrote this work, ends and means had evolved into a more complex system in which ethics are but one aspect of a more general theory of hierarchic relationships. The latter notion, in short, represents the tying-together of his scientific and social interests. The idea of a 'political spectrum', flanked by the symbolic figures of the Yogi and the Commissar, has also been refined into the duality of 'self-assertive' and 'self-transcendent' behaviour, which is a manifestation of the simultaneous 'partness and wholeness' of a hierarchic component. But the same principle also applies to the living organism, so that, for example, a single cell's principles of operation are different from those of a whole organ of which it may form a part: an isolated kidney cell behaves quite differently from a similar cell at work within the kidney itself. Hierarchic systems may be psychological, social, biological and even inorganic: in each case, the same organizing principles are at work: thus in Koestler's view it makes sense to compare organic and social hierarchic properties, just as it makes sense to relate hierarchies in the social and psychological spheres. And from the hierarchy there emerges a much more sophisticated statement of freedom.

No component of a hierarchy, no 'holon', is totally free; but by the same token, it cannot be totally determined. Freedom, for a holon, is relative to the levels of organization adjacent to it, but one encounters 'degrees of freedom' among holons relative to their level in the hierarchy. A skilled activity, such as writing a letter, reveals a whole gradient of freedoms from the almost infinite choice of content down to the muscle-contractions involved in the physical act of writing itself. In short, there is an increasing amount of determinism in one direction and an increasing degree of freedom in the other. But there is no ceiling, as it were, at which absolute freedom is enjoyed: 'there is an ascending series of levels, leading from automatic and semi-automatic reactions through awareness and self-awareness to the self's awareness of itself and so on, without hitting a ceiling.[16] In similar fashion, the inorganic universe, from macro- to microsphere, has no finite limits in Koestler's theory. Moreover, since, in a hierarchy, the 'environment' of a holon is largely comprised of the levels above it, total definition of an environment is effectively impossible. It is thus not feasible to adopt an absolutely determinist position in an hierarchic universe.

Such, then, is the tale of how a basic coherence emerges from the work of the man Cyril Connolly referred to as a 'popular polymath'[17] a term which, though kindly meant, does an injustice to the worth of Koestler's contribution, as I hope to show very shortly. If I appear to have cheated a little by importing terms from THE GHOST IN THE MACHINE, these do not in fact alter the essential theory: they are simply more economical. From

1955 onwards, Koestler's major works have all been oriented about the hierarchic concept, and have all, in some respect, maintained their concern with the issue of freedom. Thus THE SLEEPWALKERS has as one of its sub-themes the setting-up of the mechanistic notion of the universe, and closes with a discussion of the problem of causality in modern physics. Even the social theories of THE GHOST IN THE MACHINE are set within the context of a critique of behaviourism and a definition of consciousness. Even THE LOTUS AND THE ROBOT, which revolves about meditative techniques in India and Japan, is concerned with the basic irony of self-transcendent freedom: that the very regimens by which man seeks to project himself into the All-Knowing and All-One are themselves constraints upon entrepreneurism, social concern and public defence against invaders. Behind the illumination of the Hindu Atman, Koestler has seen the seedy form of the medicine-man, and heard the mumble of his incantations. Even polemics such as REFLECTIONS ON HANGING (1956) are motivated by their revulsion at the final sanction of removal of consciousness.

The most valuable ingot to emerge from this crucible is THE ACT OF CREATION (1964), which is Koestler's statement of the positive freedom of creativity. To the more cautious statements on this theme that emerge in INSIGHT AND OUTLOOK (1949), Koestler has added not merely sophistication but a vast and varied array of evidence. As in the earlier work, Koestler holds to the view that life-forms are hierarchically organized. One of the properties of a hierarchy, he claims, is its ability to make unusual adaptations under certain conditions of environmental stress. Below this level of stress, the organism (i.e., the hierarchy) will select a response from its already-established repertoire of behaviour. Above this level, its hierarchic functioning will permanently collapse. In so far as the middle stage, which Koestler calls 'regenerative equilibrium', induces a response which is outside the organism's normal repertoire of instinct, conditioning, habits or learning, it increases the scope of the organism's behaviour, particularly if the new response is capable of being added permanently to that repertoire. In this respect, the organism may be said to have greater capacity for action than before, and so, in a relative sense, is 'more free'. Such an increase in relative freedom through the workings of 'regenerative equilibrium' is at its most significant level in human mentation, Koestler believes, although he claims that a continuum of creative-like behaviour may be observed throughout other levels of evolution. On the human level, in fact, regenerative equilibrium increases the experience of free choice. And so, in part, we have the answer to the dilemma of Spartacus before the mob, of Rubashov in his prison cell, and perhaps to several dilemmas of their author, who, stretched as he was between identity and various deterministic creeds, produced them as symbols of his tension. Perhaps in hierarchy he has found an alternative creed, which his objectivity can accept, but which his inner reality, his 'sense of I', can tolerate.

KOESTLER AND SYSTEMS THEORY

Such, then, is the remarkable continuity in the work of a remarkable writer. But continuity of this kind spans not merely many years but many disciplines. Yet, were one to ignore Koestler's literary output entirely, it is still difficult to imagine any single point of view from which he may be assessed – difficult, that is, until one notes the increasing relevance of his work to General Systems Theory. In both THE GHOST IN THE MACHINE and the Alpbach Symposium, Koestler refers to his concept of hierarchy as 'an exercise' in this relatively new area of enquiry, which, in the words of its virtual founding father, the late Ludwig von Bertalanffy, 'became necessary in view of the complexities of modern technology and society in general',[18] and, according to Anatol Rapoport, seeks to find 'the most general conceptual framework in which a scientific theory or technological problem can be placed without losing the essential features of the theory or the problem.'[19] In short, and again in the words of Rapoport, the supporters of General Systems Theory see in it 'the focal point of resynthesis of knowledge.'[20] They take as their province both biological and electrical systems, linguistic and social systems and mathematical systems, indeed any pattern of organized activity in which the whole made by its components is richer in ways of behaving than what is obtained by leaving the parts isolated.[21] The Renaissance *uomo universale* spoke Latin; in the atomic dark ages the *lingua franca* is General Systems Theory.

General Systems Theorists seek to establish laws which apply to all systems, and far from regarding such laws as philosophical, have come in certain cases to view them as empirical. These laws are, says Paul Weiss in the Alpbach Symposium, 'the products of our experience with nature.'[22] Koestler would agree, and examined from a General Systems viewpoint, his theory of hierarchy not only finds support, but praise from Bertalanffy himself. In his own contribution to the Alpbach Symposium, he identifies hierarchical order as possibly the most important system problem still eluding mathematical theory, and suspects that 'considerations such as those of Koestler may eventually lead to a more rigorous theory.'[23] Had Bertalanffy looked more closely at Koestler's work, he might also have remarked that the concept of open hierarchies as described in INSIGHT AND OUTLOOK (written almost completely by 1947) is among the earliest expositions of concepts which today would be recognized as belonging to the General Systems area. As far as I can establish, Bertalanffy himself wrote little on this topic in English until after the war. It is not surprising that INSIGHT AND OUTLOOK puzzled its literary reviewers.

It is to other contributors that there must lie the role of examining the other figure – Koestler the controversialist. Let it suffice that in the realm of creativity Koestler seems to have made three powerful and original contributions. The first concerns his very existence as a man who has made such varied yet equally discussed additions to human thought. I have sought to demonstrate that a bridge exists between these, and moreover that it was one provided by Koestler himself: its framework is the lattice of General Systems Theory, yet its foundations lie in the rich soil of the humanities. In an age when division of intellectual labour seems to have led to division of wisdom and loss of perspective, the *uomo universale* is a welcome guide, all the more so because he is so rare. If he is somewhat contentious on details, perhaps we should remember the meta-theory before rising to the assaults on our respective specialisms. If, as Goegre Miller says in an otherwise hard-hitting review, he flies too high and handsome at times, 'perhaps we should not try to bring him down to earth; perhaps we should offer him flight pay'.[24]

Secondly, Koestler seems to have made an unusual contribution to General Systems literature in his demonstration that hierarchic systems may be creative. In a survey of General Systems Yearbooks from their inception to the early sixties, I was unable to discover more than one article seeking to relate creativity with General Systems – apart from some work on serendipity. Thirdly, it is worth noting that 5676 publications on creativity had been documented by the Creative Education Foundation by 1967,[25] of which 90 per cent belonged to that decade: many writers have testified to the disjointed, plural quality of the research behind them. Yet there is precious little which could be said to constitute a meta-theory, and those that do exist are generally more lightweight than Koestler's contribution. It is in this context, that of the idea which is relevant to a whole range of observations and preconceptions, that THE ACT OF CREATION should be regarded. Thus I find myself in agreement with Professor Kneller's assessment:

In THE ACT OF CREATION, Koestler has achieved a synthesis at once sweeping and detailed. Some reviewers have claimed that he has pushed his ideas too far, but all have praised the range and power of his vision. There is no doubt that THE ACT OF CREATION has accomplished the twofold task of any great synthesis: to open a host of avenues for detailed research and to describe the entire field within which this research may proceed.[26]

Whatever else Koestler may achieve with his current works, that would make a good plaque when he finally hangs up his pen.

REFERENCES

1. THE LOTUS AND THE ROBOT, Hutchinson, 1960, Preface.

2. Atkins, J., *Arthur Koestler,* Neville Spearman, 1956.

3. Calder, J., *Chronicles of Conscience,* Secker and Warburg, 1968.

4. Medawar, Sir P. B., 'Koestler's Theory of the Creative Act', *New States-man,* 19 June 1964. See also Medawar, Sir P. B., *The Art of the Soluble* (Methuen 1967), Pelican 1969, pp. 95 ff.

5. Miller, G. A., 'Arthur Koestler's View of the Creative Process', *Scientific American,* April 1965, pp. 145 ff.

6. 'Now the errors are atoned for, the bitter passion has burnt itself out; Cassandra has gone hoarse, and is due for a vocational change.' THE TRAIL OF THE DINOSAUR, Collins, 1955, p. viii.

7. Calder, *op. cit.,* p. 121.

8. THE GLADIATORS (Cape, 1939), Hutchinson, 1965, p. 232.

9. DARKNESS AT NOON (Cape 1940) and Penguin, 1966, p. 203.

10. This quotation actually occurs in a similar passage in INSIGHT AND OUTLOOK, p. 219, but I felt it summed up the sense of the earlier work most appropriately.

11. THE YOGI AND THE COMMISSAR (Cape 1945), Cape 1964, p. 13.

12. *ibid.,* pp. 11–12.

13. *ibid.,* p. 231.

14. *ibid.,* p. 236.

15. *ibid.,* p. 241.

16. THE GHOST IN THE MACHINE, p. 205.

17. Connolly, C., 'Koestler as Popular Polymath', *Sunday Times,* 31 May 1964.

18. Bertalanffy, L. von, BEYOND REDUCTIONISM, eds. Koestler, A., and Smythies, J. R., Hutchinson, 1969.

19. Rapoport, A., 'Systems', *International Encyclopaedia of the Social sciences,* Vol. 15, New York, 1964, p. 452.

20. *ibid.*

21. This is a close paraphrase of a description by Ashby, W. R., *An Introduction to Cybernetics,* Wiley, 1956.

22. Weiss, P., in BEYOND REDUCTIONISM, p. 10.

23. Bertalanffy, L. von, in BEYOND REDUCTIONISM, pp. 62–3.

24. Miller, G. A., *op. cit.,* p. 148.

25. Parnes, S. J. and Brunelle, E. A., *Bibliography of Creativity and Problem Solving,* Creative Education Foundation Inc., 1967. See also the comments of the same authors in *The Journal of Creative Behaviour,* Vol. 1, No. 1, pp. 52 ff., 1967.

26. Kneller, G. F., *The Art and Science of Creativity,* Holt, Rinehart and Winston, 1965, p. 46.

THE SLEEPWALKERS: Its Contribution and Impact

Mark Graubard

Arthur Koestler's THE SLEEPWALKERS (London and New York, 1959) appeared with an introduction by Herbert Butterfield; the classic *On the Revolutions of Heavenly Spheres* by Nicolaus Copernicus (Nuremberg 1543) appeared with an introduction by Andreas Osiander. Each work is a landmark in thought and each introduction has merit all its own. Butterfield's is based on his pioneering *Origins of Modern Science* (London, 1949) issued ten years previously, and Osiander's heralds in few words the modern notions of the role of theory, truth and reality in science. A few words about Butterfield; Osiander will be considered later.

Butterfield's book conveyed to historians of science a number of new ideas largely overlooked for understandable reasons. In the nineteenth century, science history was an integral part of many scientists' thought processes as necessary references to their antecedents. Darwin wrote a masterful historical introduction to his *Origin of Species,* and Charles Lyell did the same for his *Principles of Geology.* It was only late in the nineteenth century that the history of science gained status as a recognized discipline.

The outlook in the field was rationalist throughout, with minor exceptions. Belief in progress was an unchallengeable tenet, and with reason. Science meant expansion of horizons, clarification of concepts, and steady accretion. What could one say of Aris-

totle, Galen, Ptolemy or Albertus Magnus but that they were
'wrong' and their influence detrimental? There were some great
minds in the past who had proved 'right' and escaped obloquy
– Euclid, Archimedes, Hippocrates, Roger Bacon. Like true
visionaries they went unnoticed; obstructionists were in control.
This simplistic outlook prevailed – the eternal, pleasing dichotomy of hero and villain, Greek and barbarian, good and bad
Indians.

Butterfield's presentation was objective, erudite and persua-
sive. He showed that scientific progress was allied to other facets
of the culture, that both the pioneers and their work were not
strictly 'rational', that 'progress' came in spurts, that the 'reactionary' forces were not so inane as many claim, that besides the
salient geniuses there were others who made sporadic but ancillary
contributions, and finally that all innovators reached great
conceptual heights although their feet and their minds were
fully rooted in the heritage of the past. No organized devil
lurked to pounce upon innovators, and the hallowed formula for
the scientific method based on the sequence of facts, hypotheses,
crucial tests, prediction and verification hardly represented the
waywardness of the actual process. His book had an immediate
impact on the field.

Koestler's THE SLEEPWALKERS came as a fitting major event
along the new path, an original beacon illuminating the workings
of progress in science, with cosmology as model. Recognizing
that the path of scientific evolution was not a teleological progression from darkness to light, Koestler examines the experimental material with a fresh approach. Why 'has it followed a
zigzag course' rather than 'a kind of clean, rational advance along
a straight ascending line?' What kind of creative geniuses were
the men who gave birth to the inspiring cosmological schemes of
the past? How did they come by their generalizations? Did they
perceive, think, reason and conceive differently than the other
scholars? Were their personalities unique, and how did these
relate to the contributions? How did great minds utilize data so as
to construct theories and then go about seeking out new facts
and inventing new hypotheses? How did these men of genius

relate to the mores and beliefs of the times? To faith? To their colleagues? To society?

In the life of Johannes Kepler, Koestler struck the biggest paydirt imaginable. Here was a man of creative power in mathematics, physics and astronomy, facile in conceptualization, skilful in experimentation. Whatever was on his mind was on his tongue. As Koestler explains: 'Kepler is one of the few geniuses who enables one to follow, step by step, the tortuous path that led him to his discoveries, and to get a really intimate glimpse, as in a slow-motion film, of the creative act.' (p. 15) He was as ideal to Koestler's quest for an anatomy of a creative mind as were the data of Tycho Brahe to Kepler's quest for the orbit of Mars. In both instances the results were a triumph.

Consider Kepler the man. He studied Lutheran theology but became a teacher of mathematics and astronomy at a high school. Though devoutly religious and mystical, he fashioned his own ideas in matters of faith and ritual. He was possessed of strong passions for astronomy and astrology, wrote poetry, 'read the texts of Aristotle', enjoyed disputes, displayed broad and persistent interests in most aspects of nature, and 'liked to compare paradoxes . . . loved mathematics above all other studies', as he says of himself in his essay, 'Horoscope'. Though haemophilic and frequently ill, he never showed signs of blaming society or his fate. He embraced the ideas of Copernicus in his earliest student days and openly defended them.

His first published work, which appeared in 1596 when Kepler was twenty-five years old, was *The Cosmic Mystery,* a brilliant geometrical design that sought to explain why there were only six planets (five visible to the unaided eye and the planet earth), why they revolved about the sun and at their particular distances, and other features of the solar family. He relates how his magnificent scheme came to him in a flash while drawing a figure on the blackboard. The theme of the book is that God, the great mathematician, created the world in geometric harmony. The planets were in orbits fashioned by the five possible perfect solids called Pythagorean or Platonic, which are polyhedrons that have all their sides as well as the faces formed by them equal. In other words, the Copernican scheme was not happenstance, but an ordered geometrical creation by God, the all-wise Creator and benevolent Father and Lord.

If Kepler makes a wonderful subject because he bares his heart and mind, Koestler is a remarkable biographer for his keenness of perception and depth of understanding. He has amply displayed these skills as intellectual novelist, as critic, analyst and anatomist of psychology, society and creativity in a number of fantastic books that constitute rare X-ray tomograms of modern man and modern times. Never before has such fine dissection been applied to such an excellent patient as Kepler, and so masterfully. That section in THE SLEEPWALKERS has to be read, pondered over, and filled in with some collateral reading of Kepler's own writings to enable one to share Koestler's keenness and its exciting harvest.

The Cosmic Mystery, with its intricate design of circumscribed and inscribed spheres accommodating the perfect solids of antiquity, was an excellent mental construction of the known cosmos which a 'true believer' could insist was 'real'. (See how it fits and how deeply I feel that it must be so, and my opponents are blind and reactionary!) While small minds do act thus, Kepler, like every other creative mind, never gave a thought to its reality or unreality. He juggled all the various elements of the scheme until they fitted to his satisfaction. He naturally took it for granted that the Copernican scheme and his own additions were true. He found it easy to explain why there were only six planets, why they were placed 'where they fit in perfectly', why the cube lay between Saturn and Jupiter and the octahedron between Mercury and Venus. He included chapters on the astrology and numerology of the system and sought to relate his model to the Pythagorean harmony of the spheres. Admitting that all this was merely a scheme based on probability, he devoted the second half of the book to efforts to prove its soundness, that is, agreement with the facts, the data. The biggest task was to explain away discrepancies, and that any mind can do, let alone a mind good enough to generate a theory. In performing this task Kepler's mental cauldron raised many problems and laid bare a host of valuable relationships for the future to think about and work out.

Koestler examines all of Kepler's subsequent works and finds similar procedures. *The Cosmic Mystery* serves as a paradigm of the sleepwalker's seething visions and his use of data, logic and proof. True, Kepler's Mystery turned out to be 'false' in its entirety, but far more 'absurd' and 'fantastic' ones had in fact turned out to be 'true', that is, wholly consistent with every element they included either in their explanations or predictions. To Kepler his scheme seemed perfect and full of fascination. (One might even say that nature was too dumb to follow it, or that God had simply not thought of it, what a pity.) Yet the same mind produced the great laws which may well be said to be the first mathematically stated invariant relationships in nature. And the clever, wildly meandering paths Kepler trod to attain them, his retreats and turns, are most enlightening.

Kepler's *Astronomia Nova* offers Koestler hitherto unseen bits of information as he dissects the workings of the gifted mind in pursuit of sights and mirages. The seeker invariably begins from a base built upon the heritage of past efforts, and the resulting ideas are like gems emerging haphazardly from crude ore. These may both bedevil or illumine progress, since it cannot be known in advance how each newborn concept will function. Brahe's accurate data proved crucial because their regular disfigurement of the circle's symmetry raised questions. The plan of Mars' revolution did not oscillate as Copernicus thought, and a vision struck Kepler, who had read Gilbert's *De Magnete,* with uncanny clarity that a force like that of a magnet held and swept the planets around the sun as centre. It had been known that the further the planet was from the centre, the slower its orbital velocity; and Kepler put that into his scheme. The rest was labour. Kepler was so naive, so open-hearted, that had nature tried to reveal the secret workings of a mind it would not have improved upon his honest reporting. And had nature looked for a better analyst of the process, it could not have found one better qualified than Koestler.

In his idea-packed Epilogue Koestler suggests the complement to his notion of the theorist as visionary. Clearly, he says, progress in science is 'neither "continuous" nor "organic".

'The philosophy of nature evolved by occasional leaps and bounds alternating with delusional pursuits, culs-de-sac, regressions, periods of blindness and amnesia. The great discoveries that determined its course were sometimes the unexpected by-products of a chase after quite different hares.' Evolution in science follows the course of biologic evolution with the term progress excluded. 'New ideas are thrown up spontaneously like mutations; the vast majority of them are useless crank theories, the equivalent of biological freaks without survival-value. There is a constant struggle for survival between competing theories in every branch of history of thought. The process of "natural selection", too, has its equivalent in mental evolution; among the multitude of new concepts which emerge only those survive which are well adapted to the period's intellectual milieu.' This is an original and most fertile idea. Those mutant theories survive which lead to further experimentation and thereby to further hypothesizing, hence to inevitable enrichment. To call it progress is subjective. Natural selection probably operates in social institutions as well, such as monogamy, the family, tribe, faith, laws.

Koestler further points out that 'most geniuses responsible for the major mutations in the history of thought' display common features, particularly scepticism, 'often carried to the point of iconoclasm' and 'an openmindedness that verges on naive credulity towards new concepts'. These conspire to present old relationships in a 'new light or new context'. There is also the 'ripeness of age' and a creeping sense of 'a feeling of frustration and malaise . . . that the whole tradition is somehow out of step', leading to a 'thaw of dogma' and to an attenuation of the 'specialist's hubris'. But there seems to be hubris also in the mutant genius, who feeds on opposition by smaller minds, on a growing sense of paranoia and messianism, which in turn oblige him to apply his theory with excessive overkill, just as a nation bursting with national power and cultural efflorescence willy-nilly expands into an empire. Exaggeration and overapplication result, as well as occasional distortion of peripheral regions. Paracelsus acted thus on a vast scale, and so did Freud, Pasteur and others. In social philosophy the trend to over-expand one's theory is very conspicuous; in science, less so.

THE SLEEPWALKERS shows, no doubt, some symptoms of this overspread. So rich is the soil of Kepler and so abundant Koestler's harvest that the other visionaries dealt with, all but Pythagoras, are treated somewhat unfairly, though always with a reasonable base and perhaps legitimately in the light of the author's licence as literary and psychological craftsman and analyst. Koestler has to reconstruct the personalities of Ptolemy and Copernicus from sketchy remnants and their own theoretical productions. The outcome is personal and dimmed by the enchantment and luminous glare of Kepler. It is not really necessary to regard Ptolemy's geometrical scheme as 'completely mad' when it can in all honesty be viewed as the first truly great construction, the first scientific theory that organized, even if it did not fuse into a family as did the Copernican scheme, the sun and the planets, and accounted well for all the known data, and made satisfactory predictions to boot. It performed as well as any theory could, which was considerable when no mechanical model was anywhere in sight to the keenest genius of the time.

Examine Aristotle's *Physics* or Seneca's *Natural Questions* or Pliny's sections on physical science in his *Natural History* and you find that it is unsound and inhuman to expect of that period a physical model. One is, however, obliged to forgive Koestler his impatience with Ptolemy's 'profoundly distasteful' universe and his unkind words about a man who was the author of three best-sellers of fifteen centuries' duration (*The Almagest, Geography* and *Tetrabiblos*), when one reads Koestler's atoning words *circa* 500 pages later: 'Compared to the modern physicist's picture of the world, the Ptolemaic universe of epicycles and crystal spheres was a model of sanity.' A man who is saner than Dirac, Heisenberg, Einstein, de Broglie and Fermi, cannot be all that bad. Besides, was not Ptolemy the teacher of their masters?

Nor was Ptolemy really a dreary pedant. The sole poem attributed to him, and the knowledge of man and his fate that he displays in his *Tetrabiblos*, bear strong witness to that. And are epicycles really a lunatic's Ferris wheel? The solar system is full of them, boasting thirty-one satellites about the several planets. Also many of their orbits are practically circular. A viewer from the sun, or the earth, would see them as epicycles.

Nor is the 'sacredness of the circle' a Platonic or Aristotelian concoction. Ptolemy appears in his *Almagest* as a thorough-going empiricist, cautiously but soundly rejecting the helio-centric scheme of Aristarchus and detailing all the reasons why the sun, moon, stars and sky move in circles as actually measured by us on earth. The circle became sacred in the same way as gravity, special relativity and inertia are sacred to us. Circular motion was a fact of life in the heavens, and the few exceptions had to be explained away exactly as we explain away our own troublesome deviations.

Had Koestler viewed Ptolemy kindly as a creative mathematical theoretician, the theme of his SLEEPWALKERS would be greatly strengthened because Ptolemy was a sleepwalker *par excellence*. He is so enwrapped in his vision that he cares not the least whether it has a physical foundation, even as subsequent dreamers were heedless of the reality of negative or imaginary numbers, neu-trinos, positrons or negative energy. Better than anyone else in the field is Koestler aware of the basic principle of the student of man that it is a barbarism, nay, a crime, to judge other cultures, or our own subcultures, by the values and fashions of the present, absolute and sound though they may seem to us. To witness. He recounts in THE SLEEPWALKERS the ordeal of Kepler's mother accused of witchcraft and kept imprisoned and chained for fourteen months. Says he: 'In Weil der Stadt . . . thirty-eight witches were burnt between 1615 and 1629. In neighbouring Leonberg . . . six witches were burnt in the winter of 1615 alone. It was one of the hurricanes of madness which strikes the world from time to time, and seems to be part of man's condition' (p. 384). Compare this crisp but wise comment with the futile words of the supreme authority in Kepleriana, Max Caspar, on the same incident. Says Caspar: 'There are few expressions of human baseness not manifested in this affair', and, 'Yet stupidity is blind and does not want to see the truth, and malevolence is

deaf and does not want to be taught about that which is right.'
(Max Caspar, *Kepler*, New York, 1962, p. 252)

But it was Koestler's chapters on Copernicus and Galileo, not
Ptolemy, that roused the ire of the 'Establishment' historians of
science. Some still live in the eighteenth and nineteenth centuries
and use the word 'truth' with the sanctimoniousness of politicians.
Koestler treats Copernicus and Galileo as personalities, as gifted
human beings, as blessed mutants who dream their stirring
visions for the glory and enrichment of mankind. But Copernicus
and Galileo have sacred auras of awe and sentiment which are
real and enduring. Admittedly, sentiment can be a treacherous
guide to thought and action if not viewed in overall perspective.
Unfortunately, Koestler's original and fruitful employment of
the technique of dissection of character and his insight into the
mental metabolism of the creative mind seems to lead him into
the same troubles that led Galileo into conflict with his culture so
as to irritate it needlessly, as Koestler himself points out. Such
upsets can be serious. (Mark Graubard, 'Displacement of Scientific Theories and the Resulting "Culture Wobble",' *Proc. Minn.
Acad. of Sci.*, xxv, 1957-8, pp. 450–61) Koestler obviously causes
a wobble in the creed of his contemporaries. Much of his thesis is
needlessly sharp, some of it, indeed, is onesided or exaggerated, as
we shall see.

Let us here summarize the scheme of man's mental evolution
which his work suggests. We start with man as a highly developed
mammal that interacts with the outside world by means of
sense organs. These are locks shielding a particular sensory nerve
so as to permit effective stimulation by only one unique force in
the environment, the one having the special means of entry. The
sensory nerve impulses are then directed to distinctive sensory
brain regions where they are somehow metamorphosed into an
event we know as sensation, period. This event is novel, ultimate,
and so unique as to be untranslatable. Sensations are the alphabet
of experience and the stuff of sentiment, thought and all of man's
mental equipment. Since the vast majority of mankind possesses
more or less identical sense organs, communication is rendered
possible. Science is an aspect of human behaviour which aims at an

orderly, communicable and verifiable understanding of the world man lives in, as well as of himself. His senses supply him with the basic data. His mind also employs emotional components and invisible axioms which often confuse and obscure the very knowledge of facts and must be sought out and eliminated or accounted for.

With the emergence of *Homo sapiens,* evolution brought into the world the phenomenon of concepts as the building blocks of thought, theories, generalizations, values. Judging by man's conduct, no other animal seems to have that operational skill. Its appearance in man is new and is loaded with vast evolutionary possibilities similar to those resulting from the appearance of four legs in amphibia or wings in archaeopteryx. The human type of brain is only at its evolutionary inception. The brain, like the stomach, wings, or facial features, is under the influence of genes, acting, of course, in their inner and outer environments.

All objects man uses, ideas, books, laws, etc., are the products of uniquely gifted inventors. Leather, cotton, buttons, electric current, radio, poems, aspirin, ritual, suffrage, all are brainchildren of a particular or a few unique persons. The sum total of these mutations yields our social heritage which the culture, hence society, presents to each of us on a silver platter from infancy onward.

In history's earliest stages the searching minds dealt with facts, discerned analogies and made discoveries. Simple or complex, these were tied with an umbilical cord to sensory experience. Koestler refers to this elsewhere as the sensory, experiential stage. Aristotle clung strongly to this realistic bond and was the first systematizer of sensory-experiential science. With the advance of mathematical abstractions, more concepts came into being. Conceptual thinking, abstract symbols and relationships brought thoughtful order and a new vitality to the world of direct experience. In time, direct experience became as if exhausted, and science, particularly the physical realm, became more and more abstract. This is the conceptual stage. Koestler's sleepwalkers – the Ptolemys, Euclids, Aristotles, Copernicuses,

Keplers, Galileos, Newtons, Darwins, Freuds, Bohrs, Heisenbergs, etc. – are the mental mutants, the equivalent of Darwin's sports. Their dreams are ultimately weighed in one scale only, the scale of stimulation of other scholars and generation of continued efforts. The theory of Copernicus proved great and valuable only because it was employed by Kepler to unveil new horizons and stimulate others in the endless relay race of scientific enquiry. Aristotle and Ptolemy lost out because, like diapers, the child outgrew them. It is folly to ridicule diapers. They are extremely valuable to infants of four months, but a symptom of serious pathology if still needed at the age of eighteen.

Theories that have outlived their usefulness quite naturally demonstrate inertia and are not quickly rejected. A true student of man should respect rather than abuse his experimental animal; a physiologist should respect his dogs and a carpenter his wood. Antecedent scholars are neither stupid nor blind. If a theory like Ptolemy's dominated thought for fifteen centuries, it contained fifteen hundred *belyers,* or belief-years. Lamarck's theory of inheritance of acquired characters possessed only about one hundred such units, Darwin's pangenesis a mere ten or less. The greater the number of belyers, the more innately appealing is the theory, or the poorer are its competitors in the field, or the more difficult is the field for mastery by man. Like Darwin's great evolutionary theory, Koestler presents a mechanism for growth in all conceptual fields. In addition, Koestler succeeds in peering deeply into the very process of formation of sports, their mode of operation, their social selection and spread.

Subsequent works such as Kuhn's notion of the emergence of paradigms and their role in reorganization of a given domain of science (Thomas Kuhn, *The Structure of Scientific Revolutions,* Univ. of Chicago Press, 1962) and of other contributors (Mark Graubard, 'The Rational and Irrational in the History of Science,' *Indian Journal of History of Science* 3, p. 61-7, 1968) are logical expansions of Koestler's basic scheme. More additions and refinements will no doubt emerge in the future. In passing, it should be noted that Koestler postulates a third level of mental operation, which is manifested in the occult, the mystic, the oceanic feelings or romantic-spiritual-poetic regions of the mind. Many scientists reject or deride this notion. It remains a fact, none the less, that some minds work creatively in that zone, perform a service to many, and that meritorious results ensue from their efforts. For this wholly innocent suggestion Koestler received, sad to say, considerable abuse from professional scientists.

A few words about the reception of Koestler's SLEEPWALKERS. Reviewers in humanistic journals were almost unanimously enthusiastic. One or two were deeply impressed, though also disturbed by it. Another found it 'not entirely novel'. Of particular interest are the reviews in *Isis,* the journal of the American History of Science Society, and in the authoritative and popular *Scientific American,* both written by outstanding historians.

The *Isis* review (1959, Vol. 50, p. 255) by two erudite and diligent scholars in Galileana (G. de Santillana and Stillman Drake) was hostile to a degree rarely encountered in academic literature. The senior author, Professor Santillana, had published four years previously *The Crime of Galileo* (Univ. of Chicago Press, 1955), a work rooted in the eighteenth-century outlook enriched by a whodunit plotlet. Galileo fought for 'truth', verifiable and mandatory. But the 'Church' and her Cardinals and Bishops were 'enemies'. (Galileo also uses that term in surfeit, but then he really did live in the seventeenth century and relished disputes over interpretations, priority, and such.) The 'enemies' and 'scientific renegades', Santillana's terms, 'sought to trump up charges', 'to trap him', 'spread dark rumours', to have him 'manouevred and driven and cornered' and 'denounced by informers'. Current dullards, he says, stupidly honour Bellarmine's pleadings with Galileo to obtain more facts, rather than rebut the sly Cardinal with clever sorites because they are 'apologists' and seek to 'whitewash' the wicked churchman. To help in the battle against science, Tycho's system was 'pressed into the service of the Vatican'. Finally, being unable to condemn Galileo legally, the Church planted a faked document to prove that at his first hearings (1616), Galileo had been forbidden to teach and expound the Copernican view, which is what he later did in his *Dialogues,* in 1632. Santillana seems unaware that the powers of reason or rationalization have never been found incapable of defending anything one believed in, from concentration camps to invasions, from faith to atheism. Are tricks really needed?

What is depressing about Santillana's approach is the following. Here is the conflict of Pope Urban VIII, lover of science, long-standing admirer and defender of Galileo, but one who turned against him after the uproar over the *Dialogues*. This turnabout constitutes one of the greatest tragedies in history, a model for hundreds of such conflicts in our own times. Urban, theologian and churchman, was in love with science, the 'new philosophy of nature'. He was a Cardinal and later became Pope. He thought that he could serve both gods, had done so for years; science sang the glories of God and could go hand in hand with the Sermon on the Mount. Who better than Koestler knows that many brilliant minds in our own day thought they could serve communism and decency (or Nazism and honour), or even American party politics and moral purity? But clashes are at times unavoidable, bitter clashes of split loyalties that bite into each other, much as the twins in Rebecca's womb clawed one another. After all, Urban did owe allegiance to the Church as well, and primarily. Yet, the Church was mild and compromising, especially when compared to modern brutalities. To top it all, history shows reason and scientific rightness to have been with Bellarmine and not with Galileo, who truly had no evidence besides the phases of Venus which disproved Ptolemy, but not Brahe. There was indeed no real proof.

Koestler pictures this episode with psychological insight. Others before him saw it clearly as well, but his contribution remains unique because he is the first to employ a literary depth analysis of character to glimpse at the intricacies of personality and the creative mind re its impact on science history. The overall work of traditional historians such as Santillana, compares to the contribution of a Koestler much as the work of rat-psychologists compares to the contribution of a Sophocles, Dostoyevsky, Tolstoy or Faulkner to our knowledge of the human psyche, even though here and there Santillana does point to a slight inaccuracy of no genuine relevance.

Koestler's approach to Galileo may justly be said to have some serious weaknesses, especially since Galileo is not really a cosmology sleepwalker within his own scheme. Admittedly, Koestler's literary approach generates personal preferences and exaggerations. He obviously does not view kindly poor Copernicus who was indeed timid (what is wrong with intellectual timidity?) or Galileo, who surely deserves much of his criticism. Who can deny that Galileo disputed needlessly; unjustly took all of heaven to be his personal domain so as to accuse others of trespassing; that the entire argument over the Copernican theory was as if someone fought today tooth and nail for the steady-state as against the big-bang theory? Who does not believe today that a scientist 'places little reliance on persuading his opponent with rhetoric or driving him from the field with invective?' as James B. Conant says. (*On Understanding Science,* Yale Univ. Press, 1947, p. 7)

'Science is a process of fabricating a web of interconnected concepts and conceptual schemes arising from experiments and observations.' (Conant, *Modern Science and Modern Man.* Garden City, N.Y. 1955, p. 106.) Hence why fuss and fume and waste ten years of a rare mind over a futile issue? A theory is a scaffold to serve as platform for further experimentation. When rendered useless it is torn down and replaced by another. It is no object for combat or rage. Galileo's contributions to science lay in his turning the telescope skyward and dramatically revealing in a brief span the vast potential of the new tool to uncover hidden horizons (*The Starry Messenger,* 1609) and in his solving gloriously the problem of velocity and acceleration, a problem that gnawed at the minds of the keenest scientists for two thousand years with no solution. It was too difficult. His alone was the triumph. (*The New Sciences,* 1638.) A third contribution was his application of mathematical thinking to experimental data; in that Kepler preceded and surpassed him. Clearly, Galileo's championing of the Copernican theory, with its circular orbits, epicycles, wobbly precession and nine motions of the earth, had no scientific merit because no experimental use was to be made of it. Only Kepler used Copernicus with scientific justice and honour because it was he and his successors who proved its value. Yet Kepler was involved in no imbroglios, and Galileo was.

Koestler sees this, Santillana does not. The latter sees only heroes and villains who are so stupid that they need the aid of real 'thieves in the night'. Drake is exempt because elsewhere he publicly disavows his co-reviewer's penchant for sneakery as the key to tragedy (Ludovico Geymonat *Galileo Galilei*, New York, 1965, Appendices A and B). The difference in outlook between Koestler and Santillana is so great and so unbridgeable that the fury of the long review is inevitable. Yet it is improper to review a book without divulging what it is about, but plunge at once into invective with professorial haughtiness, as the *Isis* reviewers do. Santillana seems so obsessed with deceit that he practises some on his own. The very first quotation in the *Isis* review (for purposes of derision) is a textual falsification. Page 352 of THE SLEEPWALKERS, say Santillana and Drake, states that 'the intellectual giants of the scientific revolution *were only moral dwarfs*'. Koestler does not say that at all. He says: 'The intellectual giants of the scientific revolution were moral dwarfs. They were, of course, neither better nor worse than the average of their contemporaries. They were *moral dwarfs only in proportion* to their intellectual greatness.' What a difference the misquotation makes, which is apparently the reason for its existence.

The reviewers then proceed to present a list of indictments. First comes the popular eighteenth-century obligation to abuse Osiander for his introduction to Copernicus' *De Revolutionibus*. This ritual stems from the naivete, so brilliantly described by Conant, of those who view science in the light of 'eighteenth- and nineteenth-century misconceptions of scientific investigations'. They see science much like the work of 'the early explorers and map makers'. Their task was to uncover the hidden truth by 'improving man's accuracy of observation'. The rivers, mountains and bays lay there to be discovered and named. Science did just that. The atom, gene, electron, neutrino, positron, wave mechanics, non-Euclidean geometry lay hidden presumably until discovered as 'truth', a term used in *The Crime of Galileo* in 1955 as often as by Galileo in 1615. Hence our reviewers have no use for Koestler, whose notion of science is in line with the definitions given above and which apply to the Copernican theory as much as to Bohr's model of the atom, quantum mechanics, the uncertainty principle, complementarity, psychoanalysis and all social systems.

This is where Osiander's vision comes in. Copernicus probably believed his scheme to be 'real', for all it matters. Most people, except mathematicians, tend to reify abstract schemes. Since Koestler, like Duhem and others, fails to whip Osiander, off with his head! That this view is still prominent among many historians was seen at the XI International Congress of History of Science in Warsaw, 1965, where a summary was given of the only published study of Osiander's devotion to science and his view of the role of theory (Mark Graubard, 'Andreas Osiander: Lover of Science or Appeaser of its Enemies', *Science Education,* 48, 168–87, 1964). The audience of fifty or so historians, of the stripe of our *Isis* reviewers, were horrified, and responded with genuine rage. Admittedly the meeting took place in Communist Warsaw which attracted Soviet academics (who somehow escaped or survived Stalin's death camps), a sprinkling of American para-Leninists, a goodly sample of East Germans, and some British lumpen-bourgeois with Oxford degrees and New-Left leanings. Their overall outlook in science history was that of Brecht's play, *Galileo.* To them, too, THE SLEEPWALKERS was anathema, since their roots, both Marxist and rationalist, were in the nineteenth century.

The review in the *Scientific American* (1959, vol. 200, June, p. 187) by I. Bernard Cohen of Harvard University is of quite another genre. It is dignified, scholarly, and to the point. Cohen understands that 'Kepler makes an ideal subject for Koestler', and gives an excellent statement of THE SLEEPWALKERS' content and contributions, which, he says, are based on 'a solid job of research'. The last third of the review is devoted to Koestler's treatment of Copernicus and Galileo which Professor Cohen finds weak and 'unsympathetic'. Here again value judgements and emotional loyalties clash, as already mentioned, and some good points are made. Any sleepwalker's contribution, and Koestler's book is such, all too frequently bears roses as well as some thorns. But Koestler's contribution opens wide new windows into the nature of scientific pioneering and his technique of dissecting the creative mind in science has already borne fruit and is here to stay.

Bisociates: Artist and Scientist in The Act of Creation

Frank Barron

It is tempting at first to emphasize the hidden community that lies back of the very different countenances of art and of science, rather than to try to sharpen our sense of their divergence. Both, after all, are mind at work, and in a sense they are, like philosophy and religion, simply different positions or perspectives that mind in general occupies in the material cosmos. They are the ever-changing embodiments of mind as it imagines itself and the universe. This act of imagination is in response to the problem set by external reality: namely, to *construe* it, and to make the construction public. This is the common bond of science and art.

Yet indeed they are different, in their means and in their effects. They are bisociates in Koestler's sense of the term, for they come from afar to find their meeting ground. As a poet has put it, proudly, 'Poetry makes nothing happen; it exists in the valley of its saying . . .' (W. H. Auden). And again, 'A poem should be equal to, Not true . . . A poem should not mean, But be.' (Archibald MacLeish). Science by its method limits itself to appearance, but *about* appearances it seeks to say something both meaningful and true; and certainly some scientists pride themselves precisely on being able to make things happen. We are all by now only too painfully aware that of the things science can make happen, some are for good and some are for ill.

Pure science, one might reply, disdains consequences just as much as art does. The mathematicians of the left, as Silvan Tomkins has cogently argued,* view their science as pure play, creative play arising out of mind at its purest. Yet even pure mind may turn quite practical when the attached animal feels its survival threatened. Witness Einstein the radical pacifist when events required him to look Hitler in the eye. Suddenly pure science produced an explosion, and not for the first time, though this was bigger than the others and soon got harnessed to the biggest of all guns. Bullets to the moon is our scene today.

Yet what of art? Does it make nothing happen? Perhaps it makes science happen, sometimes if not always. Was Plato wholly amiss in his fear of the poet and artist as disturbances to the harmony of his *Republic*? Recall the phrase – 'let who will write a country's laws; I should rather write its songs'. And we need only remember the music of the 1960s and its appeal to youth to realize that the art of music can make things happen in the body politic. Bob Dylan not only tuned in to the weather that was 'a comin'', he changed the weather. He made the weather happen, or at least hurried it along.

But we might employ a less linear cause-and-effect metaphor and say simply that both science and art are part of a field of energy in which each continually acts upon the other. Think, for instance, of the interesting situation in science and in art at the end of the nineteenth century. Relativism was in the air, in painting, sculpture, the novel, music, poetry, as well as in mathematics, physics, physical chemistry, and biology. Henri Poincaré had antennae as sensitive as any poet's, surely; and in 1904 in his presidential address to the European Physical Society he called explicitly for 'a theory of relativity', with which Einstein was soon to oblige. And only five years earlier, Henry Adams had decided not to enter the twentieth century, preferring to put as bad a face

* Tomkins, Silvan, 'Left and right: a basic dimension in ideology and personality.' In *The Study of Lives,* edited by Robert W. White. Atherton Press, Menlo Park, Calif., 1963. pp. 388–411.

as possible upon the increasing complexity and contradiction, the dissolving order, of the modern world, He might almost have said, 'I'd rather be dead than relative', though of course he did gracefully live out his days to 1916, with nothing in the events of his last years to alter his verdict of 1900.

W. B. Yeats wrote, in *Nineteen Hundred and Nineteen*:

> O but we dreamed to mend
> Whatever mischief seemed
> To afflict mankind, but now
> That winds of winter blow
> Learn that we were crackpated when we dreamed.

> We, who seven years ago
> Talked of honour and of truth,
> Shriek with pleasure if we show
> The weasel's twist, the weasel's tooth.

The Great War, soon to be demoted to World War I, had shaken man's consciousness. This was not a war among or against pagans, this was a good Christian war. The control-of-consciousness business had long since been captured by Church and State, with art for ornamentation and science for the forging of instruments of power. But now more than a mere crack had appeared in the foundations. Though for most people it remained only in the background of their consciousness, the savage fact had revealed itself: insatiable intelligence in the form of science showed no sign of yielding in its assumption that there is a reason for everything *and that it must be found out, whatever the risk*; so it remained for other social institutions to seek to accommodate divided groups (nations, races, classes) with political or religious restraints upon aggression.

It would, of course, be a grave mistake to emphasize the potentially destructive effects of science at the expense of its great potential for human good. Art too may go either way, and art too may be very powerful. And in their essences, both art and science are mankind puzzling about the world and the self, and in their own ways doing something about the puzzle.

Although this too is inexact, science acts mostly upon the

object, and is objective in its methods, while art acts mostly upon the subject, and is subjective in its methods. Science supposes a nature that can best be understood through mathematics and rigorously applied common sense linked to imagination, while art supposes a nature that can best be understood (or better, its meaning evoked) through metaphor and intuition (in the sense of direct experience rather than ratiocination and proof).

If these remarks are valid as to the enterprises of art and of science, what might we expect should characterize their practitioners, as to abilities, personality, values, motives?

Here we may call empirical research to our aid. Even as Arthur Koestler was developing his monumental scholarly comprehension of the psychology of creativity through the history of ideas, the frontiers of knowledge in that area were slowly yielding to the psychometric batteries of a small army of workers in education and in cognitive and social psychology. THE ACT OF CREATION was published in 1963, and in the same year the proceedings of the US National Science Foundation's conferences on creativity, held at the University of Utah in the late 1950s, were published in the volume *Scientific Creativity,* edited by myself and Calvin W. Taylor of the University of Utah. My own work (*Creativity and Psychological Health*) reporting the results obtained by my colleagues and myself at the University of California, Berkeley, in extensive studies of creativity in outstanding contemporary mathematicians, scientists, writers, architects, and artists, appeared too in 1963. Koestler's remarkable integration of lessons to be learned from intellectual history proceeded almost entirely without recourse to the results of psychometric research and experiment, it may be added, though in certain of its major conclusions, as we shall see, it dovetails nicely with the empirical approach.

In the course of preparing an overview of established facts for a chapter in *Scientific Creativity,* I summarized the results of empirical research on the part of some eight investigators of the intellectual, motivational, and personality characteristics of productive scientists. By doing only a slight job of translation of terms from one theoretical system to another and then reducing the lot to common language, I was able to come up with the following list of traits found consistently in study after study. (These are *productive* scientists, let me emphasize, not necessarily creative or original scientists – of which, more later.)

1. A high degree of autonomy, self-sufficiency, self-direction.
2. A preference for mental manipulations involving things rather than people: a somewhat distant or detached attitude in interpersonal relations, and a preference for intellectually challenging situations rather than socially challenging ones.
3. High ego strength and emotional stability.
4. A liking for method, precision, exactness.
5. A preference for such defence mechanisms as repression and isolation in dealing with affect and instinctual energies.
6. A high degree of personal dominance but a dislike of personally toned controversy.
7. A high degree of control of impulse, amounting almost to over–control: relatively little talkativeness, gregariousness, impulsiveness.
8. A liking for abstract thinking, with considerable tolerance of cognitive ambiguity.
9. Marked independence of judgement, rejection of group pressures toward conformity in thinking.
10. Superior general intelligence.
11. An early, very broad interest in intellectual activities.
12. A drive toward comprehensiveness and elegance in explanation.
13. A special interest in the kind of 'wagering' which involves pitting oneself against uncertain circumstances in which one's own effort can be the deciding factor.

These characteristics do overlap to some extent with those of scientists who are not only productive in the convergent sense emphasized by J. P. Guilford and by Thomas Kuhn, but who are also original and divergent. In our work at the Institute of Personality Assessment and Research at the University of California, Berkeley, we found that the more original of our young scientists had these characteristics: (1) superior measured intelligence; (2) unusually unflappable independence of judgement and resistance to group-endorsed unsound opinions: (3) a strong need for order and for perceptual closure, combined with a resistance to premature closure and an interest in what may appear as contradictions, disorder and imbalance, or at least a very complex balance whose ordering principle is not immediately apparent; (4) an appreciation of the intuitive and non-rational elements in their own nature, going beyond being merely merciful towards lunatic aspects of their own thinking and approaching an embrace of the irrational in the service of novelty; and (5) a profound commitment to the search for aesthetic and philosophic meaning in all experience.

A consideration of these personal characteristics of creative scientists must be combined with an understanding of the nature of the scientific enterprise if one is to understand the bisociation of science and of art. Here is the final formulation of the scientific side of the equation in *Scientific Creativity*:

Scientific knowledge undergoes development as a living body in much the same way as human beings do: through alternating periods of crisis and of coalescence, diffusion and integration, revolution and consensus. The image of scientific advance as cumulative is not so apt as an image of it as 'development through periodic crisis which produces genuine divergence following periods of convergence.' It is precisely the point at which a strong and established consensus finds itself confronted with an unassimilable fact that the forces of revolution are set in motion. These forces, as in all revolutions, threaten the established order, and they turn the state, in this case the state of knowledge, in a radically new direction of development. Since the forces of revolution must be embodied in persons, what kind of person may serve as the vehicle for the change in thinking which must come? We would argue here that a person possessing the traits just described is the one most likely to be called to the task.

Briefly, let us consider the nature of those relationships:

1. The more highly developed a body of knowledge becomes, the more intelligence and capacity for discrimination and discipline is required for its mastery. The scientist who can respond creatively to crisis must therefore be of a high

order of intellectual ability and must be orderly, thorough, and disciplined in his acquisition of current knowledge.

2. As discoveries occur which cannot be assimilated to current conceptions of orderliness in nature, increasing effort must be made to understand the unordered and to find a new principle which will restore order. The person who pays close attention to what appears discordant and contradictory and who is challenged by such irregularities is therefore likely to be in the front ranks of the revolutionaries.

3. If such a person then embarks on the risky business of seeking and putting forth new theories, he must be prepared to stand his ground against outcries from the proponents of the previous, but in his view no longer tenable, consensus. He must possess independence of judgement and hold to his own opinion in the face of a consensus which does not fit all the facts.

4. Such a creative person in science must be passionately committed to his own cosmology and must respect his private intuitions, even when they seem unreasonable to himself; he must be able to open himself to sources of information which others deny to themselves.

5. Through such persons, who are embodiments of the creative process in nature, science remains alive and open to novelty; a scientific enterprise or organized scientific activity which does not allow free play to its own creative possibilities will shortly become moribund.

So much for science and scientists. What then of the characteristics of artists and the nature of art?

Over the years I have been able to compare many groups of artists, established masters as well as students, with scientists and with other non-artists of similar general intelligence, educational and cultural level, and social class. And within groups of artists I have been able to separate the more from the less creative (not without some risk to my life were the classifications revealed). The artists who bravely took part in these studies included writers as well as painters, sculptors, and dancers. Most of my own findings as well as those of some other investigators are summarized in my 1972 volume, *Artists in the Making*. They are expressed there in terms of standardized psychological tests, for the most part; once again let me translate the results into simpler language.

In terms of adjectival self-descriptions, here is how a group of student artists described themselves as compared with graduate students in the sciences (unselected for creativity):

> Spontaneous rather than quiet
> Hasty rather than deliberate
> Temperamental rather than pleasant
> Uninhibited rather than unassuming
> Original rather than logical
> Dreamy rather than rational
> Imaginative rather than clear-thinking
> Carefree rather than responsible
> Intuitive rather than logical
> Pleasure-seeking rather than earnest
> Daring rather than cautious
> Complex rather than simple

Evidence from the biographies of eminent scientists and artists who lived during the time span A.D. 1450 to A.D. 1850 reveal a somewhat similar pattern. In the famous studies by Lewis Terman and his associates at Stanford University, an effort was made through systematic coding of biographical data to estimate the IQs and describe the 'personal and moral qualities' of historical geniuses. In Volume II of Terman's *Genetic Studies of Genius* we find a classification of the 301 geniuses studied by Terman's student, Catherine Cox, into eleven subgroups; among them, in addition to scientists and artists, were 'imaginative writers' (poets, novelists, and dramatists). The groups were characterized in terms of sixty-seven personal and moral qualities in addition to intellectual ones.

The picture of scientists is consistent with what we have found through psychological testing in research with contemporary scientists, though it is less complete. The average IQ is estimated as probably greater than 170. When compared with all other subgroups, the scientific geniuses were disproportionately high in 'intellectual traits', 'strength or force of character', 'balance', and 'activity'. They were disproportionately low in 'excitability', 'sensitiveness to criticism' and various 'social' traits. Overall, they were described as 'the strongest, most forceful, and best balanced' group in the study.

Artists, by contrast, were notably high in 'aesthetic feeling', 'desire to excel', 'belief in their own powers', 'the degree to which they work with distant objects in view', and 'originality of ideas'. They were rated as below the average of eminent men as a whole in their 'average goodness'(!), and their average IQ was estimated to be about 135.

Imaginative writers were judged to have an average IQ of 165. Compared with their fellow geniuses, they were notably high in 'imaginativeness and aesthetic feeling', and, in a quaintly worded variable, 'amount of work spent on pleasures'.They were also higher than eminent men in general on 'originality of ideas', 'strength of memory', and 'keenness of observation'. They were significantly lower in 'soundness of common sense' and 'the degree to which action and thought are dependent on reason'.

Studies of young contemporary artists by standardized psychological testing may be summarized as follows:

Psychiatrically speaking—eccentric, unconventional, hypomanic, moody, anxious; if male, somewhat feminine, if female, somewhat masculine.

In interests—like artists (as might be expected), and also like musicians, authors, journalists, advertising men, psychologists, physicians, and lawyers.

In social adjustment—flexible, impulsive, psychologically minded, poised, confident, self-accepting, independent, not concerned about making a good impression.

In personal philosophy—independent, not conventionally religious, complex, not conservative either socially, politically, or religiously.

In abilities—strongly visual, fluent, original, able to synthesize impressions from several sensory modalities in problem-solving.

Once again, as in the case of science and young scientists, the fit to the nature of the enterprise is evident in these young artists. For what is art but the expression in gesture and image, in picture and sound and shaped form, of the felt world, of the experience of existence of the single individual, whether alone or in society? Art is singular vision, communicated so that all may see if the all are lucky, or at least one other if the artist is not altogether unlucky. It requires intensity, freedom from the blinkers of convention, daring, courage to burn the conceptual boats and strike into new territory with no hope of going back; all in a spirit of zest and appreciation, however sombre the vision, churlish the manner, anxious the mood, or doomed the voyage.

But the imaginative writer is an artist too, though words alone are his means for calling forth images and symbols and uniting them in dramatic themes and scenes. The measure of his original-ity will be the elegance of fit of evoked associations whose initial remoteness in common sense merit their being called bisociation. Bisociation as Koestler defines it in THE ACT OF CREATION is not merely an association of flat and pallid items of information, however remote, but rather the complex interlocking of matrices of meaning in an uncommon marriage. It is in this sense of the term that the community of science and art may be understood. In Koestler himself we find this unusual conjunction, for as novelist he has shown himself a great artist and as psychological theoretician he has exhibited great scholarship, an original and open mind, and an immensely detailed balancing of evidence and theory from the physical and natural sciences as well as from psychology.

Koestler as artist has had as much influence on my own career as Koestler as psychologist. When I entered the university in the Fall of 1938 it had never crossed my mind to become a psycholo-gist. My interests then were in philosophy and literature and history. But in the summer of 1941 psychology came and got me, though I had never had an academic course in it. I was spending the holiday months between my junior and senior years in college working as an attendant in what in those days was known as an insane asylum. I had been assigned to a locked back ward, on a work schedule of thirteen hours a day, seven days out of every eight. Most of the time I was the only worker on the ward, and my duties included changing of bed linens, cleaning of latrines, getting patients out of bed and dressed for the day, maintaining discipline on the ward and on the way to and from the dining hall, and even such unexpected sundry duties as barbering, showering, and serving as valet to patients who were to receive visitors. In brief, I got to know some 100 severely psychotic men very well that summer. They were a frightening mystery to me at the start, but in important ways they seemed not much different from myself at the end, while we all remained outwardly unchanged. Perhaps that should be the frightening mystery.

Meanwhile, in the evenings I was doing a lot of reading, and the book that most engaged my imagination that summer was DARKNESS AT NOON. I picked it up in the hospital library only because of its title, for I had never heard of it. The title image is, of course, a bisociation. The power of that image lies not only in the unusual juxtaposition of light and dark but in its universality and and in the primitive sense of dread it evokes: the sun eclipsed at noon; Earth's promise taken back; the light of the mind swallowed up in shadow; the young lying dead or maimed; the self in solitary confinement; the rosebush deflowered by a summer freeze; a rape of virginity; the oasis found dry. Darkness had fallen across the lives in that hospital ward where I spent my days. Was it worth more than a shrug? For thus had DARKNESS AT NOON ended, as Rubashov lay dying in the corridor – a shrug, a shrug of eternity. Yes, I thought, it was worth more, at least from me, and when I returned to school in the Fall I changed my academic course and prepared myself for advanced study in the mental sciences.

When next I encountered the work of Arthur Koestler I was already a graduate student in psychology at Berkeley, my own war service behind me and the choice of where to engage myself in professional psychology very much before me. Once again a work of Koestler's came to my hand by chance. INSIGHT AND OUTLOOK happened to be left on the library table by another student, and I picked it up and began reading. As events were to prove, it was Koestler's intellectual preamble to his major theoretical opus, THE ACT OF CREATION. The basic idea of bisociation was already there, as well as its link to metaphor. The book dealt too with wit and humour, the flash of insight, the resolving power of paradox. Its psychology was not like the psychology I had been learning, but I recognized Koestler as a fellow of mine in some remote way, and I felt free then as I do now in saying that we are both psychologists.

Yet to some writers it seems a paradox in itself that a creative artist should look both outside and inside to concern himself with the psychology of the act of creation. Poets have been known to speak of the process of intellectual analysis of the creation of a poem as 'slitting the nightingale's throat'. What reason is there for an artist to turn to analysis?

At the risk of claiming too much for my own preoccupation in psychology, I would answer that inquiry into the process of creativity through both objective and subjective engagement with it is transcendent of the limitations both of science and of art. Psychic creation is a special case of the process of generation of novelty in all of nature. And it alone of the many aspects of creation is accessible directly to the creating agent. Science and art bisociate in the psychology of creativity. If, that is, they find the right mind to cohabit in.

REFERENCES

Auden, W. H., *The collected poetry of W. H. Auden*, p. 50 (from *In memory of W. B. Yeats*, pp. 48–51), New York, Random House, 1945.

Barron, F., *Creativity and psychological health*, Princeton, New Jersey, D. Van Nostrand Company, 1963.

Barron, F., *Artists in the making*, New York, Seminar Press, 1972.

Barron F., and Taylor, C. W. (Eds.), *Scientific creativity*, pp. 387–8, New York, John Wiley and Sons, 1963.

MacLeish, A., Untitled poem in *A new anthology of modern poetry*, S. Rodman (Ed.), New York, The Modern Library, 1938.

White, R. W., *The study of lives*. Menlo Park, California, Atherton Press, 1963.

Yeats, W. B., *The collected poems of W. B. Yeats*, pp. 206–7, New York, The Macmillan Company, 1951.

Arthur Koestler and Biological Thought

W. H. Thorpe

Arthur Koestler's writings on scientific subjects are unique in several respects. The very fact that he is not himself a research worker but is at the same time immensely well informed, enables him to bring a refreshingly new and lively assessment of problems both old and new. Coupled with this his extraordinary historical erudition (so wonderfully displayed in THE SLEEPWALKERS) extends equally into the arts and the humanities. He seems to have read everything and nearly always to succeed in extracting the kernel of essential significance from every controversy, trend and argument which he discusses. Added to this his outstanding powers as a novelist and a student of humour and his uncanny ability to find *le mot juste* makes everything he writes scintillate with life. Even though a scientist may disagree with some of the detail regarding his own specialism I would say that no scientist, particularly one with real interest in the history and philosophy of his subject, can fail to get profit from reading him.

It is my aim in this chapter to consider and to attempt to evaluate those of his writings which deal primarily with the behavioural sciences (psychology, physiological psychology and ethology) and the philosophy of biology, particularly its evolutionary aspects. This means that I shall be dealing primarily with THE ACT OF CREATION (1964): THE GHOST IN THE MACH-

INE (1967): THE CASE OF THE MIDWIFE TOAD (1971) and to a lesser extent THE ROOTS OF COINCIDENCE (1972). I shall attempt to extract from these the main topics around which his writings centre and to evaluate his views, as far as I can, in to light of present day scientific opinion. I think one can say at the outset that, controversial though his views often are, recent developments in scientific knowledge tend to confirm most of them.

The ACT OF CREATION seems to be primarily motivated by his revulsion at the blinkered barrenness of some of the dominant trends in academic psychology and the philosophy of psychology, characteristic of the last fifty years or so. The first of these is, of course, Behaviourism, the primarily American School of psychology virtually founded by J. B. Watson. According to this, the behaviour of organisms, including animals and men, comprises the whole contents of psychology. It renounces all mental concepts and all ideas, innate urges or 'instincts' and seeks to explain all by a theory of a mechanical compounding of stimuli, based originally upon the results of Thorndike, and of Pavlov. B. F. Skinner is generally regarded as the present day leader of the behaviourist school.

Thorndike's main studies consisted in placing kittens in 'a state of utter hunger' in puzzle boxes which could be opened from inside by pressing on a lever or manipulating some other form of catch device. The boxes were so designed that it was in any case impossible for the animal inside to perceive the way in which the release mechanism acted; the result was that when food was placed outside the box yet in full view, the kitten would make wild scrabblings; until sooner or later it accidentally pressed the lever and escaped to get the food. As a result of such a successful accident the kitten was more likely to pay attention to the part of the cage where the lever was situated on the next trial, and so over a number of trials began to learn how to open the box. Thus, however intelligent, it was impossible that the kitten could ever solve the problem by insight or understanding but only, on the first occasion, by a lucky accident. So it not infrequently happened that experiments of this nature, far from revealing such mental capacities and intelligence as the creature may have, actually prevent these being displayed: creating, in fact, an experimental moron.

In the early days of behaviourism the work of Pavlov became known for the first time outside Russia and the Russian experiments on the conditioning of reflexes (e.g., the attachment of fairly stereotyped responses like salivations to new stimuli, such as the ringing of a bell) provided what seemed a neat and a scientific way of accounting for the process of learning. The Pavlovian technique did indeed become of immense importance as a means of studying the perceptive ability of animals; this fact is universally acknowledged: but as a general theory of behavior it was woefully inadequate. Reflex conditioning methods have indeed their uses in investigating the behaviour of man – we all know that we can often be irrationally conditioned to produce a particular response in a particular situation. But when the system is applied to the nature of man as a general theory, then man becomes reduced to a conditioned automaton. Once this position is accepted a strictly deterministic philosophy is apt to gain sway. So Koestler argues that there are only two alternatives left: (*i*) to seek refuge in dreamlike states, (*ii*) to break out of one's mental cage and display insight.

In this way Koestler is led on to creativity, conscious and unconscious; and so we come to consider evolution as a creative mechanism. From this we proceed to the consideration of creativity in both science and in art.

In THE GHOST IN THE MACHINE (p. 138) Koestler argues very cogently for the view that the creativeness of man probably results from the combination of two hitherto unrelated ideas or concepts, in such a manner as to reveal their overlap. So a new concept is born. As in art, so in science; a new inspiration is achieved. A distinguished physicist, P. W. Anderson (*Science*, 177, 393–6, 1972), argues that when, in scientific research, further microscopic analysis fails us, we need 'some combination of inspiration, analysis and synthesis'. As I have argued elsewhere (W. H. Thorpe, *Animal Nature and Human Nature*, 1974), theoretical physicists are among the most intelligent and imaginative scientists of our day and much of their strength comes from their ability to hold in mind at the same time two apparently contradictory and incompatible ideas. Koestler extends this very effectively in THE GHOST IN THE MACHINE (p. 196) where he points out that the verification of a discovery comes *after* the creative act itself. It is for the scientist, as well as the artist, a leap in the dark; and the greatest mathematicians and physicists have confessed that at such decisive moments they have often been guided, not by logic, but by a sense of beauty which they were unable to define. He goes on to claim that in art the experience of truth, however subjective, *must* be present for the experience of beauty to arise.

Another point of great importance, which I think can be amply confirmed, is that creativity often starts where language ends. I myself would put this slightly differently and say that creative ideas are basically non-linguistic. There is massive evidence from animal behaviour to suggest this. I might mention the fact that birds can 'count' in the sense that it is possible to train them to react solely to the *number* of discrete units in a pattern presented, while ignoring all the other features. In other words the understanding of 'number' up to about 'seven' has been fully demonstrated by Otto Koehler in animals which have no language in anything like our sense. And finally another point in which recent animal behaviour studies have strongly supported Arthur Koestler is the demonstration that it is primarily the investigative or exploratory drive in animals which is the motivation for much of their learning. In the 'classic' behaviouristic experiments this exploratory drive was severely limited if not excluded altogether: and again one created an experimental moron. In a sense I agree with Arthur Koestler that 'the motivation for learning is to learn'.

EVOLUTION AS A CREATIVE MECHANISM

Although this topic is dealt with to some extent in THE ACT OF CREATION, Arthur's main discussion of this is reserved for THE GHOST IN THE MACHINE where it is developed into a discussion of the human predicament and the pathology of the human mind.

These subjects are, of course, highly complex and Arthur starts one of his chapters with a delightful dictum of Poul Anderson, 'I have yet to see any problem, however complicated, which when you look at it the right way did not become still more complicated.' This is, of course, a direct reversal of the famous canon of Lloyd Morgan who argued that we should always adopt a theory which is lower in the psychological scale than one which is more elaborate. When Lloyd Morgan was writing, in the later nineteenth century, this dictum was of great value as a corrective to the anthropocentric and anecdotal descriptions of animal behaviour which were so common up to that time.

Passing to the consideration of evolution as a theme with variations, Koestler quotes Professor Waddington to the effect that 'to suppose that the evolution of the wonderfully adaptive biological mechanisms has depended only on a section out of a haphazard set of variations, each produced by blind chance, is like suggesting that if we went on throwing bricks together in heaps, we should eventually be able to choose ourselves the most desirable house'. And he argues that if we only have twenty factors governing the growth and development of organisms, which is still a modest estimate for the evolution of a complex organ, 'the odds against their simultaneous alteration by chance alone become absurd, and instead of scientific explanations, we should be *trading in miracles*'. Although he castigates the ingrained conservatism of many biologists he rightly attributes it to the understandable fault of temperament of scientists – that they tend not to ask themselves questions until they can see the rudiments of an answer in their minds. Embarrassing questions tend to remain unasked or if asked, to be answered rudely. At this point we might quote the profound remark of the American biologist George Wald, which Koestler himself brings in at a later stage. 'The great questions are those which an intelligent child asks, and, getting no answers, stops asking.' And we call that education!

Now Arthur, of course, sees that, whatever geneticists and biologists may at times have thought, there is no necessity whatever to suppose that all the variations produced in the course of the progressive adaptation of any animal or human stock are completely due to 'chance'. The very fact that an organism or a group of animals has taken the first steps along a certain line of development, has developed a certain type of structure and physiology, already means that its future potential is limited. No conceivable mutations can turn an insect grub into a tadpole nor a mouse into a man. Though it is clear that Mendelian mutations are random in the sense that most of them are lethal to the organism and nearly all deleterious in the short term, it does not imply that absolutely anything can happen at the touch of a new mutation.

At this stage Koestler goes into the topic of what is known as 'internal selection' and shows how in fact selection of a kind is proceeding right from the earliest stages and that before a mutation has a chance of being submitted to the Darwinian tests of survival in the external environment, it must have passed the tests of 'internal selection' for its physical, chemical and biological fitness. He points out that one must remember that an organ like an eye is not simply a collection of elements, such as a retina, a lens, an iris and so on, which we put together and which happens to fit. It is something which is gradually formed while the adult animal is developing from the egg; and as the eye forms, different parts influence one another. This means that there is no reason why a chance mutation should not affect the whole organ in a harmonious way and there is a reasonable possibility that it might improve it. He, of course, agrees that there is no doubt that Darwinian selection is a powerful force; and that in between the chemical changes of a gene and the appearance of the finished product as a newcomer on the evolutionary stage, there is a whole hierarchy of internal processes at work which impose strict limitations on the range of possible mutations and thus considerably reduce the importance of the chance factor.

Previously Koestler discusses the whimsical suggestion of Eddington that, given sufficient time, an army of monkeys strumming at random on typewriters would eventually, completely by chance, write all the sonnets of Shakespeare! This is strictly true; but it would require far longer than the history of the universe for a reasonable probability that it could happen. Koestler points out that we might say that in fact the monkeys work at typewritters which the manufacturers have programmed to print only syllables which exist in our language but not nonsense syllables. If a nonsense syllable occurs, the machine will automatically erase it. He says, 'To pursue the metaphor, we would have to populate the higher levels of the hierarchy with proof readers and then editors, whose task is no longer elimination but correction, self repair and coordination – as in the example of the mutated eye.'

From here he goes on to consider (THE GHOST IN THE MACHINE, pp. 135 and 137) the appallingly difficult problem of the evolution and inheritance of homologous organs. This topic, which is glibly dealt with in elementary textbooks of biology and which was thought to be easily explained on the classical genetic theory, has, as a result of recent developments, come to seem virtually impossible of explanation. He quotes Sir Alister Hardy. 'The concept of homology is absolutely fundamental to what we are talking about when we speak of evolution, yet in truth', Hardy adds wistfully, 'we cannot explain it at all in terms of present day biological theory.' What seems to be happening is that although the organ remains constant in structure and design throughout countless aeons of evolution the gene-pool, which is responsible for its development and control, is changing all the time. So it seems we have a changing genetical organization which ensures unchanging results! I myself raised this problem with Waddington (see BEYOND REDUCTIONISM, p. 392) and received what I think one might call a dusty answer. Koestler (THE GHOST IN THE MACHINE, p. 137) says; 'The only way out of this cul-de-sac seems to be to substitute for genetic atomism, which has so drastically broken down, the concept of genetic micro-hierarchy with its own built-in rules that permit a great amount of variation but only in limited directions and *on a limited number of themes.*'

Arthur then develops one of his marvellously learned and eminently readable accounts of the history of biological philosophy; and proceeding *via* fantastic similarities in structure and adaptations between two entirely different groups of animals, the marsupials in Australia and mammals in the rest of the world, returns to sum up with the words, 'The evolution of life is a game played according to fixed rules which limit its possibilities but leave sufficient scope for a limitless number of variations.' That is to say, evolution is neither a free for all nor the execution of a rigidly predetermined computer programme. 'It could be compared to a musical composition whose possibilities are limited by the rules of harmony and the structure of the diatonic scale – which, however, permit an inexhaustible number of original creations.' Then passing to the problems of the dramatist he points out that not even Shakespeare could invent an original plot. He says that Goethe quoted with approval the Italian dramatist Carlo Gozzi, according to whom there are only thirty-six tragic situations. Arthur adds that Goethe himself thought that there were probably even less; but their exact number is a well kept secret among writers of fiction! He sums it all up in a characteristic phrase. 'Evolution is not a tale told by an idiot, but an epic recited by a stutterer.'

From this point he returns to the problems of directiveness and the purposer and so makes renewed contact with the problem of learning. He stresses very effectively the importance of behavioural trends in helping to maintain a directiveness in an evolutionary stock (a point which I myself have emphasized in my 1974 book) and quotes with approval a remark by the ethologist Dr R. F. Ewer, 'Behaviour is always a jump ahead of structure'.

His discussions on Lamarckism are mainly reserved for the later book THE CASE OF THE MIDWIFE TOAD, but as Arthur is such a strong supporter of ethology as against behaviourism it seems worth mentioning a point that I have only recently fully realized. This is that the concepts of ethology really arose in France fifty years or more before they surfaced anywhere else and came to their first climax in the discussions at the Académie des Sciences in Paris between Étienne Geoffroy-Saint-Hilaire and the great Baron Cuvier – discussions which developed from the ideas of Lamarck. The main point of Lamarck's argument was, of course, that the possibility of animal evolution rests upon the inherited effects of use and disuse. It follows that it is the effect of use and disuse which are crucial in the adaptation of an organism to its environment. This at once raises the question as to what causes the use and disuse. The provisional answer is, naturally, the predilections, power of choice and 'inventiveness' of the animal itself. What then causes the inventiveness? In 1830 this was, of course, very much in doubt and has remained so until recently. But the argument of Étienne Geoffroy-Saint-Hilaire was that the close study of what we now call the 'ethology' of animals (that is the study of the capabilities, together with a detailed inventory of the actions, of animals in the wild under natural conditions) was essential before we could hope to understand how these could have become inherited. Cuvier, being essentially a creationist, was vehemently against evolution or any kind of 'transformisme' saying that we must stick to facts that can be obtained in the laboratory and the dissecting room. He was, of course, wrong, and Étienne right; but it took the best part of a century before this was fully realized and the science of ethology emerged as a fully autonomous discipline.

DIRECTIVENESS AND PURPOSIVENESS IN EVOLUTION

Arthur Koestler, of course, shares with the great majority of biologists (see several of the papers in *Studies in Philosophical Biology*, eds. Ayala and Dobzhansky, 1974) the feelings of awe and wonder and the recognition of beauty and value experienced when we look at the evolutionary process. But a great debate still centres around the problem as to how far this process can be the expression of the natural selection of random variations and how far some sort of direction is necessary. I think everyone agrees with Dobzhansky that natural selection puts a restraint on chance and makes evolution directional. Moreover selection increases the adaptiveness of the population to its environments. Many biologists, though by no means all, would agree with Koestler that Whyte's (1965) 'internal selection' (discussed above) is in a sense different from the natural selection operating upon organisms from without.

But there is another point, which has recently become clear, that helps us to draw a line between change in the physical world of atoms, molecules, stars and planets and change as demonstrated in the world of living things. In the latter we find storage of information; with this information store then issuing *instructions,* which guide the behaviour of the organisms in all its parts. Indeed it is now seen with considerable clarity that organisms are self-programming and that this feature can give perhaps the most satisfactory distinction between living and non-living. And this result and the biological concept, of the programme being something different from the purely physical idea of the programme, is fundamental; and we can now point to an actual programme 'tape' in the heart of the cell, namely the DNA molecule. Even more remarkable is the fact that the programmed activity which we find in living nature will not merely determine the way in which the organism will react to its environment; it actually controls the structure of the organism and its replication, *including the replication of the programmes themselves.* This is what we mean by saying (a statement due originally to Professor Christopher Lorguet-Higgins, that can hardly be reiterated too often) that *life is not merely programmed activity but self-programmed activity* (Thorpe, W. H., 1974, p. 26). This implies, of course, that the organism, even when only looked at as a physico-chemical mechanism is, obviously in some degree and often a very large degree, directive.

It is obvious also that similar directiveness is the characteristic of man-made machines. We can legitimately ask what a man-made machine is for; we can also legitimately ask what a particular biological structure – a limb, a feather, or a particular 'nucleus' in the brain – is for. This ties in with Karl Popper's recent conclusion that the idea of problem solving is quite foreign to the subject matter of non-biological sciences but seems to have emerged together with life. Even though there may be something like natural selection at work prior to the origin of life we cannot say that for an atomic nucleus 'survival' is a 'problem' in any sense of the term. Nor can we say that crystals have 'problems' of growth or propagation or survival. But life, as Popper says, is faced with the problem of survival from the very beginning. Indeed we can describe life, if we like, as problem solving; and living organisms as the only problem solving complexes in the universe. But it does not seem to make sense to ask of any part of the purely inanimate world, 'What is this for?'

Purpose is, naturally, an idea arising from our own personal knowledge of our aims and intentions. The word has many overtones of meaning but it involves three basic components. First, an inward awareness or sensibility – what might be called, 'having internal perception'; second, an awareness of self, of one's own existence. Third, the idea of consciousness includes that of unity; that is to say, it implies in some rather vague sense, the fusion of the totality of the impressions, thoughts and feelings which make up a person's conscious being into a single whole. As the great physiologist Karl Lashley put it, the process of awareness implies a belief in an internal perceiving agent – an 'I' or 'self' which does the perceiving. This leads inevitably to the conclusion that this agent selects and unifies elements into a unique field of consciousness.

Karl Popper (*Objective Knowledge, an Evolutionary Approach* 1972; see also 1974) agrees with, I think, the majority of students of animal behaviour in that there can be little doubt that many animals possess consciousness and that some can be, at times, even conscious of a problem. Nor can there be much doubt that consciousness in animals has some evolutionary function; and can from the viewpoint of natural selection, be regarded as if it were a bodily organ. Of course, there are many philosophers who fully deserve the sharp and searing wit which Arthur Koestler has directed against them.* Such philosophers and behaviourists tend to deny the existence of consciousness altogether and indeed one can say that in some circles, at any rate until recently, such a position has been quite fashionable. As Karl Popper says, 'A theory of the non-existence of consciousness cannot be taken any more seriously than a theory of the non-existence of matter'.

---

* See the passage on p. 202 of THE GHOST IN THE MACHINE where he deals with the Oxford School of philosophy (though, alas, not peculiar to Oxford) which treats thought as a disease, and with others who kept snickering about the horse in the locomotive, whilst superciliously ignoring those great savants whose life is devoted to the anatomy, physiology and surgery of the brain and who have become increasingly converted to the opposite view.

These theories, he says, solve the problem of the relationship between body and mind by a radical simplification. It is the denial either of body or of mind; but I agree with Popper that such a solution is, to say the least, too cheap – perhaps one should rather say 'too expensive'. In fact there seems to be no prospect whatever of reducing the human consciousness of self and the creativeness of the human mind to any other explanatory level (see also A. C. Ewing, *Value and Reality*, London, 1973). In fact the origin of consciousness is as mysterious as the origin of life itself. It is remarkable to find two people as different in their background, their training and their approach as Karl Popper and Jacques Monod,* the one a philosopher and the other a molecular biologist, in total agreement over this point. That is to say, they are both clearly convinced of the present impossibility of reduction from the living to the non-living and from the conscious mentality to the non-mental aspect and organisation of life.

This is a big step in favour of Arthur's prolonged campaign against reductionism; of which the Alpbach Symposium (which he organized and above all catalysed in his own inimitable way) is his lasting memorial in this field. Karl Popper indeed goes much further and believes that the reduction of biology to chemistry or of chemistry to physics; or the reduction to physiology of the conscious or subconscious experiences which we may ascribe to

* Monod (1971, *Chance and Necessity*) has suggested that the combination of processes which must have occurred to produce life in inanimate matter is so exremely improbable that its occurrence indeed may have been a unique event. In addition we have the extraordinary problem that the genetic code is without any biological function unless and until it is translated, that is, unless it leads to the synthesis of the proteins whose structure is laid down by the code. But the machinery by which the cell translates the code consists of at least fifty macromolecular components which are themselves coded in DNA. Thus the code cannot be translated except by using certain products of its translation. As Sir Karl Popper comments, 'This constitutes a really baffling circle: a vicious circle, it seems, for any attempt to form a model or theory of the genesis of the genetic code.' This undreamed of breakthrough of molecular biology, far from solving the problem of the origin of life, has made it, in Sir Karl Popper's opinion, a greater riddle than it was before. It may indeed prove an impenetrable barrier to science and a block which resists all attempts to reduce biology to chemistry and physics.

animals, and still more, the reduction of human consciousness itself and the creativeness of the human mind to animal experience – are all projects the complete success of which seems most unlikely if not impossible (1974 in *Studies in Philosophical Biology*).

Of course no one, and certainly not Arthur Koestler, would argue that reduction is valueless in science. Quite to the contrary, it is of immense value; and as Popper suggests, scientists have to be reductionists in the sense that nothing is as great a success in science as successful reduction. Indeed it is, perhaps, the most successful form conceivable of all scientific explanations since it results in the identification of the unknown with the known. Moreover, Popper argues that scientists have to be reductionists in their methods – either naive or else more or less critical reductionists, sometimes desperate critical reductionists, since, as he points out, hardly any major reduction in science has ever been completely successful. There is almost always an unresolved residue left by even the most successful attempt at reduction. Again Popper contends that there do not seem to be any reasons in favour of philosophical reductionism. Yet, never the less, working scientists must continue to attempt reductions because we learn an immense amount even from unsuccessful attempts at reduction and problems left open in this way belong to the most valuable intellectual possessions of science. In other words, emphasis on scientific failure can do us a lot of good. I have discussed these and other views of reductionism in my recent book (Thorpe, 1974) but Karl Popper's recent chapter ('Scientific Reduction and the Essential Incompleteness of all Science') comprising pp. 260–84 of *Studies in the Philosophy of Biology* (eds. Ayala, F. J., and Dobzhansky, T., 1974) is essential reading, for anyone concerned with any of these problems.

HIERARCHY AS THE BASIC CONCEPT CONCERNING THE
NATURE OF LIVING ORGANISATION:

A Fundamental Principle of Living Nature

The scientific problem with which Arthur Koestler has been most consistently and actively concerned is that of hierarchy. I do not propose to enter into this topic in detail here for two reasons: one, because I think that almost all theoretical and philosophical biologists either already agree with him or are coming round to his conclusions. Two, the matter is of considerable complexity and to discuss it fully would take a great deal of space.

I think there is no doubt whatever that the idea of hierarchy is fundamental to the understanding of both evolution and of the composition of organisms. The word hierachy is generally used to refer to a complex system in which each of the sub-systems is subordinated by an authority-relation to the system to which it belongs. This is to say that each of the sub-systems has a boss which is the immediate subordinate of the ·boss of the system. Arthur has himself worked this out with precision and clarity in his own contribution to the Alpbach Symposium and one cannot better what he says. As he puts it, just because reality is hierarchically arranged so the process of continuing analysis, which is what reductionism is about, can be balanced, eliminated, and to some extent superseded by this very hierarchical principle, according to which we focus our attention on the relationship between the whole and its parts (which Koestler refers to not as parts, but as sub-wholes and 'holons'). These, according to the hierarchical principle, are 'Janus-faced' in that when seen from above they appear and act in some respect as parts; seen from below they appear and act in some respect as wholes.

It is highly significant that amongst all the contributors to the Symposium edited by Ayala and Dobzhansky (which is subtitled *Reduction and Related Problems*) not a single one, whether he claimed to be reductionist, or anti-reductionist or both, appeared to have any doubt that hierarchical organization is an essential feature of living matter. Thus Dr Henryk Skolimowski refers on p. 212 to Platts' contention, which he shares with Michael Polanyi and Arthur Koestler, that acts of hierarchical growth are never rationally deducible from the smaller system structures which precede them. He also reaches another conclusion which is that hierarchical complexity in living organisms is equivalent to non-reducibility. 'When we *comprehend* the function of these organisms in terms of complexity and hierarchy we *invariably* go beyond the physiochemical rudiments of these organisms.'

THE OPEN SYSTEM

It is interesting to take the hierarchical position to its extremes and see what happens. Koestler discusses this particularly in Chapter 14 of THE GHOST IN THE MACHINE. In considering the hierarchical situation in an animal it is natural to assume that at the very top there is a governing level where the Janus-faced attributes no longer hold; that is to say, that the top level is a whole to the level below but is not a 'part' to anything above. What do we suppose in the case of a human being? A strict determinist would, of course, *say* that the situation is the same as in any animal – even a flatworm or a maggot. But no determinist, if he is outside a lunatic asylum, can actually believe that! Whatever one's philosophical convictions, in everyday life it is impossible to carry on without the implicit belief in personal responsibility; and responsibility implies freedom of choice (THE GHOST IN THE MACHINE, p. 214). Most neurophysiologists, however mechanistic their methodology of work may be, must (unless they refuse to think about the problem at all) agree with Professor MacKay that 'our belief that we are morally free in making our choices, so far from being contradictable, *has no valid alternative* from the standpoint of even the most deterministic pre-Heinsenberg physics . . .' Whatever anyone of us may say we all believe that our own consciousness is a primary datum; which would be nonsense to doubt because it is the platform on which our own doubting is built (D. MacKay in *Brain and Conscious Experience,* ed. J. C. Eccles, 1966). We cannot, of course, say what consciousness is, and we obviously cannot deny its existence; but we can and do, as Arthur Koestler suggests, say whether there is more or less of it and we can often say something about its 'fineness of texture'. Koestler suggests that the hierarchical approach turns the absolute distinction of the dualistic separation into mind and body into a serialist one because the hierarchy is always open-ended at the top. This, however, leads to complications which I cannot deal with here but which Koestler will, we hope, adumbrate later.

So we leave serialism here (it features largely in the CASE OF THE MIDWIFE TOAD and in THE ROOTS OF CONCIDENCE), but will for the moment stick to the dualism of mind and body. I was once asked how it is that I can believe that conscious phenomena can *steer* physiological brain processes; for this would surely imply that the law of the conservation of energy is infringed, because the gapless flow of causal, that is to say material, events in the brain would give additional impulses and the kinetic or potential energy would increase. It was thus suggested that I was regarding consciousness as a kind of supplementary physiological process. I answered this (*Studies in the Philosophy of Biology*, p. 137) by saying, first, that the laws of thermodynamics now bear a very different aspect to that which they presented fifty or more years ago. Secondly I argued it is now clear that such laws as these may break down at the frontiers of physical science – for instance they certainly cannot be relied upon to apply under conditions that are obtained in collapsed stars subject to hitherto unimagined pressures and in the neighbourhood of 'Black Holes'. And, if so why not at the 'mental' frontier?

Both Jacques Monod and Karl Popper have suggested, in their different ways, that the mind-brain frontier is one which must surely mark a 'discontinuity' at least as great as any other barrier facing scientific thought. This view receives support from one of the most famous neurophysiologists of the day, R. W. Sperry, who suggests, as the result of his studies on split-brain patients, that 'the present interpretation would tend to restore mind to its old prestigious position over matter in the sense that the mental phenomena are seen to transcend the phenomena of physiology and biochemistry'. (Ref. in *Studies in the Philosophy of Biology* 1974, p. 104.) Eccles, in his contribution to that volume, expresses the view that the split-brain investigations have falsified the psychoneural identity hypothesis. Moreover Eccles also points out that Schrödinger and Wigner have suggested that the brain-mind problem is likely to require fundamental changes in the hypothesis of physics. As Sperry said (1966), 'There is probably no more important quest in the whole of science than the attempt to understand those very particular events in evolution by which brains worked out that special trick that enabled them to add to the cosmic scheme of things: colour, sound, pain, pleasure, and all the other facets of mental experience.'

We thus have come, as we climb up and up the hierarchy of man's being, to an infinite regress. This is of course a concept enveloped in mystery. I quote, with Koestler, the words of Louis Pasteur, 'I see everywhere in the world the inevitable expression of the concept of infinity. . . . The idea of God is nothing more than one form of the idea of infinity.' I agree exactly with Koestler when he dubs the mechanist-determinist type of science as flat-earth science, because such science has no more use for the idea of infinity than the flat-earth theologians had in the Dark Ages. He adds: '*But a true science of life must let infinity in and never lose sight of it.*'

But it has long been obvious that if we go down in the microphysical world far below the level at which life comes into the picture, the ultramicroscopic world of the primary particles – that there too the view is open-ended. Instead of finding a bottom to the physical world, we again drop into infinity. So we seem to be approaching the thought of Whitehead, according to which, since ultimate reality is certainly not 'physical', it is more reasonable to assume that it is 'mental' – in the sense that all reality is process; all occasions are vectors.

Finally I would like to say a word about the recent views of Karl Popper because they seem to me to be so relevant to much of Arthur Koestler's thought. As is well known, Karl Popper has come down heavily on the side of dualism; for none sees more clearly than he that no explanation of the physical world can be valid which regards the self-consciousness of man as being an epiphenomenon – an accidental outcome of the mechanical working of a machine which we call a brain. There must be in fact *two worlds – the world of consciousness,* of self-knowing, and the physical world which is known by the operations of the scientific method. And, of course, the scientific method can only be operated by a 'knowing' being. Popper's recent papers amount to something more – to a *three world plan;* and this three world plan has fairly recently been developed or elaborated from the neuro-physiological point of view by Sir John Eccles (for the most recent statement of his thought see *Studies in the Philosophy of Biology,* 1974, pp. 87–107). Popper's three worlds are: *World 1* which contains *physical objects and states,* (a) inorganic – matter and energy in the cosmos; (b) biology – structure and actions of all living beings including human brains; (c) artefacts, material substrates of human creativity; tools, machines, books, works of art, music, etc.

World 2 is the world of *states of consciousness.* This contains subjective knowledge and includes experience of: perception, thinking, emotions, dispositional intentions, memories, dreams, creative imagination, etc.

Finally there is *World 3, knowledge in the objective sense.* This world contains (a) records of intellectual efforts: philosophical, theological, scientific, historical, literary, artistic, technological, etc., and (b) theoretical systems: scientific problems, critical arguments, etc.

It is clearly impossible here to give anything like a satisfactory general account of a development of a theory which is by any standards of major importance. Popper's claims on Worlds 2 and 3 suggest that a subjective mental world of personal experiences exists (a thesis denied by behaviourists) and that it is one of the main functions of World 2 to grasp the objects of World 3. This is, of course, something we all do: it is part of being human to learn a language; and this means, essentially, to learn to grasp *objective thought contents . . .* So one day we shall have to revolutionize psychology by looking at the human mind as primarily an organ for interacting with the objects of World 3; for understanding them, contributing to them, participating in them; and for bringing them to bear on World 1.

As has been made perfectly clear for many years Koestler is also a dualist and as I have said above I cannot here deal with the serialist problem, although I fancy that Popper might not be fundamentally averse to such an idea. In conclusion, however, it is worth stressing what Koestler has stressed – namely that, as Popper says, all explanatory sciences are impossible of completion; for to be complete a science would have to give an explanatory account of itself. A further result is implicit in Gödel's famous incompleteness theory which renders all physical science incomplete and which therefore, to the reductionist, must show that all science is incomplete. It seems that since the reductionist method can never achieve complete reductions we live in a world of emergent evolution and of problems whose solutions, when and where solutions are possible, simply create new and deeper problems. In this world of emergent novelty we can never prove the consistency of the whole for it is always open ended. As Margery Grene (*The Knower and the Known*, London, 1966) says, 'this is a formal admission which is philosophically of the highest importance'.

Finally, to sum up: if we come to the conclusion that hierarchies are open ended at the top vanishing into infinity we must realize that the same can happen at the other end. The present aspects of modern physics seem to indicate inevitably that we can no longer count on their being any ultimate 'entities'. To put it another way, atomicity has dropped out at the bottom and gone for ever. So the hierarchy is open ended there too. Koestler's remark about 'letting infinity in' truly presages what now seems to be happening. We have already quoted Louis Pasteur as saying 'the idea of God is nothing more than one form of the idea of infinity'. Perhaps the philosophy of Whitehead will after all be shown to provide the most complete and unified framework for philosophical biology. For some valuable thoughts on this see the paper by Charles Birch (*Chance, Necessity and Purpose*, being ch. 14 of *Studies in the Philosophy of Biology*, 1974).

What then is the ultimate conclusion? I suggest we hopefully await Arthur's next book. But in the meantime, let us follow his example and advice, and conclude that scientists, like artists, must increasingly become DRINKERS OF INFINITY.

Koestler's Philosophy of Mind

John Beloff

My first reaction on being asked to write about Koestler was to wonder what one could usefully say about an author who was so accomplished at expounding his own ideas. It is the obscure or equivocal writer, I thought, who requires an exegesis. It then occurred to me that, among the many roles which Koestler in his time has assumed, that of philosopher, in the academic sense, is not one, so that if one were to discuss Koestler's philosophy of mind it would first have to be disengaged from his varied and copious writings in which it is embodied. And this, it seemed to me, would be well worth doing if only it enabled one to see more clearly where Koestler stands in relation to others who have thought about the fundamental nature of mind. This, then, is what I propose to do in this paper even at the risk that he may disavow any of the labels that I may try to pin on him.

Before we come to the more abstruse issues let us take a look at what I shall call loosely his personal philosophy, that is his characteristic outlook on life, his attitude to the human predicament. The epithet which, I believe, best describes him in this connection is that of 'disenchanted humanist'. In calling Koestler a humanist I wish to imply that he belongs securely to the liberal-secular tradition of Western thought. By adding the word 'disenchanted' I wish to draw attention to his lack of that cosmic optimism that so often accompanies this tradition. When, as a young man, he emerged from his loss of faith in Marxism he did not, as did so many of his contemporaries, turn to religion or to some other-worldly cure for the sickness of mankind. He never abjured the values of the Enlightenment or doubted that reason and intelligence are, in the end, all that we can fall back on, however frail or uncertain they may prove to be. His disgruntled return from a pilgrimage to the East[1] made it perfectly clear that, having abandoned the commissar, he was not preparing to embrace the yogi. Nor, closer to home, did he show any enthusiasm for those drug-induced illuminations which so fascinated Aldous Huxley.[2] And, as a moralist, he has adhered to a robust tradition of rational hedonism that is never tempted to belittle the pleasures of this world.

Yet, all the while, there runs through all his thinking a deep vein of pessimism and gloom. It is not simply that the books with which he made his name deal with tragic and horrendous events or that he contrived to make himself the chronicler of some of the most appalling episodes of recent history. I am thinking rather of his tendency to extrapolate from such a basis to the nature of man in general. The insensate cruelties that have so disfigured our era are not, as might be supposed, an historical accident, the symptom, perhaps, of a civilization fast getting out of control. Rather they are the endemic effects of a blighted inheritance. Human sacrifice, Koestler reminds us, was already a feature of the scene at the dawn of history. We are, it seems, a flawed species. By a grotesque quirk of evolution our species has been endowed with a brain which combines, in precarious equilibrium, an inflated cortex of such a magnitude that even now we make use of only a fraction of its full potential with certain archaic infra-structures of mammalian and reptilian origins. It is the latter which govern our emotional and instinctive life and which, if unchecked, can so easily reduce us to a state of mindless and subhuman ferocity. Most dangerous of all are our 'self-transcending' tendencies that underlie our diverse fanaticisms. This, then, is the root of our misfortunes, an innate divorce between the intellect and the passions. Even so, the rationalist in Koestler allows him to play with the hope of a technological salvation in the form of some wonder drug that might yet be found to remedy this defect of nature, but the prospects he paints are so grim that the reader may be forgiven if he sees in this no more than a desperate after-thought.[3]

Yet, granted Koestler's interpretation of the human condition, a variety of options remain open to him regarding the ultimate nature of mind. In our attempt to elucidate his position in this respect a useful point of departure will be to consider those options which he most emphatically rejects. Here Koestler himself can be our guide since he has singled out for us three doctrines to which he takes special exception and which, indeed, he regards as the cardinal fallacies behind a world-view from which we are only gradually beginning to free ourselves.[4] The first of these is that evolution consists of nothing more than random mutations on the one side and the selective pressures of the environment on the other. The second is the idea that learning involves nothing more than the differential reinforcement of random responses. The third is the idea that the only valid explanation in science is one in which complex entities and processes are shown to be derived from simple entities and processes. To give each of these a convenient conventional label we may call the first Neo-Darwinism, the second Behaviourism and the third Reductionism.

These three theses are not logically interdependent – one could endorse one without endorsing the others – but undoubtedly they are intellectually related, inasmuch as they each contribute to the grand conception of a mechanistic universe. In a mechanistic universe there can be no room for such anthropocentric notions as meaning, purpose and value since man himself must be seen as no more than a chance product of impersonal forces. One could say that the whole drift of Koestler's later writings has been to challenge this particular image of man in nature and to replace it with the image of man as an autonomous centre of creative activity and of nature conceived on the analogy of an organism rather than a machine, an organism consisting of a hierarchy of systems within systems having no fixed apex and no known base.

Where Koestler differs from previous thinkers, like Bergson, who were animated by similar aims is that, far from stressing the limitations of the scientific approach, still less of reason as such, in favour of some superior form of knowledge such as intuition, Koestler maintains that his position can be defended on rational scientific grounds.

Perhaps the first point to be made concerning the targets of Koestler's attacks is that they do not all stand on the same footing with respect to the prestige or security which they command in the learned community. Thus, in psychology and still more in philosophy, agreement on fundamentals is so low among the professionals themselves that there is always likely to be room for an independent thinker. It is quite another matter when we move into the biological arena. Here consensus is much greater so that it takes real courage for the amateur to intervene at all. On the question of Neo-Darwinism, the fact is that it still has no serious rival. True, it has undergone modifications which would no doubt have surprised those who first combined the insights of Darwin with those of Mendel but these do not amount to an abandonment of its central tenets. It is significant that both C. H. Waddington and Alister Hardy, two eminent biologists from whom Koestler draws extensively in support of his case, are, on their own avowal, no more than mildly heterodox in their evolutionary views.[5] Some, indeed, would argue that the spectacular success of molecular biology and molecular genetics has made the orthodox position well-nigh impregnable. This, at any rate, would seem to be the view of Jacques Monod, a Nobel Laureate and one of the leaders of the new science, whose celebrated book *Chance and Necessity* can be read as an impassioned defence of the mechanistic universe in general and of Neo-Darwinism in particular.[6]

However, when we move from the biological to the psychological plane, the situation is very different. Behaviourism was already in retreat before Koestler entered the fray. It is true that Skinner, the foremost living spokesman of behaviourism, is probably better known today than he has ever been. But this is the result partly of the many applications that have been found for operant conditioning techniques in psychiatric and educational practice, and partly of the provocative tone of his books and public pronouncements which ensure them a wide publicity. In the academic field his importance is mainly didactic in the negative sense, that is to say that he is, as Chomsky discovered, the ideal foil against which to devlop an anti-behaviourist critique. Had Skinner not existed we would have needed Koestler in order to invent him.

Reductionism belongs in the first instance to the philosophy of science. There I would distinguish two different senses in which it can be taken. There is first the claim that high-level concepts and laws can be reduced to low-level concepts and laws by means of appropriate bridging operations. This I would call theoretical reductionism. Then there is the claim that all phenomena must be quantified in terms of appropriate units and the laws of their combination. This I would call atomistic reductionism and it is this more especially that Koestler is concerned about. In psychology, theoretical reductionism means, in effect, the reduction of mind to brain or, more precisely, of mental processes to brain processes. It has received powerful support in recent years from a new school of philosophical materialism as represented by David Armstrong and J. J. C. Smart, as well as from psychologists like D. O. Hebb or Oliver Zangwill, who see the future of psychology as an adjunct of brain physiology. Atomistic reductionism entered psychology via the early associationists and Wundtians, as well as via Pavlov and the reflexologists, and, today, is mainly represented by supporters of stimulus–response theory. It was, from the start, under continuous attack from anti-associationist schools of psychology like the Gestaltists and, at the present time, the rise of various new schools of cognitive psychology has left it looking very threadbare indeed. On this front Koestler is definitely swimming with the tide.

For reasons that I shall try and make clear, Koestler's preoccupation with evolution is a vital clue to his philosophy of mind. Theories of mind can be divided into two broad categories which I shall call respectively the transcendental and the immanent (or naturalistic). According to the former, mind, though somehow caught up with, and enmeshed in, the physical world through which it becomes manifest is not *of* that world but belongs to an entirely different order of being (some have called it a spiritual order). According to the latter, there is but one reality, that of the familiar natural world, and mind, however sublime an expression it may attain, is part and parcel of that reality. Now, those who hold to a theory of the former category can afford to be relatively indifferent to the question of what kind of laws govern the natural order provided only that they do not specifically exclude the possibility of a mind-matter interaction. Descartes, it will be remembered, cheerfully consigned the entire realm of nature, including all infra-human animals, to the sphere of the mechanical confident that somewhere in the machinery of our brain there was a small loophole through which the autonomy of the soul could assert itself. Those, on the contrary, who reject a transcendental theory as an outmoded relic of theology and who see in mind no more than the uppermost twist of an evolutionary spiral which has its roots in inanimate matter, cannot afford to be indifferent to the nature of the evolutionary process which brought it into being.

It is clear, even if he had not explicitly repudiated the Cartesian option, that Koestler is seeking to develop a theory within the naturalistic category. But, in so doing, he is immediately confronted with a problem because undoubtedly the most straightforward solution would be in terms of just such a theoretical reductionism against which he has firmly set his face. Thus, the first move in that direction would be to equate mind and brain, or at any rate with the brain considered in its functional aspect, with the implication that the brain is but a natural computer, subject to the same physico-chemical laws as any artificial computer and originating through the same evolutionary processes as any other natural organ. Monod fully accepts the logic of this argument but Koestler is not free to take this line. What alternative options are open to him?

According to Monod, evolutionists who depart from the 'principle of objectivity', as he calls it (i.e., the mechanistic interpretation of nature which he equates with the scientific approach as such), fall into two classes, the 'Vitalists' and the 'Animists' ('Teleologists' would, I think, better describe the latter but we can let that be). Vitalists believe in a radical distinction between the animate and the inanimate. He cites Bergson and Driesch as examples and, among living thinkers, Elsässer and Polanyi. The animists see in evolution the unfolding of a pre-ordained plan. Their whole universe is somehow imbued with an 'upward evolutionary surge' and man and the biosphere generally are the forward part of this 'ascent along the spiritual vector of energy'. Teilhard de Chardin is cited as the latest representative of this viewpoint. Where, then, does Koestler stand in terms of Monod's dichotomy? He is surely no animist; is he then a vitalist?

The answer is no, if this implies that the distinction between the animate and inanimate is the only critical discontinuity in nature. Koestler can more accurately be described as an 'emergentist'. For the emergentist, every level of evolutionary development can give rise to new principles and new entities that cannot be reduced to those that are to be found at a lower level. Life may be one such emergent principle, mind would be another, perhaps the phenomenon of language or rational thought would constitute yet another. His conception of evolution has much in common with that of von Bertalanffy or Paul Weiss.[7] Its key concept is the 'holon', that double-aspect entity that is, at one and the same time, an autonomous whole in relation to its parts but a subordinate part in relation to some higher whole. The weakness of earlier holistic philosophies like that of Gestaltism was that they ignored the hierarchical structure of the holon; the weakness of atomistic reductionism is that it ignores its unique holistic properties.

Koestler draws attention to a number of well-known problems which he believes to be insuperable within the confines of orthodox Neo-Darwinism.[8] I will mention here briefly three examples by way of illustration. To take first what is, perhaps, the most glaring difficulty for the orthodox position, any major evolutionary advance, say the development of a new organ or a new limb, must depend upon a whole series of nicely coordinated

structural changes. Now, the overwhelming majority of mutations are, if not lethal, at least highly deleterious. But, even when
a potentially favourable mutation of the required kind occurs, it
can have no survival value in isolation and would therefore soon
be bred out of the population. It is hard to comprehend, therefore,
how, on any reasonable time-scale, all the necessary mutations
would arise in one and the same individual to confer on it that
advantage in the struggle for survival upon which natural
selection could get to work. Secondly, Koestler discusses the
question of homology, that is the case of similar forms of life
that have arisen from entirely different genealogies, for example
the bizarre resemblance between certain marsupial species, like
the Tasmanian wolf, and certain placental species like the mammalian wolf. It is as if the demands of a particular mode of life
can be met by any number of strategies at the level of the genetic
code. Thirdly we are reminded of the numerous instances in
nature where changes in the habits and behaviour of a given
species must have preceded rather than followed the anatomical
changes that allowed it to specialize in a particular life-style. For
example, it would be of no advantage to a bird to possess a beak
of a shape specially adapted to feeding on a particular prey if it, or
its ancestor, had not at some time taken the initiative in exploiting
this source of food.

From these considerations, especially the last, Koestler rightly
concludes that the role of the individual in evolution goes beyond
that of being a mere source of random mutations. In any given
environment, various options and strategies are open to it that
may profoundly influence the direction which evolution subsequently takes. However, the question is whether this conclusion
is incompatible with orthodoxy. Monod would certainly deny
this. He insists that it is a 'completely mistaken conception' of the
orthodox theory to place the 'sole responsibility for selection
upon conditions of the external environment'. Similarly Waddington has argued that none of the difficulties raised by Koestler
are beyond the scope of Neo-Darwinian principles provided we
are careful to remember that natural selection operates on popu-
lations rather than upon individuals. However the arguments

soon become complex and technical and the lay reader can hardly hope to judge their validity.

At one point, however, Koestler's critique of Neo-Darwinism is quite definitely incompatible with orthodoxy. I refer to his prolonged flirtation with Lamarckism. Thus he is still troubled by the fact that, even in the embryo, there are signs of a toughening of the soles of the feet that will eventually produce callosities at just those places where the adult will tread and by other similar instances which, if not due to a Lamarckian influence, at any rate contrive an excellent imitation of it. I say 'flirtation' because, of course, Koestler recognizes perfectly well that the powerful objections to admitting the possibility of inheriting acquired characteristics makes it a definitely illicit temptation. We sometimes tend to forget that to the biologist the extraordinary stability and conservatism of living forms is no less striking a fact of nature than their evolution. Certain species have persisted successfully for millions of years with virtually no change whatever! It is hard to see how this could be possible if the mere accidents of an individual's life-cycle could affect the innate characteristics of its offspring. Nor has any conceivable mechanism yet been suggested whereby such an effect could be transmitted.

In spite of all this Koestler is reluctant to exclude entirely the possibility of a Lamarckian factor in evolutionary development. His sympathetic portrait of the heretical Austrian biologist, the ill-fated Paul Kammerer, which, in the end, leaves open the question of whether Kammerer's Lamarckian experiments were valid or not, shows clearly the fascination which the problem has for Koestler.[9] In a later work,[10] he compares the Inheritance of Acquired Characteristics (IAC) with Extrasensory Perception (ESP). The latter he takes to be factual but suggests that both may have been ignored by official science (a) because they are marginal, elusive and very difficult to demonstrate and (b) because of the lack of any known mechanism through which they could be mediated. To this I would offer the further comment that perhaps they are both of necessity marginal phenomena since, if they were not, the consequences would be chaotic.

When we turn from Koestler's biological to his psychological writings, what first strikes us is that the aspects of human behaviour that chiefly interest him are not those we share with our evolutionary forbears but those that are most distinctively human. In particular, he is concerned with man in his capacity as creator and inventor, a capacity which has enabled him to extend the evolutionary process by cultural as opposed to biological means. Koestler's first excursion into psychological theorizing was his INSIGHT AND OUTLOOK of 1949. It already contained most of the ideas which he later expanded and elaborated and in 1964 was followed by his THE ACT OF CREATION, the largest work he has ever published, which presents the mature version of Koestlerian psychology. Between these two dates, however, he published, in 1959, THE SLEEPWALKERS, his major contribution to the history of science. Koestler is, in my opinion, at his most inspired when writing about the psychology of geniuses and in his study of Johannes Kepler, which occupies so large a portion of THE SLEEPWALKERS, he succeeds in applying his psychological insights to a particular historical case with masterly effect. As its title suggests, the burden of this book was the strong irrational streak that permeated the thought of some of the greatest scientists and intellectual visionaries, an observation which THE ACT OF CREATION seeks to explain.

This trilogy of books represents, apart from anything else, a remarkable exercise in bridge-building across the two cultures. It is itself a notable instance of his own concept of 'bisociation' which forms the cornerstone of his theory of humour, his theory of aesthetics and his theory of discovery, the three legs of the Koestlerian synthesis. For my part, I am inclined to agree with those critics who saw in THE ACT OF CREATION a contribution to philosophical psychology rather than to empirical psychology in the strict sense. Its thesis lacked that vulnerability to experimental refutation which we have been taught to regard as the hallmark of the genuine scientific theory. Armed with a quiverful of Koestlerian concepts there is not much in psychology, one feels, that could not be brought under the Koestlerian rubric. To say this, however, is not to detract from its value as a seminal work of the 1960s.

Three movements, in particular, can be singled out in that decade as harbingers of a new post-behaviourist era in contemporary psychology. The first took its cue, as well as much of its terminology, from cybernetics, communication-theory and the computer sciences generally. Donald Broadbent is, perhaps, the best known proponent of this approach in this country. The second is the so-called revolution in linguistics associated with the name of Chomsky. The third, which is the one that concerns us here, is the new-found interest in creativity. Here the groundwork was laid by J. P. Guilford, working in the classic psychometric tradition, while the ideological fervour that powered the movement was largely supplied by the rise of a so-called 'humanistic psychology' a somewhat nebulous grouping also referred to as a 'third force' in psychology between behaviourism and psychoanalysis. It would be idle to pretend that it was Koestler who precipitated the spate of empirical studies that has still not abated on creative thinking or on the personality correlates of the creative individual, but there can be no doubt that his book provided some much needed intellectual ballast without which the entire movement was in danger of losing itself in a flood of trivialities.

What all these three movements had in common was a determination to make man again the centre of the psychological stage after his long banishment under the domination of 'ratomorphic' psychology, as Koestler calls it. Even those who adopted the computer analogy did so because they hoped that the study of artifical intelligences would prove a more fruitful approach to the core of human rationality than either the study of animal behaviour or that of brain physiology. As for Chomsky, I find it impossible to understand why he should have erected such an extraordinary mystique on the fact that we can talk gramatically or why he should insist that the use of language bears no relation to other skills or to other pre-linguistic systems of communication unless he were inspired by a quasi-religious belief in the distinctiveness of our species. Actually this emphasis on discontinuity was misplaced, a reaction, perhaps, to the crudities of the behaviourist analysis of language. It is very much a live issue in current comparative psychology whether primates can be taught the use of language, in a meaningful sense, and there have been some notable achievements in this field using sign-language or sets of ready-made symbols. Koestler, at any rate, with his evolutionary philosophy saw no need to present human creativity as something apart from the rest of nature; he saw it rather as the culmination of a phenomenon that can be discerned at every stage of evolution.

If Koestler's contribution to the philosophy of mind had ended with his GHOST IN THE MACHINE of 1967 I do not think that my description of his position as essentially one of emergent evolutionism would require much qualification. Thus, while he nowhere discusses the mind-body problem as such, there should be no difficulty in spelling out a Koestlerian solution whereby the relation of mind to brain would be expressed in terms of the relation of any emergent holon to its constituent base. But then comes a curious denouement. In two subsequent volumes Koestler turns his attention to the problem of the paranormal.[11] Not, of course, that Koestler is a stranger to the topic; there are allusions enough in his autobiography and essays. Indeed, it would have been astonishing if someone as intellectually omnivorous as Koestler and as sensitive to the cosmic mysteries had never been alerted to the problem. But, for whatever reason, he had re-frained hitherto from discussing it in any of his major works.

The reason, in my view, is not far to seek. Psychic phenomena cannot, as things stand, be assimilated into the framework of a naturalistic theory of mind. Indeed, those who are most anxious to preserve that framework at all costs have seized upon obvious defects in the parapsychological evidence as a pretext for refusing to acknowledge such phenomena as authentic. Koestler is too perceptive a thinker to take this easy way out but, philosophically, this lands him in something of an impasse. In the event, he attempts two different lines of defence. On the one hand he seeks to cushion the shock of accepting paranormal phenomena by dwelling at length on the paradoxes of modern physics. On the other, following Jung and, before him, Kammerer, he tries to assimilate as much as possible of the parapsychological evidence to the concept of 'meaningful coincidence' or, as he calls it, 'confluent events'. It is conceivable, he suggests, that there might be a universal law hidden in the structure of events whereby like is attracted to like. If so, then it is such a law that must be invoked to account for those cases we call paranormal rather than some kind of non-physical (magical?) causation.

Let us now examine this approach to the problem. As regards the argument from quantum theory, if I may call it that, the analogy misfires because the paradoxical element in modern physics lies in the peculiarity of the concepts which physicists have been forced to introduce in order to make sense of their data. In parapsychology, it is the phenomena themselves, at the gross observational level, that are anomalous. This is not to deny that the latter might one day be absorbed into a radically revised physics – indeed many parapsychologists, especially among the younger generation, ardently hope that they will – but, apart from its value as a warning against dogmatism, the analogy does not get us any closer to this goal.

What of the second argument? No one would wish to begrudge Koestler his fascination with coincidences – there is something compelling to the imagination about a really good coincidence – but, leaving aside the enormous logical problems involved in trying to distinguish between a 'meaningful' and a 'mere' coincidence, how relevant is the concept to the parapsychological evidence? There is no doubt that it can be made to fit snugly enough most spontaneous cases. It can, without too much special pleading, be made to fit much of the weak statistical effects like those associated with card-guessing and dice-throwing. Indeed, it might explain the notorious lack of repeatability of such effects and the well known decline curve in scoring. But it is hard to see how, without reducing the whole idea to an absurdity, it could be applied to the strong, directly observable, phenomena associated with both mental and physical mediumship. When confronted with a Uri Geller it seems we are either dealing with a deception or we are forced to acknowledge some unknown *causal* influence.

In view of these difficulties in reconciling Koestler's interest in the paranormal with his theory of mind one is tempted to ask whether, after all, he might not be some kind of a crypto-transcendentalist? At any rate the thought occurred to me that perhaps, like his own favourite mythological figure, the god Janus, Koestler has two faces, let us say that of the sage and that of the mystic. In that case his naturalistic theory of mind might belong only to the more familiar scientific face while a quite different esoteric doctrine might issue from the other lesser-known face. We know, at any rate, that, once, his whole outlook and sense of values underwent a profound transformation as a result of a mystical experience. I will conclude, therefore, by quoting from an earlier Koestler, but one that he has never explicitly repudiated, who is expounding what he refers to as the doctrine of the 'third order'. The scene is a prison cell in Spain and the time is that of the Spanish Civil War:

The 'hours by the window' . . . had filled me with a direct certainty that a higher order of reality existed, and that it alone invested existence with meaning. I came to call it later on 'the reality of the third order'. The narrow world of sensory experience constituted the first order; this perceptual world was enveloped by the conceptual world which contained phenomena not directly perceivable, such as gravitation, electro-magnetic fields, and curved space. The second order of reality filled in the gaps and made sense of the sensory world. In the same manner, the third order of reality enveloped, interpenetrated and gave meaning to the second. It contained 'occult' phenomena which could not be apprehended or explained either on the sensory or on the conceptual level, and yet occasionally invaded them like spiritual meteors piercing the primitive's vaulted sky.[12]

REFERENCES

1. THE LOTUS AND THE ROBOT, Hutchinson, 1960.

2. 'Return Trip to Nirvana' (1961) reprinted in his DRINKERS OF INFINITY, Hutchinson, 1968.

3. Part III of THE GHOST IN THE MACHINE, Hutchinson, 1967.

4. In Chapter 1 of his THE GHOST IN THE MACHINE (*op. cit.*) Koestler talks of *four* 'pillars of unwisdom'. However one of these, namely the homeo-static theory of motivation, is just another facet of behaviourism and can more conveniently be subsumed under that heading for present purposes.

5. For a brief introduction to Waddington's views on evolution, see 'The Theory of Evolution Today', his contribution to the Alpbach Symposium of 1968 in A. Koestler and J. R. Smythies (eds.) BEYOND REDUCTIONISM, Hutchinson, 1969, and more especially, his exchanges with Koestler in the discussion following this paper. Sir Alister Hardy expounds his views on evolution in his Gifford Lectures of 1963–4 (see his *The Living Stream*, Collins, 1965).

6. This book was originally published in Paris in 1970 as *Le Hasard et la Nécessité*.

7. See their contributions in BEYOND REDUCTIONISM (*op. cit.*).

8. Part II of THE GHOST IN THE MACHINE (*op. cit.*).

9. THE CASE OF THE MIDWIFE TOAD, Hutchinson, 1971.

10. THE ROOTS OF COINCIDENCE, Hutchinson, 1972, p. 134.

11. i.e., THE ROOTS OF COINCIDENCE (*op. cit.*) and THE CHALLENGE OF CHANCE, A. Hardy, R. Harvie and A. Koestler, Hutchinson, 1973. I have dealt at length with this latter volume in my review for the *Journal of the Society for Psychical Research* Vol. 47, 1974, 319–26.

12. *The Invisible Writing*. Hamish Hamilton, Collins, 1954, p. 353.

Wonderfully Living:
Koestler the Novelist

Iain Hamilton

I

Koestler in his own person is like the rest of us – only more so – a bundle of contradictions. Many of these he resolves, partially at least, in his writings. His range of interest and activity is probably wider than that of any other imaginative writer in England during this century; and his work – from the lightest of his journalism to the weightiest of his scientific synthesizing – is all of a piece. It is not so easy to break the novels off from the *œuvre* and consider them in isolation: but the effort is well worth making, because Koestler's peculiar qualities as a novelist have been underrated, or misunderstood, in England.

This stems in part from the very width of his interests, and also from his refusal to concede that there is a difference in kind between scientific and artistic creativity. Another reason is the acuteness of his political and psychological insights. He brought into the fuzzy English novel the real world of telegrams and anger at a time when the mandarin critics in England – those whose attitudes are summed up in the word 'Bloomsbury' – still proclaimed that personal relations were the only true subject for true novels. And then, above all, there was the enormous political impact of DARKNESS AT NOON, a novel which exposed the true nature of Stalinism long before the 'progressives' in the West

---

were willing to recognize the reality of Communism in practice.

The play of ideas in it is so dazzling, and terrifying, that it blinded many critics to the living reality of the characters who embodied, and expressed, and were dominated by these ideas. This ensured that Koestler would have the label 'political novelist' hung round his neck. But the connotations of the phrase in English are both too particular and too shallow to form anything like an adequate description of Koestler's quality.

He is indeed a 'political novelist', in the sense that his characters are always seen against the background of the onrush of history, caught up in those great tides of thought and feeling which dominate our lives. But he brought something new and disturbing into the English novel – an amalgam of intellectual analysis and imaginative insight which left many critics at something of a loss, although they recognized its power.

No doubt it was inevitable, given the shock which that searing book had administered to the leftist and liberal intelligentsia. There was indeed something disquieting about his intellectual passion, something alarming about his readiness to deal with many of the disagreeable aspects of the age which had not yet impinged fully on the English consciousness. Was there not too great an emphasis on these, at the expense of personal relations? Were not his characters mere mouthpieces? Did he not use the novel form for purposes foreign to the right true end of art? Besides, had not his apostasy from Communism, the god that had failed, induced in him an irrational sense of guilt?

Raymond Mortimer wrestled bravely with his awkward subject in an essay* written not long after the publication of Koestler's fourth novel, THIEVES IN THE NIGHT. He opened with a remark made by a friend in France just after the war (when the translation of DARKNESS AT NOON was enjoying – to the consternation of the Communist Party – a sensational success): 'Of all living English novelists I like Koestler the best.' To this Mr Mortimer had replied: 'He is wonderfully living, but he is not, English; he is not a novelist; and how far is he, as a writer, even

* In *Atlantic Monthly*.

likable?' The best that Mr Mortimer could find to say about
Koestler's English – in which he found no personal flavour – was
that it was fluent, neat, and highly readable. As to personal
relations between individuals, they occupied Koestler's attention
only in so far as they can be used to illuminate ideological
struggles and the nature of the revolutionary or his opponent.
Fiction was less his aim than his instrument – but one, Mr Mortimer admitted, that he used with deadly precision. Then came
the crucial objection (which was, perhaps, more to the way of the
world than to Koestler's use of it in his fiction):

If I find Mr Koestler's writing unlikable, it is because he accepts as
normal what I believe and hope is abnormal – because he treats ordinary, peacable enjoyment as trivial or even discreditable. I am a
conservative only in that I prefer old governments to new ones. Old
governments have lost their fangs; or rather, having no reason to fear
the people, they have no reason to inspire fear in the people.

And under such governments . . . men and women can, except when
menaced by foreign powers, give themselves, their day's work done, to
such enjoyments as their temperaments require – making music or
love, fishing or studying – in the confidence that neither their religion
nor their political opinions will expose them to persecution.

The notion of happiness has in Europe – and I cannot, alas, altogether
exclude England – become discredited. We have had to be stoical to
survive, and stoicism has bceome a habit. Europeans have become
addicts of calamity. Our most imperious need is to rehabilitate enjoyment . . . [Koestler] can breathe only in the climate of violence.
How far this obligation affects the man as well as the writer I do not
know; but his extraordinary talent is undeniably focused upon manifestations of cruelty and intolerance. He ends SCUM OF THE EARTH
with these sentences –

'. . . this is our unique and ultimate war aim: to teach this planet to
laugh again. At the moment we are still howling like dogs in the dark.
I wish the time of laughter had come.'

It is doubtful whether the time for laughter ever will come, ever
could come, for Mr Koestler. He has forgotten, if he ever knew, how
to laugh, except in mockery.

How clearly that essay illustrated the difference between the
insular and the continental experience. Now that events have

forced upon us a clearer understanding of the latter, we can see that the continental anglophile Koestler had a better understanding of the English mind than English cosmopolitans such as Mr Mortimer had of the continental. An old story. Mr Mortimer was also, it is clear, blind to that hedonism in Koestler which the distinctly unhedonistic George Orwell considered to be the chink in his armour; and he must also have forgotten, or overlooked, that notion of Koestler's which should certainly have appealed to Bloomsbury – that it was the duty of the civilized to create oases of civilization against the advancing desert of barbarism.

Koestler has an amusing recollection of that English reluctance to acknowledge the reality of violence exemplified in Mr Mortimer's essay. In 1941 he attended a PEN lecture in London. While a violent air-raid was in progress, Richard Church was talking about American novelists. 'Their outstanding characteristic,' he said, 'is their emphasis on violence in life.' Just then an enormous explosion shook the building. Church waited patiently until the reverberations had died away. 'Violence,' he resumed, 'plays an infinitesimal part in people's lives.'

At the 1941 PEN Congress, Koestler – who knew very well from experience the far from infinitesimal part played by violence in millions of European lives – read a paper on the novel in which he answered in advance the objections that Mr Mortimer was to bring against him six years later. During the pink decade of the thirties, he said, the author's chief temptation had been to cease to be a novelist and to become a reporter . . .

In the post-pink or Yogi decade the irrational dimension takes its revenge by outgrowing all the others. The few authors who have survived the pink era are those who, even in the heat of the battle, never forgot the irrational dimension – e.g., Silone and Malraux. But they are exceptions.

Koestler, although he did not say so, undoubtedly (and in my view justifiably) counted himself among them. There was a main road, he said, leading from *Eulenspiegel* and *Don Quixote* to *War and Peace, The Magic Mountain,* and *Fontamara;* and there were sidetracks leading to dead ends at which one found such

masterpieces as *Tristram Shandy, Swann's Way,* and *The Waves.*
It is not difficult to see why Bloomsbury was in two minds about
this strange and self-assertive foreign body in their midst. And
yet there were passages in that paper that might have been
written by Virginia Woolf:

The novelist's greatness is in direct proportion to the width and depth
of his vision. His window has to be filled with an all-embracing view
even if his subject is only a garden with a girl in it. . . . When there is
hope in the air he will hear it; when there is agony about he will feel
it. . . . Being a contemporary of ours, what he feels will be mainly
agony. In other periods it may seem that to care for politics is a temptation for the artist. In periods like the present is not to care for politics. . . . The artist is no leader; his mission is not to solve but to expose,
not to preach but to demonstrate. 'We make out of our quarrels with
others rhetoric, but with our quarrels with ourselves, poetry,' said
Yeats. The healing, the teaching and preaching he must leave to others;
but by exposing the truth by special means unknown to them, he
creates the emotional urge for healing.

Hindsight shows us that no less striking than Koestler's alarming insistence in his fiction on the more frightening aspects and
issues of the age was the fact that within only a year or two of his
seeking shelter in England he had become, in most respects that
matter, more English than the English (although the cast of his
thought was never to lose that sharp intellectualism more characteristic of the continental). Mr Mortimer got him wrong here.
Much nearer the mark was Orwell, who in 1944 had observed of
his friend that 'his main theme is the decadence of revolutions
owing to the corrupting effects of power, but the special nature of
the Stalin dictatorship has driven him back into a position not
far removed from pessimistic Conservatism'. But this too has to
be qualified. It was his accumulated experience of totalitarianism
itself, not merely of 'Stalinism' regarded as some sort of special
aberration, that had led him forward, rather (I should say) than
'driven him back', into this position. Also, due weight should be
given to Koestler's own insistence, repeated in various ways
during many of the essays he wrote in the forties and fifties, that
his pessimism was of the short-term, or tactical, variety. His

disenchantment with utopianism never hardened into ultimate despair.

The hedonism that Orwell considered a chink in his armour saved him from that, and it was Orwell who succumbed.

II

Koestler's first three novels – THE GLADIATORS, DARKNESS AT NOON, and ARRIVAL AND DEPARTURE – are all concerned (as he writes in his postscript to the Danube edition of DARKNESS AT NOON) with the central theme of revolutionary ethics, and of political ethics in general; with the problem whether, or to what extent, a noble end justifies ignoble means, and the related conflict between morality and expediency.

This may sound like an abstract conundrum, yet every politician is confronted with it at some stage of his career, and for the leaders of a revolutionary movement, from the slave revolt in the first century BC (the theme of THE GLADIATORS) to the old Bolsheviks of the nineteen-thirties and the radical New Left of the nineteen-seventies, the problem assumes a stark reality, which is both immediate and timeless.*

It was in the middle of the war, when the cult of kindly, pipe-smoking Uncle Joe was being tirelessly propagated, that I first encountered Koestler's work and through it became aware for the first time of that 'stark reality'. I was with my battalion in Scotland, running a course designed to sift out 'potential officers'. Most of the troops were young soldiers aged eighteen or nineteen, and many of them were very tough customers indeed, fresh from Borstal or approved schools. We had just completed an experiment dreamt up by a War Office psychologist, designed, I suppose, to test the attitude of the troops towards authority. It took the form of a mock election, with candidates offering themselves directly or by nomination for commissioned rank, and campaigning freely, with whatever help they could muster, throughout a week. Barrack-room lawyers were well to the fore, of

* Postscript to Danube Edition of DARKNESS AT NOON, p. 257.

course, together with many politically-conscious youths of the kind who might today be looking forward to shop-stewardship or junior-executive status. One or two half-wits had been pushed forward by their malicious comrades, and there were a few English and Scottish public and grammar schoolboys in the running.

Came polling day, and by secret ballot my tough charges elected the public schoolboys by an overwhelming majority, ditching others who might well have made good officers. A pity; still, I thought as I walked back to the mess that evening, there was no smell of revolutionary fervour in the old mill of Monifeith, if that was what the War Office psychologists were sniffing out.

A few days earlier, a friend of mine had been posted abroad, leaving with me a box of books. After dinner I pulled out one of them: THE GLADIATORS by Arthur Koestler, an exotic name quite new to me. For the first few pages I was on my guard. The only historical novels that had hitherto made much impression on me were those of Walter Scott and his later followers, Robert Louis Stevenson and Neil Munro – deep plunges into a romantic dreamland from which my youthful Scottish nationalism had drawn sustenance. In THE GLADIATORS I could recognize something quite different. On the surface it was certainly about that remote Latin past which had occupied much of my schooldays, not far behind me. Clearly it was solidly grounded in that doomed servile revolt led in 60 BC by the Thracian gladiator Spartacus, whose dream of founding a utopian Sun City had gone sour long before the disastrous dénouement which had helped to alter the course of Roman history, shunting it off the rails of republican and senatorial democracy towards caesarism – and so eventually towards the rise and decline of imperial grandeur. But there was nothing dreamlike about the prose, which had a hard, bright poetic quality of immediacy which I found strangely exciting.

As I read on, I realized that Koestler's vividly imagined antiquity spoke also of the recent past and present. This was not merely a kind of fictional history but also a kind of politics that meant something vital in the here and now. In Scott, Stevenson, and Munro I had lost myself. In THE GLADIATORS I began to find myself – or, at any rate, to ask myself for the first time some searching questions about the greater world I had ignored in adolescence.

In the entourage of Spartacus there is a sceptical, philosophizing lawyer, Zozimos, who sees very clearly why and how things are going wrong. 'I tell you again,' he says at one point to a young zealot, 'there is nothing so dangerous as a dictator who means well.' Suddenly I could hear the voice of my Highland grandfather, who, in the course of many a long discussion, had counselled me to avoid like the plague anyone who parades his good intentions. Now I knew what he had meant.

Soon I was devouring the pages, breaking off occasionally to think of how our own potential Spartacists had voted for their upper-class mates. The results of the election had been in some respects disappointing; but at least there were no embryo Hitlers or Stalins among the elect. How much wider was the Channel, I thought complacently, than the twenty miles of sea-road between Dover and Cap Gris Nez. But complacency vanished as I raced on through the bloody story, my mind shuttling between past and present, fascinated by the intellect and imagination behind the pages – all at once realistic, poetic, romantic, tragic, sceptical, ironic.

That was how I first encountered Koestler, and that no doubt is why, although I have re-read THE GLADIATORS many times since then, I have never been able to look at it quite objectively. I can see its weaknesses, to be sure; but, in spite of them, for me it remains a great, and underrated, novel.

There was another book by Koestler in the box my friend had left me – DARKNESS AT NOON.* The shock it administered was aesthetic rather than political: never having adhered to the Communist faith, I was not disillusioned by Koestler's exposure of the true nature of that religion in action.

What astonished me (and thirty odd years later astonishes me still) was the force that had lifted such material out of the par-

* For a full discussion of thi snovel, see the essay by Goronwy Rees, page 102. Editor.

ticularities of time and place and transformed it into a work of art
that had something to say of permanent value about the darker
side of human nature.

From that point I was hooked – for only the analogy of addic-
tion will do – on Koestler's writings.

The third novel in the trilogy, ARRIVAL AND DEPARTURE,
is more conventional in form than the others and has a considerable amount of autobiographical content. After his escape from
France in the autumn of 1940, Koestler had spent six uneasy
weeks in Lisbon waiting for an entry-permit to arrive from
London, where he intended to join the forces. He put his Kafkaesque experiences to effective use in his story of a young ex-
Communist, Peter Slavek, who, after fearful torture at the hands
of the secret police, has escaped from his Eastern European home-
land and arrives in Lisbon as a stowaway. His aim is to get to
England and join the army. He declines the sympathetic British
Consul's suggestion that he should go to America and have a good
time, 'like other young people'. While he waits, he is befriended
by a psychoanalyst of his own nationality and has an affair with
the French girl who is staying with her, waiting for her American
visa to come through. When the girl leaves, abruptly and without
warning, Peter has a nervous collapse which paralyses him.

The analyst cures him by dragging out of his unconscious the
fact that his revolutionary Communism had been rooted not in
any rational belief in Marxist ideology: it had, rather, been the
product of a guilt complex arising from his repressed memory of
an attempt he had made as a child to blind his younger brother.
Thus cured, Peter sees no reason why he should not go to America
(which is willing to have him) and have a good time, 'like other
young people'. But just before the ship sails he runs back down
the gangway. Eventually he gets to Britain, and the book ends
with Peter descending by parachute into his native land, there to
join the Resistance.

Why does Slavek choose embattled Britain instead of the
United States; and, once there, why does he choose the gap of
danger rather than the citadel of safety? Because, to put it crudely,
he is a man who has discovered that he is not a conditioned robot,

that he has freedom of choice; and he chooses to obey an ethical imperative undistorted by his former Communism, unexorcised by psychotherapy.

Throughout ARRIVAL AND DEPARTURE, Koestler's powers of description, analysis, and synthesis are at full stretch. There can be few more illuminating illustrations in fiction of the nature of heroism. In it he swims against the current of Marxist dogma (remembering that Marx himself was not a Marxist), and against the current of Freudian dogma (remembering also that Freud was not himself a Freudian). He signals in it the beginning of that campaign which he has waged ever since against mechanistic explanations of that inviolable core at the centre of the mystery of the human mind, the war against those whom Louis MacNeice had in mind when he wrote:

> *Let them not make me a stone and let them not spill me.*
> *Otherwise kill me.*

The novel had a good press. Even the hack reviewers could not fail to acknowledge its power; and many of its more percipient critics recognized its central point. (Orwell, oddly enough, was not among them. In making Peter Slavek take his final decision not to shirk action and danger, 'from a mere instinct', Koestler, he wrote, had in fact made him suffer a sudden loss of intelligence – an uncharacteristically shallow judgement.) But it was not at the time a popular success. Perhaps too much of its subject-matter was too disagreeable for the larger public, which wished to escape from rather than be confronted with the real terrors of the age. Also, Koestler was (as he has consistently been ever since) well ahead of his time. Perhaps it seemed altogether too clever, too paradoxical, too 'continental'. 'WHY SNEER AT THE INTEL-LECTUALS?' asked the headline over the review by Michael Foot who, having remarked the 'horrifying detail' of the story (mild enough in hindsight, years of horror later), went on to say that 'one page of Koestler is more convincing than a thousand atrocity accounts, however substantial. . . . He is the greatest foreign novelist since Joseph Conrad who has paid us the compliment of writing in the English tongue.'

Time and the common reader have proved Foot right, and
ARRIVAL AND DEPARTURE is established as one of the great
novels of the century, devastating in its insights into the ills that
continue to plague the civilized world.

III

If I forget thee, O Jerusalem, may my right hand forget its cunning.

During his early days in Palestine, in the twenties, Koestler had
been an enthusiastic disciple of Jabotinsky, the romantic and
flamboyant founder of the revisionist faction of the Zionist
movement which aimed at the transformation of all Palestine
into a Jewish state with an Arab minority. When he returned in
the late thirties, on a journalistic assignment, he changed his mind.
The gulf between Jews and Arabs was too wide, he saw, for the
communities to live harmoniously together. Partition, as proposed by the 1937 Royal Commission, was not an ideal solution,
but in the circumstances it was the only possible one. 'The
prospects', he wrote in the *News Chronicle* on his return, 'for the
future of the Holy Land are one colossal nightmare. . . . Britain
must act and act quickly.'

But Neville Chamberlain's government had other matters on
its mind, and Palestine moved deep into the predicted nightmare.
Jewish immigration was cut, to appease the Arabs. The British
government announced that Palestinc could look forward to
independence in ten years' time, by which time (so said London)
the Jews would constitute no more than a third of the population.
Refugee ships were turned away from the ports of Palestine.
None of this appeased the Grand Mufti of Jerusalem and his
followers. Arab attacks on Jewish settlements increased in
intensity. In the towns there was rioting against the mandatory
administration. The watchword of the Jewish Agency's illegal
military arm, Haganah, was self-restraint, and in general it
observed it. From time to time there was unofficial cooperation
against Arab terrorists between Haganah and the British forces.
'We shall fight with Great Britain in this war', said David Ben-
Gurion, 'as if there were no White Paper. And we shall fight the

White Paper as if there were no war.' That was the voice of official Zionism.

But as the war went on and the National Socialists began to implement their policy of extermination of European Jewry – and the British still refused to increase the immigration quotas laid down in the White Paper – more and more Jews turned in despair to violence. Out of Jabotinsky's revisionist movement came the Irgun Zvai Leumi and, later, the Stern Gang. While Haganah limited its operation to defence of the Jewish settlements, the Irgun hit back against the Arabs with terrorism. As time went on, both groups also increased their anti-British operations, the Irgun generally giving prior warning, the Stern Gang specializing in assassination and random destruction. Such terrorism was officially denounced by the Jewish Agency, but in fact there was considerable collaboration between the Irgun and Haganah.

By 1944 the Jewish terrorist campaign was in full swing. The situation in Palestine was ugly, and growing uglier; and in London, Koestler, through his work for the Ministry of Information and membership of the Anglo-Palestine Committee, knew the details, most of which were concealed by censorship from the public. He grew increasingly impatient. He was obsessed by an itch to return to Palestine, to see for himself what was happening, to contact the terrorists and try to persuade them to accept the idea of partition. Donald Tyerman, deputy editor of *The Times,* gave him a letter of accreditation as a special correspondent; and Chaim Weizmann, the leader of the Zionist Movement, got an entry permit for him from the Colonial Office. 'Talk to those mad friends of yours', Weizmann told him, 'and try to make them see that partition is the only chance of a peaceful settlement.' Just before he left England, Koestler heard from the International Red Cross that his aunt and cousins had been sent to an extermination camp; there was no definite news about his mother, who had been staying with them, but he assumed that she too had been deported to one of the death-factories.*

Koestler arrived in Palestine early in February 1945, and stayed

* In fact she survived.

until September, travelling widely, meeting British officials, Arab representatives, members of the Jewish Agency, and (clandestinely) leaders of the Irgun Zvai Leumi and the Stern Gang. During those seven months he collected a huge mass of material. Some if it he condensed into articles for *The Times*. Much of it eventually found its way into his account of Palestine between 1917 and 1949, PROMISE AND FULFILMENT. And during his last months in Jerusalem he drafted at white heat the novel, THIEVES IN THE NIGHT. This he sub-titled 'Chronicle of an experiment'.

The experiment is the establishment of a Jewish settlement called Ezra's Tower in 1937. The chronicle covers its development, virtually under siege conditions, between then and 1939. Koestler took as model for Ezra's Tower the *kibbutz* En Hashofeth of Galilee which was the home of his friend Teddy Kollek (now mayor of Jerusalem).

Against the richly detailed background of the settlement, the Arab village in the valley below, the intrigues in Jerusalem, Koestler demonstrates the classically tragic nature of the clash between the Zionists and the Palestinian Arabs. The point of view is, of course, Zionist, but he gives full weight to the resentment kindled in the feudal Arabs by the noisy, vulgar, graceless, and (in their eyes) shameless intruders from the Western world of modernity.

Britain might have averted the larger tragedy by forcing the issue in 1937 and imposing partition. By 1939 it was too late.

The central theme of Koestler's first three novels was the ethics of revolution: that of THIEVES IN THE NIGHT, as he writes in the postscript to the Danube edition, is the ethics of survival: 'If power corrupts, the reverse is also true: persecution corrupts the victim, though perhaps in subtler and more tragic ways. In both cases the dilemma of noble ends begetting ignoble means has the stamp of inevitability.'

At the time of its first publication (in 1946), THIEVES IN THE NIGHT foxed many of Koestler's admirers – largely, I think, because (like Mr Mortimer) they disliked its 'climate of violence' – and they sought refuge from the reality it mirrored in the explanation either that it was not so much a novel as a brilliant example of 'high journalism' or that it was simply a work of propaganda. Edmund Wilson heaped praise upon it as 'one of those rare feats of journalism which make you feel that you have been there yourself'; as 'one of the most valuable reports that have been written about the recent events of our bewildered and appalling period'; and as a 'book . . . full of the psychological insights which are the only things that make history intelligible and the writing of it a humanistic art'. But he could not bring himself to describe it as a satisfactory *novel,* as compared with the works of Malraux and Silone.

Too many ideas, in short; too little 'character' and 'personal relations'. But what precisely is the universally acceptable definition of that elastic literary form we call 'the novel'? Wilson's reservations begged the question.

In his contribution to a symposium published during that year in *New Writing,* Koestler expanded Elizabeth Bowen's definition of the novel as 'the non-poetic statement of a poetic truth'. Any true novel, he wrote, 'that is to say, a novel in which the conflict arises from the interplay of character and environment and bears the stamp of inevitability, [has] a mythological core. The leit-motifs are timeless, but the orchestration is period-bound. The modes and moods of a given period form a pattern; the individual threads in it must be seen both in the light of their archetypal origin and of their social context. If one of these conditions is missing, the novel will be a failure. But if both are fulfilled, something strange will happen. As with every living organism, you will get more out of it than you put in. It will not only describe, it will point. The novelist should never aim at more than stating; but if his echo does not bear a message, he has failed. Every philosophical, scientific, or artistic statement which is true, not only describes the world but changes it.'

The writing of THIEVES IN THE NIGHT (as of the later PROMISE AND FULFILMENT) was for Koestler a harrowing and painful experience, involving him, as he was later to recall, 'in an acute conflict between conviction and inclination, for I have had my fill of terror and violence, and was yet compelled to explain and defend the cause of the Jewish terrorists'. Now, thirty years later, THIEVES IN THE NIGHT is essential reading for anyone who seeks to understand why and how the gentle Zionism of Herzl and Weizmann was hardened into today's harsh intransigence of Israeli nationalism. That, for the moment, is answer enough to the critics who objected to Koestler's Three Rs (realism, relevance, rhythm) on the grounds, however expressed, of art for art's sake. 'Novels', as Koestler had written, 'which are not fed from archetypal sources are shallow or phoney. They are like a house with elaborate plumbing, bathrooms, cold- and hot-water taps which the builder forgot to connect with the mains.' The continuing life of THIEVES IN THE NIGHT is adequate proof that Koestler, however 'contemporary' his subject-matter and urgent his handling of it, had not forgotten Goethe's injunction to connect, only connect.

IV

When DARKNESS AT NOON was published in France after the end of the war as *Le Zéro et l'Infini* its success was sensational. Its qualities as a major work of literature were immediately recognized by a far wider public than (at the time) in England, and its political impact was enormous. In Koestler the French Communist Party, tightly organized and operating under the control of Moscow, recognized a deadly enemy. Having attempted without success to intimidate Koestler's publisher, they then spent large sums of money buying stocks of *Le Zéro et l'Infini* and destroying them. Reprint followed reprint, however, and soon the sales of the novel passed the quarter-million mark, many copies changing hands at five times the original price. When the Communists eventually recognized that their attempt to suppress it had failed, they launched a coordinated campaign of vilification both of the book and its author. This, too, failed, and the sales steadily climbed to nearly half a million.

Although the Communist Party was the strongest political force in France, both openly and through its dominance in the trades unions and the media, and although it had the support of innumerable fellow-travellers in the intellectual community, it failed to have its way in the referendum on the constitution. *Le Zéro et l'Infini* was widely recognized as the most important single factor in the defeat of the totalitarians. Koestler was a household name throughout the country, a hero in the eyes of democrats, a hate-object in those of the Communists and their dupes. During his visits to France he renewed old acquaintances, throwing himself wholeheartedly into the social and intellectual ferment of post-war Paris: some of those encounters were sad, some heartening, some bitter, some funny. He and Camus became close friends, but he soon drifted away from the fellow-travelling Jean-Paul Sartre and Simone de Beauvoir, in whose autobiographical *Force of Circumstance* and *roman a clef, The Mandarins,* the reader will find Koestler the celebrity entertainingly described and, from the stubbornly blinkered leftist point of view, caricatured with malicious relish.

In 1948, after his return from the Middle East, where he had reported the Arab–Israeli war, he decided to exchange the deadening exasperations of decent, unimaginative England and its grey austerity for the dangerous stimulus of France, still struggling out of moral decadence towards a new self-respect, still threatened by Communist subversion and the possibility of revolution and civil war. In his villa at Fontaine le Port on the Seine, he was more than ever the target of a non-stop campaign of abuse and intimidation. There he wrote his fourth novel, THE AGE OF LONGING. Fearing the worst (and with reason, as all who remember that testing time can recognize), he looked forward and set it in the mid fifties, with France and the rest of the non-Communist world awaiting the cataclysm. But like most novels set in an imagined future it is in fact a vivid and penetrating account of the recent past and present.

Around the story of a love affair between the daughter of an American diplomat and a Soviet agent (in due course recalled and liquidated) he assembles a sequence of dramatic scenes in which are portrayed, singly and in groups, vivid portraits of the Parisian intelligentsia. 'The characters in this book are fictitious . . .' says the customary disclaimer, but at this distance in time it is far from difficult to recognize behind the disguises the *doppelgängers* of Malraux, Sartre, Camus, Merleau-Ponty, Ilya Ehrenburg (the Soviet Union's licensed 'liberal'), and most of the others who can also be picked out from the wordier pages of Mme Beauvoir's *The Mandarins*. Every page is informed by the distilled essence of Koestler's own experiences – physical, moral, psychological – and the pessimistic tone of the story is brilliantly offset by Koestler's delight of the phenomenal world – women, food, drink, music, talk, nightclubs, the smell of French black tobacco, the long evening light warming the stones of Paris. It is a novel loud with warning signals, but between the klaxon alarms are passages of exquisite lyricism and elegy.

Its prophecy, happily, was unfulfilled. Oddly enough, Koestler put the finishing touches to the novel in Fontaine le Port in July 1950, just as it was growing clearer that the will of the West (for all the pusillanimity of so many of its intellectuals) had not been fatally weakened, and that general war had been averted. But for all its vivid contemporaneity (or perhaps because of the pyschological and ideological insights which inform it), there is nothing dated about THE AGE OF LONGING, in many ways the most haunting and deeply personal of Koestler's novels.

In the early fifties Koestler decided that he had had more than his fair share of political involvement. '. . . I felt', he wrote in his preface to the first edition of his collection of essays, THE TRAIL OF THE DINOSAUR, 'that I have said all I had to say on these questions which had obsessed me, in various ways, for the best part of a quarter-century. Now the errors are atoned for, the bitter passion has burnt itself out; Cassandra has gone hoarse, and is due for a vocational change.'

We had thought him lost to the novel. But in 1973, a year after the publication of BEYOND REDUCTIONISM, the account of the Alpbach Symposium on the life sciences which he edited in collaboration with the academic psychiatrist, J. R. Smythies, there appeared THE CALL-GIRLS, a brief but comprehensive satire on those peripatetic academics who can never resist the temptation to air their well-worn ideas at foundation-sponsored conferences. Its setting closely resembles the Austrian Alpine village of Alpbach, the conference centre in which the symposium that yielded BEYOND REDUCTIONISM had been held. But it would be a mistake to read it as a mere *reductio ad absurdum* of that particular gathering. It is, rather, a superbly funny (and alarming) distillation of all the symposia Koestler had ever attended; and, without weakening the narrative or reducing its characters to caricatures, it succeeds in comprehending within the narrow compass of 190 short pages an astonishing wealth of scientific and ideological interest.

The conference has been called by a nuclear phycisist, Niko Solovief, and the twelve distinguished participants represent all aspects of contemporary science, quasi-sciences such as sociology, and art. Niko's hope is that the deliberations may result in a document which will benefit mankind as much as Einstein's famous letter to President Roosevelt in 1939 (which led directly to the making of the atomic bomb) had threatened it. No such luck. Each of the 'call-girls' listens only to his or her own words, and after a horrifyingly tragi-comic climax the conference breaks up, nothing achieved. The last participants to leave look back at Niko (in whom there is much of Koestler) standing in the doorway. 'He looks like the captain of a sinking ship,' says one of them, 'determined to go down with it.'

It could be described, in a sense, as a pessimistic work, but the pessimism is offset by many passages of plain and powerful humour, just as the satire is offset by Koestler's sympathetic insight into those who propagate (in his opinion) the larger lunacies of our dangerous age – and by other passages in which he celebrates simple human tenderness. A modern amalgam of Peacock and Aldous Huxley, say, with a dash of Orwell, would have had difficulty in condensing such a wealth of ideas and characterization into such a cautionary tale, the total effect of which can be summed up by quoting a line from a poem by W. B. Yeats: 'Gaiety transfiguring all that dread.'

That famous hedonism of Koestler has served him well, and served us well too, providing in THE CALL-GIRLS an unexpected bonus of fiction, twenty-three years after THE AGE OF LONGING.

May there be more to come!

DARKNESS AT NOON and the 'Grammatical Fiction'

Goronwy Rees

Habent sua fata libelli; books have their own destinies. No doubt this is true of all books, but there are some, of which DARKNESS AT NOON is one, to which the phrase seems to have particular relevance. They are those books which, for some special reason of time or circumstance, from the moment of publication seem to assume a life of their own, almost independent of their author's original intentions, so that henceforward the world takes possession of them and makes of them whatever it wishes or pleases.

It would be hard to say what common quality confers upon such books their appeal to all kinds and conditions of men and women, of all times and in all countries. But even if we cannot define their secret, they have certain characteristic features which are worth noticing, and these DARKNESS AT NOON also shares. One, paradoxically enough, is that though their appeal is not limited by time or space, they have their origins in a narrowly circumscribed historical situation, sometimes indeed in a particular historical incident which by now has been long forgotten. It is hardly possible to understand the references in *Pilgrim's Progress* or *Gulliver's Travels* or *Robinson Crusoe* without a fairly thorough acquaintance with the ideas and controversies which agitated Englishmen in Bunyan's and Swift's and Defoe's day; yet a child

© Edito-Service S.A. Geneva 1970. This essay is adapted from the introduction and appreciation in the Heron Books edition of DARKNESS AT NOON.

can read the books with delight though he learns nothing of their origins.

Again, and perhaps as a consequence of this paradox, it is a characteristic of such books that they can be read as myths or fables of the human condition in its most universal form. For this reason, they concentrate on the life and adventures of a single person, for whom other characters are in the nature of foils, challenges, sometimes simply arguments. These are the hero's other possible selves, and his problem is to come to terms with them, which is in fact a way of coming to terms with himself. Since this is a situation of universal application such books make a very direct and personal appeal to us, and this is reinforced because the stories they have to tell, the events they narrate, are in essence simple and uncomplicated, even though the hero's reaction to them may vary between the extremes of naivete and sophistication.

DARKNESS AT NOON is, then, both a historical novel and a spiritual and intellectual biography. It is very firmly rooted in a particular time and place in history, the Russia of the Great Purge conducted by Stalin from 1936 to 1938. It is true that Koestler never names Stalin in his book, in which he is referred to throughout simply as 'No. 1', nor the Soviet Union, nor does he give precise dates to the events of his story, but there is never any doubt about what those events were, nor when and where they occurred. Indeed, we can identify them precisely because the trial of Koestler's hero, Nicolai Salmanovitch Rubashov, follows very closely the scenario devised by the Soviet secret police, the GPU, for the trial in 1938 of Nikolai Bukharin, the last and in many ways the most brillliant of the Bolshevik Old Guard, 'the darling of the Party' as Lenin described him.

DARKNESS AT NOON is also primarily the story of a single individual, who, under the circumstances of exceptional pressure and strain, both personal and political, tries to draw up a balance sheet of his life and to explain why it is that, at the end of it all, there is something wrong with the accounts. Its hero tries to solve the problem by introducing into the figures of profit and loss a factor which he has hitherto ignored, as inadmissible in strict accounting procedures. He calls it by a number of different names, and makes use of a number of analogies, often mathematical, to illustrate its nature and behaviour; but he never succeeds in identifying it to his complete satisfaction, chiefly because its mere existence, once admitted, seems to make nonsense, or worse, of his entire life and of everything it has been devoted to. At the same time, he has to confess to himself that only by accepting its existence can he understand how it is that he, and the revolution which he has helped to make, should have been reduced to the disastrous condition in which they find themselves at the moment when, without hope and without faith, he goes to meet his executioners.

It might be said that the dilemma in which the hero of DARK-NESS AT NOON found himself was one that had become distressingly familiar to its author, Arthur Koestler, in his own life; and though in Rubashov's case it acquires a political, and a philosophical, significance which transcends any purely personal experience, the autobiographical element in the novel is a very strong one and no doubt contributes to the intensity with which it is written. Koestler's life, up to the period when he wrote DARKNESS AT NOON, provides the background of the experiences out of which the novel is made; at the same time, his early life was so much a product of the characteristic social and political conflicts of the first half of this century that it has a wider interest than the biographical material which helps to explain the origins of most novels. The two volumes of his own autobiography, indeed, ARROW IN THE BLUE and THE INVISIBLE WRITING, form an invaluable contribution to the history of our own times.

In December 1931 Koestler applied for membership of the KPD, and in July of 1932, having resigned from the Ullstein Press, in which he had made a spectacularly successful journalistic career, he left Germany for the Soviet Union with an assignment to write a book and a series of articles which would present the Fatherland of Socialism in the best of all possible lights to the liberal bourgeoisie of Western Europe.

It would be difficult to analyse the reasons, conscious and unconscious, for Koestler's conversion to Communism. They would include the breakdown of the capitalist system under the strain of the world economic depression; the threat of war and dictatorship implicit in the rise of Fascism in Germany, and the inability of the democratic parties to offer any effective resistance to National Socialism. But commitment to Communism also involved irrational and emotional elements which were deeply rooted in Koestler's character; a deep sympathy with the down-trodden and oppressed, the 'wretched of the earth', with whom he identified himself; a yearning for a discipline as of some monastic order which would subjugate the warring impulses of his own nature, a desire for self-sacrifice and self-abnegation which would assuage his sense of guilt; the hope and belief that in the ranks of the Communist Party he would renew that sense of fellowship, of 'belonging', which he had only previously found as a member of his *Burschenschaft,* the student duelling society which he had joined at his university in Vienna.

But in addition there was also the attraction of Communism as a closed and all-inclusive intellectual system which not only offered a complete answer to all the problems of human existence but claimed to show that the answer could be applied in practice. Communist policy had the same relation to Marxist theory as applied science to pure science, and in both Koestler found an answer to his search for the Absolute. Communism reconciled Science with Faith, Thought with Action, the Individual with the Community, and in each of these aspects it made a profound appeal to Koestler's deepest instincts.

Its appeal, indeed, was so powerful, so much a matter of emotional need, that it made of his visit to Russia something very nearly approaching a farce. At that time, the Soviet Union, as a result of Stalin's policy of collectivizing the land, was experiencing a crisis which was even more acute and severe, and with far more terrible results in human suffering, than the parallel econ-omic crisis in the capitalist world. But of all this Koestler apparently saw nothing, or if he saw refused to believe the evidence of his eyes, though his travels took him from Kharkov, in the Ukraine, into Georgia, Armenia and Azerbaijan, across the Caucasus and through Turkestan down to the Afghan border, up to Bokhara,

Samarkand and Tashkent and through Kazakstan. He travelled through a land in which millions of people were dying of starvation and in some areas had been reduced to cannibalism, while other millions were being forcibly deported to the most intemperate regions of the Soviet Union; and yet nothing disturbed his conviction that in this vast and tormented territory he had at last arrived in the Promised Land.

Thus his visit was more in the nature of a hallucination than a journey through a real country, and he himself notes that not a word of the reality of life in the Soviet Union escaped into anything that he wrote about it, which differed in no way from the work of any Party hack. But he also notes that beneath the frozen crust of ideology which protected his illusions, in the darkness of the subconscious, the seeds of doubt had already been planted, though it was to be many years before they germinated and came to harvest.

Koestler left the USSR in the summer of 1933. By that time Hitler had come to power in Germany, the Reichstag fire had taken place, and the Communist Party of Germany had been driven underground and had ceased to have any existence as an organized political force; this total defeat and destruction of a party which even a year earlier had commanded over 6 000 000 votes was described in official Communist propaganda as a 'strategic retreat'. In the new Germany of Adolf Hitler there was no place for Koestler. Though still a devoted and active member of the Party, and faithfully performing the tasks assigned to him, he was in fact the prey of obscure impulses which fought a long and protracted struggle with the orthodoxies imposed on him by his beliefs. Some unconscious instinct of self-preservation prevented him from becoming a paid functionary of the Party, though his entire life was bound up with it, and being at the same time almost totally isolated from bourgeois society, he was debarred from any regular form of employment.

The years which he spent in Paris, from 1933 to 1936, were years of desperate poverty and at times of semi-starvation and homelessness. Yet they were also particularly fruitful years, in

which his long protracted adolescence finally came to an end and
his strangely divided personality gradually came to terms with
itself and he began to realize his true vocation, not as a journalist,
but as a writer. Nevertheless, his day-to-day activities continued
to be dominated by the Party. In 1934 the Comintern, reversing
its previous policy of refusing all collaboration with other
parties, embarked upon the policy of a Popular Front of all
radical and progressive forces in the struggle against Fascism. Its
most effective agent in the West was the great Communist
agitator and propagandist Willy Muenzenberg, who as head of
the powerful IWA (International Workers Aid) and of the
western section of AGITPROP, the Comintern's department of
agitation and propaganda, founded a bewildering variety of
Communist front organizations through which to conduct the
Popular Front's struggle against Fascism; his activity was so
multifarious and ubiquitous that in a sense it would be true to
say that the great anti-Fascist crusade of the thirties was an
invention of Muenzenberg's.

From 1934 to 1936, Koestler worked in close collaboration with
Muenzenberg and with his assistant, Otto Katz, alias André
Simon, and his association with these two remarkable men both
deepened his understanding of the intellectual processes of the
dedicated Communist revolutionary and of that curious combination of moral fervour, selfless devotion and lack of scruple
which is the basis of Communist ethics. The success with which
Muenzenberg prosecuted the Party's policy of collaboration and
alliance with everyone willing to fight under the banner of
anti-Fascism was all the more remarkable because, in the Soviet
Union itself, Stalin, having in all probability instigated the
assassination of Kirov in 1934, was preparing for the Great Purge
of the Communist Party which so completely exposed the
hollowness of the Soviet Union's pretensions to be the champion
of democracy and freedom.

On August 31st there opened in Moscow the first of the great
series of State trials which culminated in 1938 in the trial of
Bukharin; by a further irony, 1936 also saw the promulgation of
the new Soviet Constitution, 'the most liberal constitution in

the world', largely drafted by Bukharin and Radek, who, to-gether with almost every other member of the original leadership of the Bolshevik Party, were themselves to become victims of the Purge. Thus the period of the Soviet Union's collaboration with the radical and middle-class opponents of Fascism was also the period in which the dictatorship of Stalin assumed its most savage and ruthless form.

It was Koestler's privilege, or misfortune, to observe this process from within the ranks of the Communist Party, to watch its progressive deterioration as the Purge assumed more and more hideous forms and follow its repercussions as they penetrated down to the Party's smallest cells, not only in the Soviet Union but abroad. Yet, once again, his 'closed system' of beliefs for some years more proved impervious to the Great Purge as it had been to the Great Famine; the truth is that it so completely circumscribed his intellectual and emotional life that he could not conceive of existence beyond its limits.

It was to survive one more test. On July 18th, 1936, General Franco raised the flag of insurrection against the legitimate Republican government of Spain, and his revolt was followed by one of the most curious and tragic episodes in modern European history. On the one hand, it inspired a heroic struggle by the Spanish people to defend their liberty and independence against the reactionary forces, both internal and external, which were allied to destroy all their hopes for the future. On the other hand, it also inspired what might be called a Children's Crusade of volunteers, from all over the world, who saw in the Civil War the last chance of halting the triumphant advance of Fascism and to avert the world war to which it was the preliminary. It was the policy of the Soviet Union to place itself at the head of that crusade, to bring it under its own control, and to use the Civil War itself as a means to advancing its own foreign policy and to winning for the Communist Party the monopoly of political power in Spain.

Koestler, like thousands of other members of the Party, hastened to join the crusade. For him, as for others, the issues in Spain were so absolutely clear that the Civil War offered an opportunity, perhaps the last, for the Party to demonstrate that, in spite of the mutilations and deformations it had suffered, it was still the only force capable of defeating Fascism. In Spain, however, the policy of the Party revealed the same contradictions, the same conflict between propaganda and reality, the same combination of moral fervour and cynical hypocrisy, the same perverted logic, as it had already shown in Germany and in the Soviet Union itself. Its degeneration had proceeded so far that it transformed even the Civil War into an incident in an internal party struggle, of which the final victims were those of its members who had most wholeheartedly believed in the cause they thought they were defending in Spain.

Yet it was not the realization that the Party had become a hideous travesty of everything that it professed to be which provoked Koestler's final break with it. To abandon a faith, it is necessary to discover the means of living without it, if one is to go on living in any real sense at all. In Spain, Koestler underwent an experience which provided at least the basis for such an hypothesis. His own part in the Spanish Civil War took the form, after consultation with and direction by Willy Muenzenberg, of becoming an agent and observer for the Comintern under the cover of an accredited correspondent to the Franco forces of the liberal English newspaper the *News Chronicle* and, somewhat precariously, of the reactionary *Pester Lloyd* of Budapest. The operation was conceived in a curiously clumsy and amateurish fashion and five months after his arrival in Spain, in February 1937, Koestler was arrested and condemned to death as a spy. He spent three months in solitary confinement, in daily expectation of execution, before he was released in exchange for a Franco hostage in Republican hands.

The confrontation with death which Koestler underwent in his cell in Seville is closely related to the experience of Rubashov in his cell in Moscow. It was significant, not because it provided any further evidence of the corruption of the Communist Party, but because it released in him feelings, instincts, perceptions, which had been rigidly excluded from the boundaries of the 'closed system' of Marxist ideology. In this respect, Koestler's own experience offers a close parallel to that of Rubashov in DARKNESS AT NOON. In both cases, what is significant is the sudden and explosive eruption into consciousness of experiences which hitherto have been successfully repressed in the interests of a system of thought with which they cannot be reconciled.

It might be said that those experiences were, in both cases, the product of the abnormal psychological condition induced, in Koestler and Rubashov alike, by the shock of arrest, solitary confinement and imminent confrontation with death. This may well be so. But the truth is not a function of psychological states, and the validity of any experience is not to be judged by the conditions by which it has been induced. The dilemma of Koestler-Rubashov in his cell is precisely what kind of validity to attribute to an insight which threatens to shatter the coherence of a system of thought on which the whole of his life has been based. His dilemma is intensified by a heightened receptivity stimulated by a sense of release from a burden of guilt which has been borne for too long. In his cell in Seville, Koestler recognized that there was a kind of rough justice in his sentence to death, not only because he was in fact, as his judges claimed, a spy, but even more because he had for years, in his role as a convinced and committed Communist, been impersonating a character in which he fundamentally did not believe. He had become one of those 'people in prison who revalue their lives and discover that they are guilty, though not of the crimes of which they are accused'. Like Rubashov, he almost felt relief in the admission: *I must pay*.

The history of a loss of faith is a long and complicated one, and it was not until 1938 that Koestler formally resigned from the Communist Party.

In March of that year there took place in Moscow the last of the great State trials of the Bolshevik Old Guard, including Nikolai Bukharin, President of the Comintern, Christian Rakovsky, Krestinsky, Rykov, and Yagoda, head of the Soviet security police, the GPU. This last trial was a kind of monstrous *reductio ad absurdum* of the Great Purge, in which it was proved to everyone's satisfaction that not only the whole of the original leadership of the Bolshevik Party had become spies and traitors but that the case against them had been conducted by one who shared in exactly the same crimes. DARKNESS AT NOON, which is an account of the historical process of which this trial was the culmination, was begun in the Autumn of 1938 and was finished in April 1940, a month before the German invasion of France; in the meantime Koestler had been arrested, and released, by the French police, and the page proofs of the book were delivered to him in Pentonville, in England, where he had been imprisoned after the fall of France and his subsequent escape across the Channel.

Much of the material of the novel is drawn from Koestler's own experiences, and from the experiences of friends and acquaintances within the Communist Party. It is important to remember that the tragedy which was enacted in Russia in the thirties was one which penetrated to every level of the Party; for every case, like Rubashov's, which was exposed in the glare of publicity of a State trial, there were thousands of others, including those of many of Koestler's friends and colleagues, which were conducted in silence and in darkness.

The tragedy which was thus enacted had two distinct acts: the Great Famine and the Great Purge, and the second act was in some respects the logical consequence of the first, because it was in the Famine that the Party discovered and adopted the methods of repression which were brought to perfection in the Purge. Gletkin, the interrogator in DARKNESS AT NOON, describes how he discovered almost by accident during the famine the technique of extracting a false confession from a recalcitrant and unco-operative prisoner.

At the time of Rubashov's arrest, such techniques had been developed into a universal system of terror, of a scope and violence which had never previously been seen in Europe, even in the Germany of Adolf Hitler; the legitimacy of terror as a political weapon is of course one of the problems which pre-occupy Rubashov in his meditations in his prison cell. Terror had been recognized as a legitimate political means since the French Revolution, and had been accepted as such by Marx and Engels and by Lenin himself. But in the Great Purge, and even earlier, not merely terror, but torture had become an established and approved instrument of government, and this was something which was unique to the Soviet regime, until it found a willing disciple in the National Socialist government of Germany.

The use of physical torture as a political weapon plays a large part in Rubashov's meditations in prison, because it raises problems which are almost insoluble within the terms of his own revolutionary beliefs. There is the question whether its universal application during the Great Purge is merely an aberration due to No. 1's sadistic instincts, or rather a logical consequence of a doctrine which holds that revolution is an end which justifies every means. There is the irrepressible feeling that, however logical and rational its operations, a regime in which torture is not the exception but the rule has achieved something new and unique in the degradation of man by man. There is an even more difficult question: whence do such feelings arise, and with a force which cannot be ignored? For by the dialectic of the revolution, they should be judged as merely sentimental weaknesses which serve to disguise the vestiges of bourgeois moral prejudice. At the beginning of DARKNESS AT NOON, Koestler has placed a quotation from Dostoyevsky: 'Man, man, one cannot live quite without pity'. For a revolutionary, what kind of meaning can such a sentence have?

The question of physical and mental torture is of crucial importance in DARKNESS AT NOON, for several reasons. In the first place it provides the most striking demonstration of the degeneration of the Soviet State, and how and why this could have come about is one among the most urgent questions with which Rubashov torments himself in his prison cell. In the second place, it vitally affects the nature of the 'confessions' made by Rubashov himself, and by the accused in the Soviet State trials, on which his own is modelled. DARKNESS AT NOON has frequently been interpreted as offering a 'psychological' explanation of the confessions, so bewildering to the Western mind, based on the inability of the accused, as convinced and devoted Communists, to resist the authority of the Party, even when what it demands of them is the sacrifice, not merely of their lives, but of reputation, honour, dignity and self-respect.

Certainly such a motive plays a large part in Rubashov's final surrender to Gletkin, but it is only one motive among many others, and Koestler makes it abundantly clear that, in inducing his final decision, the relentless physical pressure brought upon him by Gletkin, the lack of sleep, the deprivation of the privileges accorded him by Ivanov, the blinding glare of the lamp, have also had their effect. Indeed, it is an essential part of Gletkin's creed, as a representative of the new 'Neanderthal' type of the Soviet man, that a person like Rubashov cannot be brought to capitulate without the use of such methods. Gletkin's armoury includes a multiplicity of weapons, which can be adjusted and combined to suit each particular case. What they have in common is the manipulation of the human being as material for use and a subject for experiment.

The importance of torture in DARKNESS AT NOON is that it exposes in its most naked form the fundamental problem with which the novel is concerned. That problem, at its simplest, is: how far is it justifiable to use human beings as a means and not as an end? And it is because this question has a universal application that Koestler's novel has a certain timeless quality which is independent of the particular place and time of the story it has to tell. Even to ask such a question is to assume a utilitarian ethic in which both ends and means can be quantified in a universal calculus which assigns only an infinitesimal value to the experiences of the invididual. From his own Marxist, Communist, point of view Rubashov can see no escape from this conclusion; and both his interrogators, Ivanov and Gletkin, are agreed with him in this, which is why he can find no answer to their arguments. It is important to realize that even before he has been surrendered into the merciless hands of Gletkin, Rubashov has already capitulated to the 'vivisection morality' of Ivanov: the difference between them is that out of old affection and friendship, Ivanov wishes, if he can, to save Rubashov's life. This is a sentimental weakness on Ivanov's part, and it is a part of the logic of the novel that therefore Ivanov should be shot and Rubashov be handed over to Gletkin.

One of the great merits of DARKNESS AT NOON is that Koestler should have been able to reduce the enormous complexity of his material, historical, political, and psychological, to an almost classical simplicity of form and structure; and indeed there are other elements in the story, of Fate, of Hubris, of the individual entangled in a more-than-human conflict, which recall the classical parallel. The three long sections which form the main part of the narrative unfold like the three acts of a play, each with its appropriate curtain; the short final scene of Rubashov's public trial and confession is simply an epilogue to a tragedy that has already been played out. Within this severe structural scheme, the narrative, varying continually and with great subtlety between the objective and the subjective plane, advances with compelling force, and like Rubashov himself one is caught up in a storm of events, memories, feelings and ideas which is only finally resolved in the peace of death.

The sheer pace of the narrative, indeed, is so exhilarating that one is almost tempted to overlook, or at least to underestimate, one element in the story which is of equal importance with the political problem which it presents for our consideration, though it is in a sense the key to its solution. Formally, the drama of the story is compressed into Rubashov's three confrontations with his interrogators; in the intervals between them, in the silence of his cell, Rubashov recalls incidents of his past which have a particular and sinister reference to the ordeal to which he is being subjected.

Yet in addition to Rubashov, Ivanov, Gletkin, there is always present another principal actor in the drama, who, while having no name or, in the proper sense of the word, personality, has a decisive influence in its development; one might almost call him, not Rubashov, its hero. He is like that shadowy character whom the disciples encountered on the road to Emmaus, shapeless and featureless in the dusk and yet, as they all felt, the real centre of the great event in which they have taken part.

'Who is that third who always walks beside you?' This character never, or hardly ever speaks directly, except in certain phrases which involuntarily force themselves to Rubashov's lips in his long monologues in his cell, in particular the recurrent phrase: *I must pay*. The phrase makes no logical sense to Rubashov; but it is accompanied by a sense of being at peace, as if it contained a promise of release from suffering. He hardly knows where the phrase comes from, but it transforms his meditations into a monologue *à deux*, in which the other partner cannot be identified.

To this presence, a kind of *Doppelgänger* which reverses all Rubashov's normal processes of thought, he finally gives the name of the 'grammatical fiction', the first person singular denoting the 'I', the self, to which the Party refuses to attribute any significance because it appears to have, or to claim, an existence independent of any social reality, which is the only reality which the Party recognizes. Of its nature or its mode of being, its ontological status or its psychological or intellectual procedures he knows nothing; it has something of the amorphous, floating character of the Latin poet's *animula blandula vagula*, the 'simple soul', the passive recipient on which experience imprints itself as on a photographic plate. Yet gradually he becomes uneasily aware that by his refusal to recognize its existence he may have betrayed himself, and millions of others – and for this treachery also, *I must pay*. As much as any of the arguments used by Gletkin, it is this recognition of guilt which finally persuades him to accept the shameful role for which he is cast in the scenario prepared for him by Gletkin and his superiors, and it is this recognition which finally brings him a kind of peace before the bullet in the back of his head finally puts an end to him; his last hours he reserves for converse with the 'grammatical fiction'.

The intermittent, yet decisive, appearances of the 'grammatical fiction' make of DARKNESS AT NOON something of a Hamlet without the Prince of Denmark. They also introduce into it, and especially into Rubashov's tenacious but futile struggle with his interrogators, a certain note of ambiguity. For the mute but major premise of Rubashov's argument is suppressed; the 'grammatical fiction' has no existence in Gletkin's vocabulary or syntax, nor has Rubashov himself any means of introducing it into their murderous interchanges. If, in the end, Rubashov surrenders to the idea that the Party still has a use for him, it is because, blinded by the confusion of his own mind and feelings as much as by the glare of Gletkin's lamp, he no longer has the strength of mind or will to reject the temptation out of loyalty to something whose existence he still hardly acknowledges and whose nature he has not had time to understand. It is at this point that we realize, with sympathy, that Rubashov is old, that he is intellectually and emotionally exhausted; that he is, in fact, beaten.

The 'grammatical fiction' also involves a noticeable, though perfectly justifiable, distortion of the historical material on which Koestler based his novel. This is indeed one of the reasons why we feel it to be fiction, or a work of art, rather than a political *roman à clef,* to be judged primarily by its fidelity to the particular historical situation which was its direct inspiration. Koestler tells us that Rubashov is deliberately based on the early leaders of the Bolshevik revolution. His personality and even his physical appearance, the pince-nez, the wispy beard, the incisive gestures, come from Trotsky and from Radek; the sophisticated dialectical processes from Bukharin, who had a scintillating intelligence which melted the mind and the heart even of Lenin. In his dedication to the novel, Koestler says that 'N. S. Rubashov is a synthesis of the lives of a number of men who were victims of the so-called Moscow trials. Several of them were personally known to the author.' Indeed, he follows his model Bukharin so closely that Rubashov's confession at his trial very nearly repeats *verbatim* Bukharin's at his. But there is nowhere, so far as I know, any evidence in any documents of the revolutionary period, or of the Great Purge, that any of the veteran leaders of the Bolshevik Old Guard ever fell a victim, like Rubashov, to the seductions of the 'grammatical fiction'. Its introduction into the novel is a brilliant feat of imagination on Koestler's part.

Rubashov's interrogation by Gletkin, however, is conducted entirely in terms of the revolutionary dialectic of which they are both, in their different ways, masters. The difference between them is that while Rubashov applies it as a living body of thought, capable of new insights and new developments, for Gletkin it is strictly an instrument for use, in this case in a singularly brutal way. But he is not, for that reason, any less skilful in applying it than Rubashov; indeed, he shows himself more consequent than Rubashov in pushing it to its conclusions, so that in the struggle between them Rubashov meets with total and unconditional defeat and the last vestiges of his self-respect are stripped away from him. There are readers of DARKNESS AT NOON who have come away from it with the feeling that, in the end, Gletkin's arguments are so irrefutable that Koestler has acted as a kind of devil's advocate who has succeeded in making the bad cause appear the good.

To feel this is only to acknowledge the nightmare quality, the A ... in-Wonderland kind of reality, with which Koestler has endowed his novel. This feeling is intensified by the admirable economy of detail with which its physical context is portrayed; the huge beehive of a prison, with its two thousand prisoners, each thinking his own thoughts in the solitary confinement of his own cell and each equally exposed at any moment to physical mutilation or final extinction; its long corridors where the lights forever burn nakedly and dimly and the silence is only broken by the shuffling of a jailor's shoes, the clanging of cell gates and the screams of those who are tortured in the night; it is as if one had been admitted to some vast laboratory designed to strip the skin from the flesh of its human guinea pigs and expose to pitiless examination their raw and bleeding nerves.

All this is admirably suggested; but despite the screams of the victims, the whimpering cries in the night, it is not physical brutality which Koestler dwells on, but the torture which can be inflicted by ideas, of which physical brutality is a consequence. One of the triumphs of the novel, and one which is very rarely achieved in fiction, is to make ideas living, real and actual as if they were as vital to those who thought them as the circulation of the blood. It is also a part of its horror that in it ideas are so deeply imbued with the smell and taste of blood; but it also offers a saving grace by which, perhaps, their stain can be washed away.

Proust says that it takes a very long time for a truly original work of art to be properly understood, and certainly, in the case of DARKNESS AT NOON, there was a long delay before the full significance of the novel was realized. Indeed, it required a world war, and the profound changes it brought about in political attitudes in the West, before men's minds became receptive to what it had to say. By the end of the war the hidden contradiction between the aims of the Soviet Union and those of its allies had already begun to make itself felt, and after the war the Soviet Union and the indigenous Communist parties of liberated Europe showed that the nature and the methods of Communism were indeed such as Koestler had described them in DARKNESS AT NOON. For the first time, Western countries learned by bitter experience what it was to live under Communist rule, and it confirmed in every detail the terrible picture which Koestler had drawn in his novel.

Within the Soviet sphere of influence, Communism became the permanent way of life of the countries to which No. 1 had extended his dictatorship, but even beyond it, for a short time, Communist parties, and the partisan armies which they had inherited from the resistance movements, secured a monopoly of power over large areas; it is true to say that they exercised that power in a way which would have earned the complete approval of a Gletkin and did earn them the detestation of those who suffered under it.

In France, in the period immediately following the liberation, the Communist Party, and the resistance groups it controlled, for a short time enjoyed a liberty of action which they used to carry out, wherever possible, a ruthless purge of their opponents. DARKNESS AT NOON was published there in 1946, when it was still doubtful whether General de Gaulle would succeed in establishing himself as the effective ruler of France, and the result of the forthcoming referendum on the French Constitution was in the balance. It was this situation which explains the immediate and spectacular success of the French translation of the novel, which sold over 400000 copies and broke all pre-war publishing records in France. There were some who claimed that the novel had a decisive influence on the Communist defeat in the referendum.

Since that time DARKNESS AT NOON has established itself as one of the essential documents of the political life of our time, and it has maintained that position in spite, or perhaps because of, the immense increase in recent years in our knowledge of the particular period of Russian history with which it is concerned. But DARKNESS AT NOON does not only refer to the past; it has had the peculiar distinction of appearing to predict and influence the future, as if even Communists had accepted it as a scenario by which to direct their behaviour.

Some fifteen years after the Great Purge, there took place in Prague a re-enactment of the drama which was played out in Moscow in the thirties; and the imitation repeated with a sickening fidelity the details both of the original and of the account given of it in DARKNESS AT NOON. Indeed, by a strange concatenation of events in which nature seemed to imitate art, at one point it appeared as if Rubashov himself had returned to life to repeat the message of the novel.

The culmination of the purge in Czechoslovakia was the trial in 1952 of Rudolf Slansky, general secretary of the Czech Communist Party, Vlado Clementis, the Foreign Secretary, and twelve other defendants, who all duly confessed to the charges falsely brought against them and were condemned to death or life imprisonment. Among the accused was Koestler's friend and former colleague in the 'Muenzenberg trust', Otto Katz, alias André Simon; his public confession of guilt was an ironic parody of Rubashov's final speech at his trial, which in turn was a repetition of Bukharin's confession in 1938. Simon's last words were: 'I . . . belong to the gallows. The only service I can still render is to serve as a warning example to all who by origin or character are in danger of following the same path to hell. The sterner the punishment . . .' At this point his voice became inaudible. According to Koestler, Simon's parody of Rubashov was both an indication, for those who could understand, of the falsity of his 'confession', and perhaps a last desperate appeal to his friends outside Czechoslovakia to organize the kind of rescue operation by which he and Muenzenberg had helped to save Koestler's life in Spain.

It was not only Simon's confession which recalled DARKNESS AT NOON. Our knowledge of the proceedings in, and the preparations for, the Slansky trial has by now been greatly enlarged as a result of information published during Czecho-slovakia's tragic bid for freedom in the summer of 1968; some of that information has been summarized in an article entitled, significantly enough, 'Koestler Revisited', and introduced by a quotation from the Czech historian, Jaroslav Orpat: 'A remark-able novel exists, known all over the world except in our country, the novel DARKNESS AT NOON by Arthur Koestler, which accurately describes the mechanism of the Soviet trials in the second half of the thirties, the logic of the interrogators, the judges, the prosecutors and the accused, who themselves become the collaborators of the investigators and the prosecution . . . The most tragic thing is that a decade later these events repeated themselves with the force of a natural law.'

A natural law; the phrase emphasizes that DARKNESS AT NOON not only describes a particular stage in the development of the Soviet Union, but is also an analysis of certain essential features of Communism wherever it establishes itself in power. It is a story of the past which remains valid in the present and foreshadows the future. 'Koestler Revisited' also emphasizes that the use of terror as a political instrument is not an exclusively 'Russian' phenomenon but is applied with equal ruthlessness wherever Communism judges it necessary. Indeed, it shows that, if any-thing, Koestler has understated rather than exaggerated its merciless inhumanity. All the weapons in the armoury of a Gletkin were applied to the victims of the Slansky trial. They were held without trial in solitary confinement. They were beaten into insensibility. They were subjected to arbitrary and bizarre methods of punishment that disorientated them in time and space. They were exposed to starvation and alternations of intense cold and intense heat. Their personality was disintegrated by the use of hallucinatory drugs and forms of degradation designed to reduce them to the status of animals; they were placed in Kafkaesque situations created in order to induce a sense of the unreal and the absurd.

Reading of such experiences, one can do no more than repeat Kurtz's exclamation after his reversion to savagery in Conrad's *Heart of Darkness*: 'Oh, the horror . . . the horror!', and it is this same sense of a vast and unnameable evil which one feels in reading DARKNESS AT NOON. What is remarkable is that Koestler achieves this effect, not by dwelling on physical horrors, but by exposing the moral evil which it reflects. It is an effect, not of documentation, but of art. The physical horrors occur in the honeycombed cells and corridors which lie beyond Rubashov's field of vision between his prison bars. The screams in the night go unheard; it was precisely the triumph of DARKNESS AT NOON that it made the world listen to them.

DARKNESS AT NOON, says Koestler, was the second in a cycle of four books devoted to examining the morality of revolutionary ethics. The first was THE GLADIATORS; the third and fourth were ARRIVAL AND DEPARTURE and THE YOGI AND THE COMMISSAR. With the completion of the cycle, Koestler turned away from the problems of political morality which had been the main inspiration of his writing, as if he had exhausted the subject by the very intensity of his experience and by the finality of his rejection of Communism both in theory and in practice. Thereafter, his main interest has been in science, which has inspired a long succession of books. It is worth noticing, however, that despite his withdrawal from politics and the reversal of interests which it involved, there is, in one respect at least, a marked continuity between his early and his later works; just as, indeed, his later writings are inspired by a revival of the scientific interests which were so important to him in childhood and youth, before politics ever touched him.

For in our day, it is not only totalitarian political systems which threaten, or deny, the existence of that 'grammatical fiction', the self, which forced itself into Rubashov's consciousness while in prison. It is equally threatened, or dispensed with, by forms of scientific thinking which refuse to take cognizance of any experiences which cannot be quantified, and, more especially in the field of experimental psychology, reject the hypothesis that there is anything in human nature which cannot be identified by the normal processes of scientific observation and, potentially, cannot be changed as a result of scientific research.

There are indeed Neanderthalers of the laboratory as well as of the torture chamber, inspired by the same 'vivisection morality' as Gletkin. Koestler's later writings have been very largely an attempt to defend the claims of the 'grammatical fiction' against those types of scientific thought which regard it as no more than an unnecessary hypothesis and human beings as no more than a collection of sense data. In essence, this is the same problem with which Rubashov wrestled in his cell; and it is because of his final, even though reluctant, awareness of the 'grammatical fiction' as a hypothesis without which human life ceases to have any meaning or value, that DARKNESS AT NOON is not only a terrible vision of evil, but a vision also of the sources through which the evil may ultimately be exorcised.

The Do-Gooder from Seville Gaol

John Grigg

Many writers who have had a rough time have turned their experiences to good account in their literary work, but have not otherwise exerted themselves to make the world a less nasty place. This could never be said of Arthur Koestler, whose experiences have resulted not only in major literature but in practical philanthropy and intense, if intermittent, crusading effort.

In a short essay one has to take for granted the biggest causes that have claimed his allegiance – his Zionism, his Communism and his anti-Communism. They have shaped his life in its successive phases and have revealed the essential character of his mind, which is at once rational and mystical. But while he has been converted to, or with equal fervour reacted against, all-embracing secular faiths, his desire to improve the world has never been satisfied with cosmic generalities. He has also been attracted to more limited and specific causes, as a rule directly inspired by what has happened to him personally, and in working for them he has deployed all his resources of intellectual concentration and moral passion.

In the immediate post-war period he was conscious of being a refugee who had made good, while other victims of Continental Europe's agony were struggling for mere survival. Having known, himself, what it was like to be an impoverished and disorientated exile, he wanted to do something to help others in like case without impairing their self-respect or their will to make a new life for themselves.

The device that he hit upon was a fund to enable exiled writers from Eastern Europe to continue writing while they were in the process of finding their feet in an alien environment. He called it the Fund for Intellectual Freedom and for about a year in the early 1950s he devoted half his working time to it. The idea was that Western writers should assign to it not less than 10 per cent of their royalties from a given territory. Many responded to his appeal, including Aldous Huxley, Richard Rovere and Stephen Spender. His own contribution, apart from the work he put in, was the whole of the royalties from the dramatized version of DARKNESS AT NOON, which ran for eighteen months on Broadway. This amounted to about 40000 dollars.

The Fund provided refugee authors with the tools of their trade (such as typewriters), made advance payments to them for work in progress, gave them grants for research and, if they were ill, paid their hospital fees. It also established outlets for their work. For instance, a Russian-language literary monthly, *Literaturny Sovremennik,* was launched in Munich, at that time the centre of Soviet emigration. Its 260 octavo pages contained poems, short stories, memoirs, translations and reviews.

In the mid-1950s another cause monopolized Arthur's crusading talents and energies. No writer has better reason to regard capital punishment as an abomination. As a prisoner in Franco's hands during the Spanish Civil War he spent three months under sentence of death. Alone in his cell he heard and saw (through the keyhole) other people being led off to execution. Night after night he expected to share their fate. On one occasion in the gaol at Seville, when the inmates of neighbouring cells had been marched off, the warder's key was momentarily put into his lock and then withdrawn.

In DIALOGUE WITH DEATH, written immediately after his release, he has given a detailed account of his Spanish prison experience, which – along with several of his other books – is likely to endure as a classic of the twentieth century. And in

THE INVISIBLE WRITING he describes in retrospect how, when he 'heard the familiar oily voice read out the lists' of prospective victims in the prison corridor, he 'felt an obsessive urge to share in imagination the fate of those who were taken out, to live and re-live the scene of their execution in every detail', for he was 'convinced that this act of solidarity and identification would make death easier for them'.

THE INVISIBLE WRITING was published in 1954. Early the previous year Derek Bentley, a nineteen-year-old grade four mental defective, was hanged as accomplice in the murder of a policeman. His companion who actually committed the murder was, at sixteen, too young to be executed. There were grounds for believing that Bentley, weak-minded though he was, had tried to prevent the fatal act, and the Home Secretary's refusal to recommend a reprieve for him was widely deplored.

In the early part of 1955 public feeling was further aroused by the case of Ruth Ellis, who was hanged for shooting her lover when she was in an emotionally unbalanced state three weeks after having a miscarriage. At the same time there was growing disquiet about the case of Timothy Evans, who had been convicted and hanged on the evidence of a man who subsequently turned out to be a multiple murderer.

It seemed to Arthur that the time was ripe for a full-scale assault on the institution of capital punishment in Britain. In the summer of 1955 he approached Victor Gollancz with the suggestion that they should together organize a national campaign. Gollancz had never been an intimate friend but he had published Arthur's first book in English, SPANISH TESTAMENT, and they had worked together as Zionists. Arthur admired Gollancz's enthusiasm and his prowess as an impresario of good causes. Their joint efforts for abolition were to prove fruitful but stormy.

The National Campaign for the Abolition of Capital Punishment, whose executive committee held its first meeting on 11 August 1955, was (and is) rather too grandiloquently named. It did not unite in its ranks all who were working to get the death penalty abolished, and it was more of a pressure group than the mass movement, that its name implied. Sydney Silverman, the leading exponent of abolition in the House of Commons, was not invited to join the executive committee and was not even among the speakers at the Campaign's first big rally, in the Central Hall, Westminster, on 10 November 1955.

Arthur did not speak there, either, but from his own choice. 'I do not', he wrote at the time, 'wish to talk in public on the subject. A foreign accent and a foreign name would be an added liability in a campaign basically directed at irrational, emotional prejudice.' Actually he did speak at least once during the winter of 1955–6 – to the Cambridge University Conservative Association, which to his pleasure and surprise showed a 75 per cent majority for abolition on a show of hands after his speech.

The National Campaign may not have been quite as formidable as its name, but its impact on public opinion was by no means insignificant. By the end of 1955 it had nearly 17000 declared supporters, and by February 1956 the number had risen to 26500. It promoted much active lobbying of MPs and other opinion-formers. But probably its most effective weapons were two books, Gerald Gardiner's *Capital Punishment as a Deterrent, and the Alternative*, and Arthur's REFLECTIONS ON HANGING. In their different ways these two books provided an overwhelming statement of the case for abolition, and though their influence cannot be measured it must have been very considerable.

Arthur's was almost certainly the more influential, if only because its message reached a far wider public through serialization in the *Observer* early in 1956, in five instalments of 3000 words each. To write the book Arthur had to interrupt his work on THE SLEEPWALKERS, but he did so without hesitation or regret. Victor Gollancz was the publisher, but there was a delay in bringing it out after the *Observer* serialization, which annoyed Arthur and contributed to the virtual rupture between him and Gollancz in 1956. The book was eventually published in April of that year.

Beyond question it is a polemic of extraordinary power. Arthur showed Britain's persistence in clinging to a barbarous penalty, abandoned by most civilized countries, as contrasting strangely with the generally liberal and humanitarian spirit of modern British history. He did not spare the judiciary and was particularly caustic at the expense of Lord Goddard. Nor did he spare his readers' feelings, evidently intending that they should share in imagination, as he did in Seville gaol, the fate of the poor wretches who were executed. Some critics complained that the book was too gruesome and too lacking in charity towards retentionists, whom he described as 'hanghards'. But Ian Gilmour put the opposite view well when he wrote in the *Spectator*:

As he was once himself under sentence of death, his attitude is perfectly understandable, and if there are any disadvantages in his emotionalism they are outweighed by the power it brings to his writing. Indeed his moral fervour combined with his usual literary grace and distinction may conceivably penetrate the cocoon of complacency which protects many retentionists from the realities of the case. . . .

Besides, there is plenty of hard matter in the book, as well as moral fervour. Gerald Gardiner, whose style of advocacy, on this and other issues, is markedly more restrained, wrote to Arthur after reading the proofs for him: 'I thought that I knew pretty well everything that there was to be known on the subject but I find that I have learned a lot from it.'

REFLECTIONS ON HANGING was followed by a summary of the case-histories of executed murderers from 1949 to 1953, compiled by Arthur and by Cynthia Jefferies (now Mrs Koestler), which was published in the *Observer* and afterwards reprinted as a pamphlet under the title *Patterns of Murder*. Authorship was concealed in the pseudonym 'Vigil', which Arthur himself said he wished to be the 'collective pseudonym for a team' in which he had 'no vested interest'. But most people would regard 'Vigil' in this context as essentially another manifestation of Arthur, and *Patterns of Murder* was, in fact, included as an appendix in the American edition of REFLECTIONS ON HANGING. The case-histories show convincingly that most murderers are not the calculating villains of crime fiction, but are either psychopaths or people caught in tragic personal circumstances, acting under the stress of sudden violent emotion.

The effectiveness of controversial writing can often be judged from the asperity and unreasonableness of the reactions it provokes, and it was, perhaps, a high compliment to Arthur that he was intemperately attacked by government spokesmen in both Houses of Parliament. But the *Observer* stood by him when, far from making any apology, he demanded one himself. Dissatisfied with grudging amends made by Lords Mancroft and Hailsham, he took the matter to the Press Council, which in a statement on 1 May 1956 vindicated him and the *Observer* while administering mild rebukes to the two peers.

Another paper which enabled Arthur to communicate his abolitionist arguments to a mass readership was *Picture Post*, then nearing the end of its creditable career. But undoubtedly it was through the *Observer* that he was able to make his biggest contribution to the cause, which the editor, David Astor, generously acknowledged as being a no less substantial boon to the paper. 'I don't want to sound sententious,' he wrote to Arthur, 'but want to say all the same that I believe your "hanging" journalism – the book extracts, the Vigil pieces and your handling of the attacks – have contributed something of real value to this country and to this newspaper. It is the episode that most deserves to be recorded in the history of this paper, since I've been here. I'm very proud of being associated with what you've done. . . .'

Meanwhile, in mid-February, the House of Commons had voted for abolition. This was not a completely new departure brought about by the National Campaign and its leaders, though of course they played a noticeable part. As early as 1938 the House had voted for an abolitionist motion. Victor Gollancz was convinced that the Commons vote in 1956 would be decisive and that the death penalty was on the way out. He felt that even if the Lords voted against abolition the government would be bound to carry out the will of the Commons, and it is only fair to say that his optimism was shared by many other abolitionists at the time.

It was not shared by Arthur. Immediately after the February vote in the Commons the difference of opinion (and personality clash) between him and Victor Gollancz came to a head. As they were leaving the Houses of Parliament together V.G. told one of the Campaign's provincial organizers, who happened to approach them, that there would be no need for further meetings in the provinces. Arthur was horrified and soon afterwards, after he and V.G. had circulated rival letters to their fellow-members of the executive, the breach between them was formalized without, however, being made public. In a letter to V.G. on 14 March Arthur announced his *de facto* resignation to avoid further 'painful and embarrassing arguments', while undertaking to 'continue to write and work for abolition as before'.

He was as good as his word in at least one vital respect. The Campaign's finances were at a desperately low ebb, and to rectify this state of affairs Arthur took an initiative which led to the raising of a large fund. He suggested to his friend June Osborn (now Mrs Jeremy Hutchinson) that she should organize an auction sale of literary manuscripts and works of art, the proceeds to go towards abolition and penal reform. June, recently widowed, threw herself into the work with her own peculiarly infectious gusto and ruthless powers of persuasion. With the help of a few friends she assembled a remarkable collection of objects, including the works of many famous contemporary artists, presented by themselves. These were sold in London on 30 May at an auction conducted by her cousin, Peter Wilson of Sotheby's. The sum raised was about £4400, and though some of this was in due course given to the Howard League for Penal Reform, most of it was devoted to keeping the National Campaign in being.*

Arthur's sceptical view of the prospects for abolition was, in

---

* It is interesting to record some of the prices paid at the sale – £270 for an Epstein bronze head, £34 for an Edward Lear water-colour, £52 for a John Minton gouache, £250 for a Henry Moore bronze group, £30 for a John Piper pen-and-ink and purple wash, £165 for a Matthew Smith pastel, £100 for a Graham Sutherland gouache; and among the manuscripts, £45 for a Henry Green novel, £47 for a Rosamond Lehmann novel, £265 for a Somerset Maugham short story, £38 for a George Orwell piece on capital punishment (written just before his death), £28 for a Bertrand Russell essay, £18 for an Oscar Wilde letter and £55 for a Virginia Woolf essay. The market for such things was indeed a buyer's market in those days.

the short-term, wholly justified. Though the House of Commons carried the measure through all its stages, the House of Lords threw it out; and the government then introduced a 'compromise' measure on lines that the Gowers Commission had shown to be logically indefensible. Only when the Homicide Act had been tried and found wanting was the death penalty first (in 1965) suspended and then (in 1970) abolished. Arthur played little part in the later stages of the Campaign, though an abridged and updated version of REFLECTIONS ON HANGING was produced in 1961 as a Penguin Special, under the title *Hanged by the Neck,* with C. H. Rolph as the editor and joint-author.

The singular beastliness of killing a human being in cold blood – singular because human beings, unlike animals, can apprehend their own slaughter – was not the only lesson that Arthur learned from his period of incarceration in Spain. He also became vividly aware of the demoralizing, dehumanizing effect of captivity when the prisoner is denied occupation and the means to express himself. It was some time before Arthur was given a book to read or paper to write on. Frustration of his living faculties was thus added to the ever-present fear of death.

One summer evening in 1960, while he was reflecting on his prison days at Seville, the idea came to him of a practical way to help at least the more creative inmates of British gaols. The idea was to give prizes for literature, painting, sculpture, craftsman-ship and musical composition, and by March of the following year the Arthur Koestler Award scheme was agreed with the Prison Commission and approved by the Home Secretary (R. A. Butler). Arthur covenanted for an annual £400 to be distributed in prize-money, ranging from £100 for a work of outstanding merit to consolation prizes of £5. In addition his friend and literary agent, A. D. Peters, who became the first chairman of the Koestler Trustees, provided £100 a year to cover administrative costs.

The scheme came into operation in 1962 and has since not merely continued to operate, but has developed steadily in scope and prestige. The original panel of adjudicating 'experts' ('judges' was not thought to be an appropiate word) consisted of Henry

Green, J. B. Priestley, V. S. Pritchett and Philip Toynbee for literature; Sir Kenneth Clark, Eric Newton and Robert Rowe for arts and crafts; and Sir Arthur Bliss for music. Volunteers of the same high quality have never failed to give their services for what, with the growing number of entries, has become increasingly arduous and time-consuming work. The first year's entries were not up to much, though two of the poems were good enough to be published, anonymously, in *Encounter*. But by 1971 Laurie Lee could write of the poetry alone:

Owing to the remarkable increase in the number of entries this year, and to the power and originality of so many of the poems – even among the work of some who I would guess have seldom tried their hand at poetry before – I have had a heavy problem judging the competition. I have been faced by so much that is compelling . . . that one can only wish that there were more prizes to distribute.

The arts and crafts entries have shown a similar buoyancy, and every year a selection of the best work is exhibited in London. These exhibitions are normally opened by somebody with a special reason for sympathizing with the Award scheme's purpose, and one particularly memorable opener was Sir Geoffrey Jackson, who said that he had been able to keep sane during his eight months' captivity at the hands of terrorists in Uruguay, because they had allowed him pencils and paper and even encouraged his first groping efforts as an amateur artist.

The Koestler Awards can already boast a number of success stories, of which perhaps the best-known is that of the writer 'Zeno', who while serving a life sentence received his first award for a short story and another for his novel *Cauldron,* later published by Macmillan. But the success of the scheme is not really to be judged by its success stories. The chief benefit of it to prisoners is that it gives those with very slight talent, but with some desire for self-expression and self-improvement, a motive for work in prison and – if they win a prize, however small – a sense of achievement. This, moreover, is not only a benefit to the prisoners themselves; it is also, obviously, a potential benefit to society.

In 1968, when Arthur's covenant was due for renewal, Lord Stonham was Minister of State at the Home Office, and at his suggestion the Trustees – under the chairmanship, then, of Sir Hugh Casson–launched an appeal for further funds to enable the scheme to be extended to cover industrial and vocational work in prisons. The response from those approached was generous and their donations and covenants, added to Arthur's renewed covenant, provided a sound financial base for the scheme in its wider form. Seeing that others had joined him in the financing of it Arthur tried to have his name removed from the awards, but the Trustees and Lord Stonham were adamant that his name was indispensable to the standing of the scheme, which in any case was his brainchild. His scruples were eventually overborne, though not without difficulty.

The scheme is capable of still further development, and the most recent step has been to bring musical performance, as well as musical composition, within its scope. The Koestler Awards are a good example of what can be done when the imagination of an individual, and the voluntary service of other private citizens following his lead, receive wholehearted backing and cooperation from the State.

As a serio-comic pendant to this brief account of Arthur's do-gooding activities something must be said of his valiant, but abortive, attempt to mitigate the rigours of the British animal quarantine regulations. Here, too, the inspiration was subjective. He has always been fond of dogs. During his life so far he has owned an Alsatian, a pie-dog, several Boxers, a St Bernard, a black Labrador, a Dalmatian, and his present Landseer New-foundland and Lhasa Apso, not to mention a few mongrels. Moreover, in spite of his profound love of Britain – the country that he has chosen to belong to – he still likes to spend some months of every year outside it, normally on the Continent. He has thus been vulnerable to the rule that dogs taken abroad by their British owners must expiate the offence and purge themselves of foreign contamination during six months behind bars.

At the end of 1961 Peregrine Worsthorne announced in his *Sunday Telegraph* column that Arthur would soon be starting a campaign against dogs' quarantine. The Worsthorne column brought a flood of letters, mainly from members of the Foreign Service and of the Forces stationed abroad, and from representatives of British firms in Europe. There was also a letter from Arthur himself to the *Sunday Telegraph*, explaining that his demand was not that 'canine aliens' should be let in, but simply that 'dogs born and bred in this country' should be allowed to return without undergoing quarantine, provided they had a certificate of inoculation against rabies. (The letter was accompanied by a picture of Arthur with two dogs, one rather ominously called Attila.)

In April 1962 he stated his case more fully in the *Observer*, quoting some of the letters he had received from business men, diplomats and serving officers, and showing that the new Flury vaccine was foolproof against rabies, which was anyway (he said) virtually extinct in the West. But he emphasized again that he was not proposing free entry for foreign dogs (or cats, which were included in the argument though very little mentioned). He ended with an appeal for common sense and compassion. The existing system was adhered to by no other country; it involved

a painful deprivation which cannot be justified on any conceivable grounds except stubborn prejudice; and nobody who has seen his once lively dog slowly going to pot in its solitary lock-up, and had to pay fifty-odd pounds for it, will break into cheers at the august pronouncement of the spokesman for the Ministry of Agriculture ... 'After the experience of thirty years it is proved that this country is far in advance of any other country in this respect.'

For several weeks Arthur devoted himself to the campaign. A committee was formed, a petition got up and a star-studded letter written to *The Times*. Arthur's supporters included Peter Scott and Sir Julian Huxley, as well as generals and ambassadors. But it was all to no avail. Officialdom stood firm and the quiet world of British veterinary medicine, finding itself suddenly under fire from a literary big gun, reacted with nervous indignation. Even the RSPCA was opposed to Arthur, though he received a warm letter of approval from its Gibraltar branch. The Minister of Agriculture, Christopher Soames, at first made seemingly hopeful noises, but in the event did not budge; and an attempt to enlist the support of his aged father-in-law, Winston Churchill – on the apparently false assumption that he took his poodle with him to the South of France – met with a polite but negative response from his private secretary.

The *Observer*, for its part, was far less enthusiastic than it had been about the abolitionist campaign. David Astor advised Arthur not to expend too much time and argumentative effort upon an issue which many might regard as relatively trivial. Though somewhat resentful of this advice, Arthur seems to have acted on it, because three weeks after his original article he wrote another replying to criticism but in effect withdrawing from the campaign. (The two articles are reprinted in his collection of essays, DRINKERS OF INFINITY.)

One day his proposal will almost certainly be adopted, but in the short run a combination of conservatism and xenophobia defeated him. The British have always prided themselves on knowing better than anyone how animals should be treated, and it was galling for them to be lectured on the subject by an intellectual of foreign provenance, citing the example of foreign countries. He may also have had to contend with some class feeling against 'the doggy doggy few'. Most British dog-lovers do not go abroad for long periods and have no desire to take their dogs on short holiday trips to the Costa Brava. Above all, the limited character of Arthur's proposal was imperfectly grasped and his opponents were able to exploit the British fear of mass foreign immigration, scarcely more welcome when the immigrants are dogs than when they are human beings.

In conclusion, a few general comments should be made on Arthur in the capacity of do-gooder. He has a conspicuous talent for working on the conscience as well as the affection of his friends. This talent is very necessary for a philanthropist and Arthur possesses it in a marked degree. After his second *Observer* article on the quarantine issue, when he had disappeared to his house in Austria, Lady Beckett – a friend and member of the still-functioning committee – wrote to him there describing a lunch of the campaigners at which a letter from him was read and 'a slight shudder of fear and guilt swept the table'.

Partly because he is so good at mobilizing friends he can be a formidable campaigner. But he shuns the limelight. Television interviews and oratorical displays are not for him. Though he is unduly sensitive about his foreign name and accent, he is probably wise to concentrate upon the less superficial forms of persuasion at which he excels – private conversation, the written word and the techniques of permeation that come naturally to him as an ex-Communist.

If he will never be a full-time do-gooder, it is not because he lacks the idealism or the staying-power. His practical endeavours are restricted only by the imperious demands of his true calling, which is that of an original writer. His good works are very good indeed, but the works of his that matter most are his literary works, and they are even better. Arthur is, after all, the most distinguished Continental-born English writer since Joseph Conrad.

Twenty-five Writing Years

Cynthia Koestler

In the summer of 1949, when I first started working for Arthur, he was in between books, always an unhappy time. Outwardly he looked the opposite of unhappy: lots of friends came to see him at his house on the Seine near Fontainebleau, and he was near Paris, his favourite city. It was a hedonistic summer and that made him feel even more miserable and guilty.

However, he did manage to write the introduction to ARROW IN THE BLUE, which he worked on in 1951. During a visit to London he had looked up *The Times* published on his birth-date, and this had inspired him to do the introduction to his auto-biography, two years before he started to write the book.

When autumn came he settled down to writing THE AGE OF LONGING. Every week I came out to Fontaine le Port from Paris and typed a new instalment. I could hardly wait for the next one. It reminded me of my childhood when every Thursday my father used to bring home my favourite comics – *Tiger Tim, Bubbles* and *Puck.* In no time I had read them and then had to wait another whole long week to see whether Pat the Pirate would have to walk the plank. I wondered what would happen to Fedya, the hero of THE AGE OF LONGING, and to the heroine, Hydie. One day I saw on Arthur's desk a chapter called 'Love in the Afternoon' which began: 'Wait,' cried Hydie, 'wait! You are tearing my blouse to pieces.' But I was only given this chapter to type in its proper order, which turned out to be a hundred pages after Fedya had taken Hydie out to dinner.

THE AGE OF LONGING was finished in the summer of 1950. In the autumn Arthur went to America and in December bought an island in the Delaware River with an old Pennsylvania Dutch house on it. I went to live and work in London.

In February 1951 I got a letter from him, asking me to come to America and be his secretary. In ten days I had given up my job and flat and was on my way. He had just begun ARROW IN THE BLUE. He dictated large chunks to me, which I took down in shorthand. The dictated part was narrative, but the more difficult passages he wrote in longhand. The book was finished in the autumn.

The second volume of the autobiography, THE INVISIBLE WRITING, was begun in the spring of 1952 and finished in the spring of 1953. It was written in his present London house which he had just bought. I worked part-time again for him, in the mornings. When the book was finished I returned to America and stayed there for two years. His essay volume, THE TRAIL OF THE DINOSAUR, came out in 1955, and early in that year I had a funny letter from him, saying that he was writing a long, scholarly book which would take him two years and that he was looking for a rich Brazilian widow to keep him. This was THE SLEEP-WALKERS.

In the summer of 1955 I came to England on a long holiday and to see my family. This holiday was spent working for Arthur, and the book which he told me he was 'burning to write' was REFLECTIONS ON HANGING. Ruth Ellis had just been hanged – the last woman to be hanged in Britain. Shortly afterwards, Arthur went to see Victor Gollancz at his country place, and the National Campaign for the Abolition of Capital Punishment was founded.*

In the Preface to THE TRAIL OF THE DINOSAUR he had made a vow not to write about Communism and politics any more. By the summer of 1955 he had found this new obsession, and a pretty overwhelming one it was too. He was like somebody possessed; the subject was never far from his mind. If we went to

* The campaign is described in greater detail by John Grigg in his article on page 123 – Ed.

a pub for a drink, he would start up a discussion with the publican. All publicans were hangers in those days, which, of course, was just what Arthur was hoping, and he would present a diabolically reasoned and objective case for abolition. Although he never managed to persuade a single die-hard publican, he never gave up hope. At the end of a working day, the obsession would continue to buzz maddeningly round his head, and he would spend the evening dictating notes to me for the following morning's work. One night he decided to have a fictional chapter in the book. It would be a dialogue between a young abolitionist and a wise old hanging judge. In the cold light of day this idea was rejected.

In September I went back to America only to return to England about a month later because Arthur had resumed work on THE SLEEPWALKERS. He thought it would take another six months to finish. He had written the Copernicus part of a hundred pages before REFLECTIONS ON HANGING. Now he hoped to get on with it and finish it. However, this was not to be, for he continued to be involved in the abolition campaign for a further six or seven months.

In 1956, Lord Kennet – then Wayland Young – lent Arthur his cottage in Wiltshire, The Lackett, for the summer. Here, surrounded by the ghosts of the Bloomsbury set, he was at last able to settle down to writing about his beloved Johannes Kepler.

Kepler had been one of his heroes since the time of his youth. In ARROW IN THE BLUE he writes: 'The heroes of my youth were Darwin and Spencer, Kepler, Newton and Mach . . .' In THE CALL-GIRLS Kepler is mentioned in a clearly autobiographical part – the intellectual development of the hero, Nikolai Solovief:

Later on he was to discover that the Pythagorean fantasy of musical harmonies governing the motions of the stars had never lost its hold on mankind . . . Eventually it produced one of the most astonishing feats in the history of human thought: Johannes Kepler, mathematician and mystic, built the foundations of modern astronomy on similar speculations . . .

He found he had many things in common which endeared him

to Kepler – including a love of gnawing bones and crusts of dry bread. I came across the name of Kepler first when typing THE AGE OF LONGING: at Monsieur Anatole's party the French 'novelist-knight errant' (affectionately modelled on Malraux) mentions in passing that 'Kepler's search for the planetary laws was more an aesthetic than a pragmatic pursuit' and that the law governing planetary motion is 'a particularly elegant gesture of God'.

Even earlier, in DARKNESS AT NOON, one cannot help thinking of THE SLEEPWALKERS when one reads at the very end of the book the poignant exchange tapped between Rubashov and No. 402:

DON'T LISTEN. I WILL TELL YOU IN TIME WHEN THEY ARE COMING ... WHAT WOULD YOU DO IF YOU WERE PARDONED?
Rubashov thought it over. Then he tapped: STUDY ASTRONOMY.

And indeed, after the last piece he ever wrote on Communism – the title essay in THE TRAIL OF THE DINOSAUR – Arthur began THE SLEEPWALKERS.

He had originally intended the book to be a biography of Kepler, but had found it necessary to go back to Copernicus. Then REFLECTIONS ON HANGING had intervened. Now that the time had come to write about Kepler he found that it was not easy at all; the incubation period (more than a year) had been too long. It took several weeks before he found the right style and the complicated and contradictory character of Kepler began to emerge. He worried about the sort of reader he was writing for. Was it to be a scholarly book purely for the specialist or one for the intelligent layman? This problem was eventually solved by relegating parts which were only of interest to the specialist to voluminous Notes at the end of the book. Now the flow of the book was undisturbed by technicalities and pedantry.

Back in London in the autumn, he decided that he must go further back in the history of science. He went back to the Middle Ages, then wrote Part I, the cosmology of the Greeks and Egyptians. I remember one bleak winter's night when his obsession with Plato and Aristotle, 'the twin stars' as he called them, became unbearable. He had to talk to somebody about it. Henry Green lived round the corner and had studied Classics, so we went to see him. Arthur, alas, got little out of the visit, except perhaps letting off steam. But Henry did: he had nothing to say about Plato and Aristotle, but he looked on and listened, obviously bemused by the sight of a man with a burning obesssion. Sebastian, Henry's son, plied Arthur with vodkas, but even they did not help. When at last we left he was as tormented as ever by the twin stars; somewhat the worse for wear and staggering slightly, he wondered if his mind would give him any peace to sleep.

THE SLEEPWALKERS grew longer and longer. After Kepler came Galileo and then Newton and the Epilogue. Most of the book was written in another house haunted by the Bloomsbury set – Long Barn in Kent – which Arthur owned for three years. It was at last finished in the spring of 1958. Then he was between books again. We spent the summer in Alpbach, looking for a piece of land to buy. Arthur worked on an idea he had for a novel, but it came to naught. He told me that to visit India and Japan was 'on the cards', and spent the autumn reading up and preparing for the journey. His main purpose was to visit holy men and psychiatrists. He left in December, returned in April 1959, and then wrote three pieces on India for the *Observer* and two on Japan for *Encounter*. They were to be part of a book to be called THE LOTUS AND THE ROBOT. We went to Alpbach again, this time to supervise the building of the house. It took all summer. Arthur managed to write the chapter on Baiji and Ananda Mayee Ma, but the house-building prevented him from finding the peace he needed. Besides, that burning obsession, which accompanies the writing of all his books, was lacking. It had all been wastefully channelled into the building and the usual frustrating dealings with elusive builders.

By the autumn the house was finished. When he got back to London, Arthur started work on three long lectures on creativity which he had been invited to give at Manchester University. This encouraged him, and he decided he would at last write Volume Two of INSIGHT AND OUTLOOK (later called THE ACT OF CREATION). He abandoned THE LOTUS AND THE ROBOT;

there was not enough material for more than a further two pieces for *Encounter*.

Arthur was a great admirer of Jayaprakash Narayan, whom he had met in India. He told me he was a 'prince among Indians'. He now invited him to come and stay with him in London, an invitation which included his return air fare. J.P. accepted. He came at the beginning of December and stayed for three weeks. The visit was a disappointment for Arthur. Among other things he hoped that an urban Bhoodan movement could be set up to do something about the homeless who sleep in the streets of Bombay and Calcutta. Hopes were high, but that was all, and as usually happens with Indian projects, nothing came of it.

However, J.P.'s visit inspired Arthur to write THE LOTUS AND THE ROBOT after all. He finished it in four months, to meet his publisher's deadline. Whilst writing the part on Japan he took three or four times a week a 'happy pill' (Drymamil) as he was working against time. It made writing easier; but he found that passages which he had thought were good whilst writing them were, on a second reading, purple-patchy.

Installed for the summer in his new house in Alpbach, Arthur began to write the book which he dreaded and had shelved for so long – since Volume I, INSIGHT AND OUTLOOK, which was written in 1945-7. This was THE ACT OF CREATION. Disheartened by the reception of INSIGHT AND OUTLOOK in 1948, he was now returning to the subject after thirteen years. The book took three and a half years, and he began by re-writing the humour part in INSIGHT AND OUTLOOK. This was difficult as he was sick of the subject and hated having to chew the cud. He was also unable to find any suitable new jokes. Once this torture was over, he was launched on the book. He was so immersed that he did not look at the 'Urgent' file (letters to be answered) for weeks, nor did he care, which was unusual. And he gave up do-it-yourself repairs around the house – carpentry and electrical – which he enjoys. He even stopped studying wine-lists and ordering the wine himself.

At the beginning of 1963 he rented for a month a friend's villa near Gassin, a *village perché* up above St Tropez. Here, cut off from the world by heavy snowfalls, he wrote the chapter on the psychology and physiology of weeping – an area of human behaviour almost completely neglected by the psychologist.

However, after two and a half years, he came up for air and more or less shelved the book for a time – from the end of 1962 till May, 1963 – when he became involved in a cause which he has felt passionately about since the war. The *Observer* asked him to contribute to a series of articles on 'What's Left For Patriotism?' Arthur wrote a piece about the decline of Britain, the class barrier (Them and Us) and the disrupting and unpatriotic attitude of the trade unions. During the war, when he was a private in the Pioneer Corps 'digging for victory', he had met with a phenomenon which was quite unlike its counterparts on the Continent – the British working class. He had kept a file called 'Suicide of a Nation' ever since he returned to England in 1952. In it were newspaper cuttings about wildcat strikes, about the royal yacht being repaired abroad (where it was quicker and cheaper), about demarcation disputes. A typical cutting (from the *Guardian*) was: 'Britain Bottom of the Class'. The *Observer* were not at all happy about Arthur's piece; they felt it had nothing to do with the subject of patriotism. But they printed it. This resulted in Arthur being invited by Melvin J. Lasky to edit a special issue of *Encounter* on the state of Britain. Arthur hoped it might open the nation's eyes to the present crisis – which has now gone from bad to worse. The *Encounter* issue, with the contributions of sixteen other writers, was published in July 1963, and later that year in book form.

THE ACT OF CREATION neared its end. I dreaded the post-book depression. Would Arthur ever write again? This was his *magnum opus*. Perhaps the post-book depression was worse than past ones. I shall never know because he never talks about them. But one can detect the signs. After the publication of the book in May 1964, Arthur received a great many invitations to symposia on psychology, biology and neurophysiology. He was excited by this because he enjoyed above all hard-headed – and hot-headed – discussions in overlapping fields of science, which were the purpose of such symposia. He was to be sadly disappointed in the lack of communication between the different branches – one of the tragic themes in THE CALL-GIRLS.

In 1964 he was invited for a year as a Fellow of the Center for Advanced Study in the Behavioral Sciences at Stanford, California. It was here that his next book, THE GHOST IN THE MACHINE, started to take shape. He formed a Workshop with the neurophysiologist, Professor Karl Pribram, which met for discussion twice a week, and he delved more deeply into the subject of evolution. He found that evolution, through paedomorphosis, could be fitted into his theory of creativity – in the act of *reculer pour mieux sauter*. The seed of an idea was also sown at the Center for the book which he was working on in 1974.

In the autumn of 1965, at the Bicentennial Celebration of the Smithsonian Institution in Washington, he met Paul MacLean for the first time, and read his papers on the old and new brain. He must have formulated his theory, based on Paul MacLean's work, at this time; he had been studying, whilst at the Center, books on cannibalism and human sacrifice, and Paul MacLean's work came at the right moment when a number of ideas on this theme were in chrysalis form.

On his return to London, Arthur began to write. THE GHOST IN THE MACHINE, he said, was going to be as light as a soufflé. He was cheered by this thought, having spent so much time in recent years wading through heavy-handed scientific jargon and even having to resort to it himself. The book took a year and a half to write. As I typed the first hundred pages I wondered what had happened to the soufflé; it had become as heavy and solid as a dumpling. It was only when he reached Part III that one began to see that this dumpling was the massive foundation on which the alarming theory propounded in this Part was built. As he neared the end of the book, Arthur became more and more tormented with the thought that it was not one book, but two. Where was the bridge between Parts I and II and Part III? It *was* two books. Many a time he discussed this awful problem with me, late at night when his torments always worried him most. I was a bad listener, rubbing my eyes, my head nodding. And how could I possibly say whether a book had a 'bridge', as he liked to call it, or not? In the end the two books became one. Afterwards Arthur felt he had made the wrong decision.

THE GHOST IN THE MACHINE was finished in the spring of 1967. In the summer, among other things, he put together a volume of essays written over the years 1955–67 – DRINKERS OF INFINITY. In the autumn he began to organize the Alpbach Symposium, which was held in June 1968. The summer was spent in editing the discussions and getting the Symposium into book form.* The year ended with a trip to Australia, the South Pacific and the Caribbean. As always on journeys to unknown countries, Arthur did an enormous amount of reading up beforehand.

Returning to London at the beginning of 1969, he began a year in which he had several ideas for a new book but they did not work out. One was to be about Semmelweiss, the doctor who abolished puerperal fever in his hospital in Vienna by insisting that all the doctors and nurses wash their hands before tending to patients in childbirth. But this novel idea was not accepted by the medical profession and Semmelweiss came to a tragic end. As Semmelweiss was a Hungarian, Arthur had the advantage of being able to read material in Hungarian, a secret language to most people. Alas, the documentation was sparse. A biography of Mesmer against the background of the times was another still-born idea – the material, too, was scant, and Arthur was disappointed in Mesmer as a person. In February 1969 he thought of writing a novel about the call-girl circuit at scientific symposia; he would call it 'The Parameter of Urgency'.

During the summer of 1969 he wrote, among other things, two short stories ('The Chimaera' and 'The Misunderstanding'), which later became the Prologue and Epilogue to THE CALL-GIRLS. 'The Misunderstanding' he sketched out entirely one evening after dinner over a bottle of wine. After-dinner ideas were frequently rejected the morning after. But 'The Misunderstanding' was an inspiration which he dashed off in the heat of the moment the following day – a rare thing for a slow writer like Arthur. The idea that Christ had wanted to die to draw

* BEYOND REDUCTIONISM (Hutchinson, 1969).

God's attention to the sad state of the world was one he had had at the back of his mind for several years. I heard him trying it out one evening on an old friend, a Jungian analyst, and had thought he would one day write an essay on the subject.

In November 1969 Arthur started to write THE CALL-GIRLS. He also had an idea for an essay: 'Kammerer and The Law of the Series'. By January he had written thirty-five pages of THE CALL-GIRLS but was still uncertain whether it would come off. As we were spending four weeks in January and February in Alpbach, he decided to ask a research student and translator at the University of Innsbruck, who had transcribed the tapes for BEYOND REDUCTIONISM, to see what material she could dig up on Paul Kammerer, starting with the obituaries. The obituaries from the Viennese papers arrived a week later. The suicide note alone showed that Paul Kammerer was no ordinary person. The quest for Kammerer became an intriguing work of detection, and grew into a book – THE CASE OF THE MIDWIFE TOAD. His obsessive feelings were divided between the figure of Kammerer and the background – the birth of Neo-Darwinism. When he had told the story of the forgery of which Kammerer was accused, Arthur then turned to Kammerer's fat book, *The Law of the Series*. He had read it as a student and always been intrigued by it. As he delved into 'confluential events', he got more and more involved in ESP and in ESP and physics. He had not studied the progress of physics beyond the 1920s; when he brought that knowledge up to date, it made his mind boggle. The book began to grow, but it grew out of hand. It seemed to be turning into two books. Once more, Arthur could not make up his mind what to do. He thought he could solve the problem by having two parts: Part I – The Case of the Midwife Toad, and Part II – Psi. But still he was not happy. And where did the chapter on 'The Law of the Series' go? He was reminded of his mistake in making one book out of Parts I and II of THE ACT OF CREATION (to solve a publishing difficulty) and of THE GHOST IN THE MACHINE. And the same was the case with SPANISH TESTAMENT (the first part political, the second – DIALOGUE WITH DEATH – introspective). In December, when he was well into the ESP bit, he at last cut the nerve between the two intended parts. He revised the first draft of THE CASE OF THE MIDWIFE TOAD, put 'The Law of the Series' into an appendix, and finished the book by the end of the year.

Part II – 'Psi' – became THE ROOTS OF COINCIDENCE. He now gave this a rest and went back to THE CALL-GIRLS. It was not until March 1971 that he was to take up the threads again of THE ROOTS OF COINCIDENCE, at a time when he got stuck with THE CALL-GIRLS. THE ROOTS OF COINCIDENCE was finished at the end of March. Since 1937, when he was in prison in Spain, Arthur has been interested in ESP. The chapter 'Hours at the Window' bears witness to his long-standing belief in the power of mind over matter. In THE SLEEPWALKERS he describes the mysticism of Kepler which led him to formulate his Three Laws. Kepler's 'universe is the symbol and "signature" of the Holy Trinity: the sun represents the Father, the sphere of the fixed stars the Son, the invisible forces which, emanating from the Father, act through interstellar space, represent the Holy Ghost'. And: 'Thus a purely mystical inspiration was the root out of which the first rational theory of the dynamics of the universe developed.' In the Epilogue he writes: 'At the beginning of this long journey, I quoted Plutarch's comment on the Pythagoreans: "The contemplation of the eternal is the aim of philosophy, as the contemplation of the mysteries is the aim of religion." For Pythagoras as for Kepler, the two kinds of contemplation were twins; for them philosophy and religion were motivated by the same longing: to catch glimpses of eternity through the window of time.'

Tucked away in Appendix II of THE ACT OF CREATION is an essay on 'Some Features of Genius' (both this Appendix and Appendix I were almost thrown out altogether, as they did not fit into the mainstream of the book). This part deals with the mystical or metaphysical quest of the scientist – from the Greeks to Pasteur. Arthur calls the Greek attitude to science 'a quest transcending the mortal self'. In Benjamin Franklin's case, like Kepler, 'a mystical conviction gave birth, by analogy, to a scientific theory'. And Maxwell: 'In his case, too, religious belief became a spur to scientific activity. . . . The connection between Maxwell's religious and scientific views is indeed just as intimate as in the case of Franklin or Kepler.' Lastly, Pasteur: 'In old age he would often browse in his earlier publications. Turning the pages of his writings, he would marvel at the lands that he had revealed by dispelling the fogs of ignorance and by overcoming stubbornness. He would live again his exciting voyages, as he told Loir in a dreamy voice: "How beautiful, how beautiful! And to think I did it all. I had forgotten it." '

During the time of Pope John, Arthur was attracted to Roman Catholicism. I remember one evening his brother-in-law, Arthur Goodman, who was a Catholic, expressing doubts about his religion. Arthur made such a moving dissertation about the beauty of symbolism in the Catholic faith that his brother-in-law, whose doubts were real, was quite overwhelmed. Arthur was equally vehement about not taking that symbolism literally.

On the other hand, as he says, with his head in the clouds, he likes to keep his feet planted firmly on the ground. Mysticism *per se* is not enough for him; indeed it disgusts him. In a discussion with a Jungian friend, he once said that he believed in wading into the sea with one's feet in the sand as long as one could. Only when the water got too deep was it permissible to float. He divided people into waders and floaters.

Not long ago, in conversation with the author of a book on reincarnation, Arthur said that the idea did not appeal to him. He liked to imagine that after death the self became a minute part of the whole universe – a grain of salt in the ocean upon which a ray of sun occasionally shone.

When he settled in London in 1952, he became a member of the Society of Psychical Research, went occasionally to lectures, subscribed to all the serious journals, and even dabbled in the occasional experiment – including one involving levitation. After his return from India he bought a huge weighing machine of the kind to be found at railway stations, and conducted a series of experiments in the hope of getting his subjects to lose a few ounces of weight. The results, alas, were neither here nor there.

THE CALL-GIRLS was only finished in the spring of 1972.

In 1971 the Alpbach house had been sold, and the house-moving and looking for a second, country place caused many interruptions which made writing impossible.

In April 1972 Arthur started work on his part of the book written jointly with Sir Alister Hardy and Robert Harvie –THE CHALLENGE OF CHANCE – which he finished in February, 1973. In it he extended the themes elaborated in THE ROOTS OF COINCIDENCE.

He then prepared a volume of essays written in between work on books over the years 1968–73 – THE HEEL OF ACHILLES.

After that an unhappy, between-books year went by. He worked for a while on a novel or short story which he has taken up from time to time over many years only to abandon it again. He decided to write a book summing up his philosophy in the trilogy (THE SLEEPWALKERS, THE ACT OF CREATION and THE GHOST IN THE MACHINE), but shied away from it. A book on euthanasia, and its connection with capital punishment and abortion, was also considered. Since he could never remember these painful times, I had to remind him that this was not the longest between-books period that he had suffered and that he had gone through similar discouraging phases in the past. Perhaps this so-called record will comfort him a little during future inevitable between-books times.

At the time of writing, he is at work on another book and lives again. But what I find puzzling is this: if he is so unhappy when he is not writing, why is he always in such a tormented hurry to finish the book he is working on? It almost seems as if the agony of writing were the more unbearable. Then follows the misery of the after-book depression. So one paradox succeeds another in his cycle of writing.

Arthur Koestler and George Orwell

T. R. Fyvel

At first sight, it may be somewhat puzzling that Arthur Koestler and George Orwell should have become close friends, in view of the sharp differences in their origin and spiritual make-up. There was Orwell, in so many ways an English islander, tall, gaunt and melancholy (in appearance, as I remember him, like a 'seedy Sahib'); by heritage, a trifle suspicious of Central European Jews; a writer of a great but in some ways narrow talent, struggling hard for anti-imperialism and internationalism and, above all, truthfulness and decency in politics. And there was Koestler, his outward opposite: small, compact, sanguine, with his past rooted in the Communist Party; a gifted linguist, a truly multinational writer with almost too many divergent talents and an enthusiasm for testing any new idea. The explanation is that with all their national and temperamental differences, Koestler and Orwell had ultimately arrived at similar views about the world; they had the same nose for the horrific news of their times, and in this identification lay the basis of their friendship.

The first meeting of minds, I suppose, took place when Orwell, on 5 February 1938, reviewed Koestler's SPANISH TESTAMENT in *Time and Tide*. Orwell himself was newly back from Spain and the experiences he was to relate in *Homage to Catalonia*. In his review, after recounting Koestler's adventures in

General Franco's prison, he touched on the point made by Koestler that no one who had lived through the hell of Madrid under bombardment could remain objective about it; if those in control of Europe's press remained objective about such bestiality, then Europe was lost. Orwell's comment was sad and emotional, prophetic for our time:

I quite agree. You cannot be objective about an aerial torpedo. And the horror we feel of these things has led to this conclusion: if someone drops a bomb on your mother, go and drop two bombs on his mother. The only apparent alternatives are to smash dwelling houses to powder, blow out human entrails and burn holes in children with lumps of thermite, or to be enslaved by people who are more ready to do these things than you are yourself; as yet no one has suggested a practical way out.

As Koestler has said, he realized from this review that a quite unusual mind had been scrutinizing his work, a mind worrying agonizedly over the dilemma of impending modern war.

Koestler and Orwell actually first met in the spring of 1941 when Orwell asked Koestler to contribute to the Searchlight Books series. This was a series of short books which had been dreamed up by Orwell and myself and F. J. Warburg as publisher, to be a forum for the discussion of British war aims. The series had been led off by Orwell's *The Lion and the Unicorn,* which had impressed Koestler greatly. The idea now was that Koestler should write about Britain's allies on the European continent. This idea, in fact, came to nothing because Koestler was very soon called up for war service in the Pioneer Corps. Koestler's view was that Orwell thought this call-up quite proper. He was surprised to learn much later from the posthumous publication of Orwell's war diaries that this was not so at all. As Orwell had written – angrily – in his diary on 12 February 1941:

Arthur Koestler is being called up this week and will be drafted into the Pioneers, other sections of the forces being barred to him as a German.* What appalling stupidity, when you have a youngish,

* Orwell was, of course, in error about Koestler's nationality – Ed.

gifted man who speaks I do not know how many languages and really knows something about Europe, especially the European political movements, to be unable to make any use of him except for shovelling bricks.

So much for the military authorities. Before this, however, in December 1940, DARKNESS AT NOON had been published and on 4 January 1941, Orwell reviewed it in the *New Statesman*. (This review is not included in the edition of Orwell's collected essays and writings.) From this Koestler learned one thing: that where reviews of the books of friends were concerned, Orwell would bend over backwards to be 'objective' – i.e., he would write from such a loftily stern and critical standpoint that one could not possibly suspect any strand of personal feeling affecting his literary integrity. Orwell's review was, indeed, quite magisterially severe. After stating that Koestler's past in prisons and concentration camps had no doubt fitted him to write a prison novel, Orwell outlined the plot and seemed particularly taken by Koestler's delineation of the character of Gletkin, the hero Rubashov's second interrogator. Gletkin is one of the Soviet state's new barbarians, a man totally severed from the past, who feels that in the interests of the Party Rubashov had best confess to plotting to assassinate Stalin. As Orwell wrote:

The only form of criticism that Gletkin was able to imagine is murder. As he sees it, anyone capable of thinking a disrespectful thought about Stalin would, as a matter of course, attempt to assassinate him. Therefore, though the attempt at assassination has perhaps not been made, it can be held to have been made . . . When Rubashov gives in and confesses, it is not because of the torture . . . so much as from complete inner emptiness. 'I asked myself,' he says at his trial, almost in Bukharin's words, 'for what am I fighting?'

For what, indeed? Orwell went on to express rather less sympathy with the old Bolsheviks than did Koestler:

The Moscow trials were a horrible spectacle, but if one remembered what the history of the Old Bolsheviks had been, it was difficult to be sorry for them as individuals. They took to the sword, and they perished by the sword.

So there!

DARKNESS AT NOON, said Orwell, though in some ways brilliant as a novel, was probably most valuable as an interpretation of the 'confessions' at the trials. While torture had clearly played some part here, said Orwell, it was not the whole story:

Mr Koestler thinks, like Souvarine, that 'for the good of the Party' was probably the final argument; indeed, his book is rather like an expanded, imaginative version of Souvarine's *Cauchemar en URSS*. As a piece of writing, it is a notable advance on his earlier work.

It was rather a severe, schoolmasterly review, and one which quite failed to bring out that DARKNESS AT NOON was, after all, a one-time great achievement, a classic of its kind. So much so that two issues later Kingsley Martin, editor of the *New Statesman*, saw fit to review DARKNESS AT NOON all over again, and with quite a different enthusiasm:

Mr Koestler's DARKNESS AT NOON is one of the few books written in this epoch which will survive it. It is written from terrible experience, from knowledge of the men whose struggles of mind and body he describes. Apart from its sociological importance, it is written with a subtlety and an economy which class it as great literature. I have read it twice without feeling that I have learned more than half of what it has to offer me.

A reaction very different from Orwell's. 'Orwell's reviews of his friends' books were so deliberately dour,' Koestler has said, 'that even his praise did not sound like praise.'

At some time later during the war, Koestler was able to leave the Pioneer Corps and to sit down to write. Orwell had first run the Indian Service of the BBC, then resigned, and when Aneurin Bevan took over the Left-wing weekly *Tribune,* Orwell in 1943 became *Tribune's* literary editor, remaining there until 1945. During this period, Koestler wrote several notable articles for Orwell, published simultaneously in *Tribune* and the *New York Times Sunday Magazine.*

One which attracted particular attention was about the defects of English book-reviewing, called 'A Reader's Dilemma', written in April 1944. (I must have got hold of a copy of *Tribune* on the Italian front, because I can well remember reading the article.) Replying to a British corporal who had written for advice on what to read, Koestler attacked the desperately low standards of some British reviewing, above all the undisicriminating praise handed out by novel-reviewers like Ralph Straus. Koestler gave an imaginary example:

Let us assume that among the newly-published novels of the week there is one called *Roses from a Kentish Garden* by a Miss Edwardes and another called *Crime and Punishment*. Each would get about twenty lines, approximately thus:

'. . . of the delightful Kentish landscape. Her characters are neatly drawn and the story, if somewhat halting, is gracefully and adroitly drawn.

'Mr Dostoyevsky, a Russian, lacks Miss Edwardes' delicate humour. An excitable young student kills a usuress with an axe . . . somewhat morbid effect. But the characters are neatly drawn, the dialogue is fluent, and, on the whole, the story is told with adroitness and skill.'

Orwell, a few weeks later in *Tribune,* followed up the article in his characteristic style:

Arthur Koestler's recent article in *Tribune* set me wondering whether the book racket will start up again in its old vigour after the war, when paper is plentiful and there are other things to spend your money on . . .

Orwell sardonically concluded that the big publishers would no doubt resume their racket of book-promotion as before. But meanwhile he was brooding about Koestler's work. When in 1944 Koestler published what was not one of his best novels, ARRIVAL AND DEPARTURE, about a young man who discovers from being psychoanalysed that his revolutionary ardour was due not to his love of the masses but to his unconscious opposition to his father, Orwell took the opportunity to survey this work in an article he called simply 'Arthur Koestler', published in *Polemic* in September 1944.

This time, Orwell took Koestler's life-style more seriously. True anti-Fascist literature, he said, could be written only by

Europeans with direct experience of Fascism and Communism, like Malraux, Silone, Borkenau and Koestler himself – 'no Englishman could have written DARKNESS AT NOON'. But there was something that worried Orwell. It had been the sin of nearly all Left-wingers, he wrote, that they wanted to be anti-Fascists without being anti-totalitarian. Koestler had, for instance, been a member of the Communist Party, which fact had introduced a false note into his early writings. But this false note had been recognized by Koestler, and this recognition made his present writings all the more valuable. After dealing with Koestler's novel, THE GLADIATORS, where the gladiators in revolt strive for an ideal 'City of the Sun' but as soon as they become a community are themselves beset by quarrels, cruelty and injustice, Orwell turned again to DARKNESS AT NOON and this time took this novel more seriously. 'DARKNESS AT NOON reaches the stature of tragedy whereas an English or American writer would at most have made it into a political tract.' Analysing the novel again, Orwell thought that Koestler seemed to be saying that all revolution was a corrupting process:

It is not merely that 'power corrupts'; so also do the ways of attaining power. Therefore, all efforts to regenerate society *by violent means* lead to the cellars of the OGPU, Lenin leads to Stalin and would have come to resemble Stalin if he had happened to survive. Of course, Koestler does not say this explicitly, and perhaps is not altogether conscious of it. He is writing about darkness, but it is darkness at what ought to be noon.

But should it ever have been noon? Looking at Koestler's work as a whole, Orwell concluded that 'the chink in Koestler's armour was his hedonism.' It was this hedonism which had prevented him from finding a new political line after breaking with Stalinism and which apparently caused Koestler to believe that at some time in the future life would cease to be brutish (as in the gladiators' 'City of the Sun'), so that it was all right to be a 'short-term pessimist', temporarily keeping out of all politics. Whereas might not the long term be equal to the short term, might not life in the long term remain brutish? It was Koestler's hopes to the contrary which worried Orwell:

At the basis of his choice [i.e., to be a 'short-term pessimist'] lies Koestler's hedonism which leads him to think that the Earthly Paradise is desirable. Perhaps, however, whether desirable or not, it isn't possible. Perhaps some degree of suffering is ineradicable from human life, perhaps the choice before man is always a choice of evils, perhaps even the aim of Socialism is not to make the world perfect but to make it better. All revolutions are failures but they are not the same failure. It is his unwillingness to admit this that has led Koestler's mind temporarily into a blind alley.

The last reference was to ARRIVAL AND DEPARTURE. Koestler has remarked that he told Orwell again and again that what he, Orwell, considered 'the hedonist chink in Koestler's armour' was, in fact, his love of life, but to no avail. Orwell had his bone and would worry over it.

Not long after the war, in March 1946, Koestler wrote his last article for *Tribune*. It happened to be a prophetic one: it dealt with the gigantic puzzle of desirable relations between the West and the Soviet Union, a question which for a while brought Koestler and Orwell into close cooperation.

After an interval they had met again in London in the summer of 1945. Orwell's first wife, Eileen, had died suddenly just after they had adopted a baby boy, Richard. Talking after drinks, Orwell remarked that he was desperately lonely, an admission which took Koestler aback. He was not used to such frankness from Orwell, he once told me, adding: 'The closer one came to him, the more there seemed to be a barrier against warmth and personal contact.'

This renewal of contact occurred, however, during the heady first months immediately after the end of the war and Koestler and Orwell between them thought up a project. This was to found a successor organization to the pre-war League for the Rights of Man, a body with something of the aims of today's Amnesty or International Jurists, which had taken up individual cases of religious, racial and political persecution. Just before the war, however, the League had been taken over by the Stalinists and become a fellow-traveller front, thus losing validity.

In view of the decline in democratic feeling caused by the war,

Koestler and Orwell decided in late 1945 that a successor organization to the League was called for. It should aim to protect the individual in all countries against arbitrary arrest without trial and deportation or restriction against his free movement, to promote freedom of speech and of the press and the right of each individual to vote democratically for the candidate of his choice. A possible name for the organization would be 'League for the Defence of Democracy'. The first task was to find people who could become members of the League and its committee. Koestler recounts how he and Orwell went over a long list of liberals, saying 'he's reliable' and, more often, 'he's not' – reliable in the sense of holding anti-totalitarian views which inevitably included anti-Communist views.

In the prevailing post-war climate, such liberals were not easy to find. It was then that Koestler, after discussions with Orwell, wrote a striking article for *Tribune* (10 March 1946), entitled 'A Way to Fight Suspicion'. In it, he stated how for historic reasons the Soviet government had built up the Soviet state on the basis of the isolation of the Soviet people from the outside world and on the idea of being perpetually at war with the outside world. Soviet citizens had, for instance, heard almost nothing about the Western war efforts except for complaints about Western shortcomings. The Soviet Government had achieved a State monopoly not only over the production and distribution of goods but over that of ideas, opinions and emotions: and this monopoly was geared to maintain suspicion against the West. To achieve better relations, palliative gestures by the West were therefore useless unless the Soviet government could be induced to turn off the master-switch of its hostile anti-Western propaganda. In any negotiations for an East–West détente, the Western powers should therefore put forward demands for Soviet psychological disarmament, including:

(a) Free access of foreign newspapers, periodicals, books and films to the USSR;

(b) Such modifications of the Russian censorship (if censorship there must be) as to permit the free circulation of information about the outside world throughout Soviet territory;

(c) Free access for accredited journalists, parliamentary committees, etc., to Russian-occupied territroy;

(d) The abolishing of restrictions on travel for foreigners in Soviet territory and for Soviet citizens abroad;

(e) Active cooperation with the Western Powers in the organization of 'vacations abroad' schemes, on a mutual exchange basis, for students, teachers, writers, workers and professional men.

Such psychological disarmament, wrote Koestler, would automatically lead to military disarnament. Although such measures would enormously raise the living standards of the Soviet people, one could not expect the Soviet leaders to agree easily to them. The demand for Soviet psychological disarmament should therefore be raised at every East–West meeting and on every forum.

Koestler spelt all this out in *Tribune* in the spring of 1946. It is the stage which the East–West debate has reached today.

Meanwhile Koestler and Orwell were busily sounding out people as possible members for the League for the Defence of Democracy and discussing its constitution. It could seem a difficult task. Koestler and his wife Mamaine had gone to live in North Wales, near Bertrand Russell, and Orwell wrote to him on 1 January 1946:

I saw Barbara Ward and Tom Hopkinson today and told them about our project. They were both a little timid, chiefly I think because they realise that an organisation of this type would in practice be anti-Russian and they are going through an acute phase of anti-Americanism. However, they are anxious to hear more and certainly are not hostile to the idea. I said the next step would be to show them the draft manifesto, or whatever it is, when drawn up. I wonder if you have seen Bertrand Russell, and if so what he said.

A little later, Orwell wrote that he had met the representative of the International Rescue and Relief Committee, an American organization with aims somewhat similar to those of the projected League, and had obtained valuable American addresses from him. 'Obviously we should have comprehensive lists of sympathizers in all countries.'

Russell had, in fact, at first sight liked the idea of the 'League for the Defence of Democracy' and suggested convening a conference in North Wales for Easter, 1946. Orwell came to visit Arthur and Mamaine Koestler to discuss this – Koestler told me recently that he remembers the weekend vividly. As Koestler had discovered, Orwell had in that week's issue of *Tribune* written a long review of what Koestler in retrospect considered 'a lousy play', TWILIGHT BAR. Orwell's review had been merciless. Koestler asked half-jokingly: 'Why didn't you just say that the play was not worthy of a gifted writer, why did you have to say that it was all muck, why did you write such a stinking review?' 'Well,' said Orwell, 'it was a stinking play.' So much for that.

Koestler had recently returned from Palestine, where British troops were engaged in futile military actions in the last stages of the Mandate. The discussion that evening turned to colonial policy and Orwell stated his view that Britain should immediately and unconditionally withdraw her troops from India. When Koestler said that on the day of such withdrawal there would be 100000 dead in Calcutta, Orwell replied that no matter, this would at least be the Indians' affair, at least there would be no more of the hated concept of the white man's burden. He similarly favoured an immediate British withdrawal from Palestine. On this issue his sympathies were completely with what he considered the underdogs, the natives, the Arabs.

Koestler and Orwell decided that there was no point in arguing further about Palestine. Koestler remembers drinking a good deal that evening. The following morning, when he went walking with Orwell across the Welsh mountain landscape, he remarked that he had slept badly and had nightmares – when he drank he often woke up with guilt feelings. After considering this, Orwell remarked: 'When I wake up, I think of all the tortures I could inflict on my enemies.' Koestler says that this odd remark stuck in his mind – it was there when he read the more sadistic pages of *Nineteen Eighty-Four*.

As it happened, the project for the 'League for the Defence of Democracy' came to nothing: the conference in North Wales for founding the League was never convened. The immediate reason was that at the last moment the expected sources of finance proved to be not forthcoming. The second reason, of course, was that British liberal intellectuals were going through their phase of severe anti-Americanism. Bertrand Russell, for instance, wanted the projected League to put as much stress on political persecution in the USA as in the Soviet Union – he had hated the Americans ever since they put him in prison for advocating free love. But such a picture of considering the USA and the Soviet Union as equally anti-democratic was precisely the 'false equation' Orwell and Koestler wanted to fight against. A third reason why the project came to nothing was that both Koestler and Orwell were writers, not organization men. Orwell was turning over *Nineteen Eighty-Four* in his mind, while Koestler was writing the essays which appeared in THE YOGI AND THE COMMISSAR. So their ways parted. The last time they met was in 1947, after which Orwell went to the Isle of Jura to write his savage novel, while Koestler went on travels in France, Italy and America until in January 1950, when he was staying in Paris, he was telephoned by David Astor, the editor of the *Observer,* with news of Orwell's death.

Koestler remembers this telephone call clearly. 'I had first brought Orwell and David Astor together by inviting them both to dinner at the Hungarian Csarda,' he told me. 'I noticed on that occasion that Orwell's shirt collar was not, well, discreetly frayed, but truly in tatters. Since Orwell was no longer in financial need, this was like a defiant gesture against the bourgeoisie. But David Astor and Orwell took to each other immediately. When David Astor telephoned me in Paris to break the news of Orwell's death he asked me to write a personal memoir of him for the *Observer* of 900 to a 1000 words. Why not 1600 words? No, it had to be 900 to a 1000. These days, of course, what with the Supplements, one could have written such a memoir at much greater length.'

Koestler duly wrote his memoir of 900 to a 1000 words about his friend. He began:

To meet one's favourite author in the flesh is mostly a disillusioning experience. George Orwell was one of the few authors who looked and behaved exactly as the reader of his books expected him to behave.

This exceptional concordance, wrote Koestler, was a measure of the exceptional integrity of Orwell's character:

His uncompromising intellectual honesty was such that it made him appear almost inhuman at times. There was an emanation of austere harshness around him which diminished only in proportion to distance, as it were: he was merciless towards himself, severe upon his friends, unresponsive to admirers, full of understanding for those on the remote periphery.

That is, for the masses of the ordinary people. Koestler went on to say that Orwell was incapable of self-love. His life was a constant series of rebellions – rebellion against the condition of humanity as it drifted towards 1984 and, in his own case, against the lung disease that had plagued him since adolescence. As a last act of such rebellion, instead of going to a sanatorium, Orwell had gone to the wilds of the Isle of Jura, to write down his savage vision of the future in *Nineteen Eighty-Four*. Then Koestler went on to give Orwell rare praise:

The urge of genius and the prompting of common sense can rarely be reconciled; Orwell's life was a victory of the former over the latter. For now that he is dead, the time has come to recognize that he was the only writer of genius among the litterateurs of social revolt between the wars.

This obituary was the end of Koestler's relationship with Orwell, or nearly so. A few years later, as he has related, he was lunching with F. J. Warburg, Orwell's publisher. 'He asked me to write Orwell's biography. I refused, of course, but under the influence of Stilton and Burgundy, I dreamed up the idea of setting up an Orwell Archive. David Astor, and with him John Beavan on behalf of the Nuffield Foundation, came in to support the idea and so an Orwell Archive was officially set up at University College.'

To sum up, Orwell had said that after his break with Stalinism, Koestler found no real new political position. This is not quite true, but what is the case is that after having written DARKNESS AT NOON and SCUM OF THE EARTH, Koestler had arrived at a changing point in his life. He had to make England the focus of his life and to become an English writer, and in the course of this he gave a great deal to England, but the change was not easy; and one can say that in helping Koestler to effect his transition into becoming an English writer, his friendship with George Orwell played a considerable part.

The Trojan Horses: Koestler and the Behaviourists

Kathleen Nott

In 1967 Arthur Koestler uncovered the conspiratorial ramifications of a very secret society: the SPCDH. The revelation appears in a witty and biting Appendix to THE GHOST IN THE MACHINE, the third of his remarkable trilogy, whose main theme is the nature of creative innovation, both in individuals gifted either scientifically or artistically, and the way in which it has given structure to our evolutionary development. The acronym stands for *The Society for the Prevention of Cruelty to Dead Horses*: and the Society, whose general influence is directed towards the maintenence of conventional good taste and the elimination of malaise in our intellectual and academic life, aims at persuading us that most of our 'Causes' and reasons for social and moral agitation have been outgrown or remedied and that there is now no point in harping on them.

In this Appendix, Koestler rebuts a particular charge of cruelty on the amply sufficient ground that the Horse is after all alive and kicking. The Horse is, of course, Behaviourism and, significantly, the accuser of necrologic impiety, whom Koestler here chooses to answer, was previously identified with a long-standing and 'almost passionate' opposition to Behaviourism – the tradition in

---

academic psychology of Pavlov, Watson and, more recently B. F. Skinner and H. J. Eysenck, which treats human beings as automatic systems of reflexes to environmental (and sometimes genetic) conditioning and, in effect, tries to eliminate the concepts of 'mind', 'consciousness' and 'purpose'.

In a review of THE ACT OF CREATION, the first of the trilogy, Professor G. A. Miller of Harvard wrote:

When one attacks strict stimulus-response Behaviourism these days one is on the side of the big battalions. Yet Koestler writes as though it were still the 1930s and Behaviourism were in its prime.

And he continues that, on the contrary, most psychologists who would call themselves Behaviourists would be 'angered by Koestler's sarcastic misrepresentation', believing that they have moved away from the rigidly mechanistic account of human organism (and mind) in terms of mere response to the stimuli of environment and are in fact 'working on exactly the kind of processes Koestler calls bisociation'. Broadly, in this particular context, Miller means that they agree with Koestler that the reactions of organisms are far from automatic and random, but, on the contrary, are governed by structures of perception and response which are both ordered and flexible, both in-built and innovative: and that what makes an individual organism (including that kind of cerebral and nervous organization we call human) is precisely that capacity for self-ordering through which it in part also orders its environment.

That contemporary psychologists, as Miller claims, have thus rejected all the old hat in scholastic Behaviourism and bought themselves a new one, I believe, with Koestler, to be dangerously mistaken. Even if some of the old Horses have been slaughtered and buried, their elements are refertilizing and reinvigorating an ancient soil. The intellectual soil and climate persist and are so familiar that we no longer notice them.

Moreover the influence and errors of the old Behaviouristic orthodoxy are by no means limited to the philosophical and theoretical. In both Skinner and Eysenck, of whom more must be said, the psychosocial engineer is on the point of breaking out.

They both regard the scope for reconditioning and manipulating the human subject as in theory limitless: and they appear to have few qualms about interference where they are persuaded – rather easily – that it is well-intentioned.

It is true that in these two cases, the approach and the proposed method may vary: in his odd novel, *Walden II,* and in his recent book *Beyond Freedom and Dignity,* Skinner proposes that all our main psychological and moral difficulties are environmental and that therefore we should concentrate on manipulating the environment – tailor it to fit Man; while Eysenck is more inclined to try and adapt individuals to their environment or to those existing social conventions and arrangements which form such an important part of it. While frequently protesting his concern for individual freedom of choice, Eysenck has little interest in radical or really critical social reform or in investigating the rationality of society's attitudes and conformities. His method is Procrustean: for those who cannot get along with their social environment, his advocated method is not *psycho*therapy but Behaviour-therapy. 'There is no neurosis, only the symptoms*': and by various methods, often physical, you remove the symptoms.

Variations of method and approach are nevertheless insignificant compared with an underlying consonance. Eysenck does not believe that psychoneurosis indicates choices and attitudes on the part of an individual with a personal history, or indeed that it has any existential meaning at all; while Skinner believes that even the normal individual's efforts to struggle with environmental odds and to try to insert some effects of choice and preference are merely so many ways of fighting one's shirt with one's head in it, thus disguising from oneself the fact that one is at all times strictly determined – unwittingly and inexorably shoved along one's course of life by 'inconspicuous contingencies'.†

I am not immediately concerned with the endless metaphysical battle about free will versus determinism, but rather with a vital

---

* *Behaviour Research and Therapy:* Vol. I, No. I, May 1963.

† Skinner means that our behaviour is entirely shaped by the flow of accidental events: it is only because we mostly don't notice them that we can maintain our illusion of 'freedom'.

example as evidence that the Behaviouristic Horse looks more like a winner than dead; anyway in good health and training, with viable prospects. In the particular case it does not much matter whether Skinner and Eysenck are philosophically right or wrong. Whether or not human beings have some innate capacity or potentiality for freedom, it is certain that freedom is limited not only by educational conditioning and by the rules which all societies have to impose in order to maintain themselves, but also by the use which individuals commonly make of that 'freedom' – most commonly to elect their masters, or the technical and psychological 'experts' who will find solutions for them. It is a likely prophecy that psychosocial engineering will intervene with ever-increasing complexity and involvement in our individual and formerly private concerns, and moreover that the gap between the 'expert' and the layman will widen beyond bridging; and that this oncoming situation will be more and not less favourable to Behaviouristic attitudes and techniques, particularly to Behaviour-therapy as an engineering instrument.

It is true that dealing with behaviour or 'symptoms' by methods which can be classed as behaviouristic – drugs, shock or surgery – can be and has been of limited benefit to individuals, and that because the methods are mass–techniques, they work, if they do, comparatively quickly and cheaply. But as we know from the strictly medical analogy, they can be operated in a very oracular if not high-handed fashion; the individual patient-victim doesn't have to know what is being done to him, or why; and admittedly often cannot know and doesn't even wish to. Thus, in the particular example, the 'individual' can be said to have only himself to blame if he accepts being phased out, and perhaps ought to feel grateful to the expert who, rather like Dostoyevsky's Grand Inquisitor, has taken on the burden of his difficulties and similarly may reward himself with a sanctimonious sense of duty done.

Koestler describes the development of Behaviour-therapy in English clinical psychiatry – still more in American – as 'the most ominous influence' of Behaviourism, no doubt because of the social implications I have just referred to and the authoritarian path they indicate. But for his own purposes the theoretical background matters most, and he sees Behaviourism and its secular arm, Behaviour-therapy, in the context of modern psychology in general, and that again (with all its divisions, conflicts and schisms) as embedded in the post-Cartesian mechanistic philosophy. The want of agreement or of any fundamental common conceptions among schools of psychology is often commented upon; the relative 'youth' of scientific psychology is, in public relations, the common apologia. It is ironic, therefore, that a kind of unity should have been imposed upon them by the unconscious conditioning that derives from a persistent philosophic climate. Willy-nilly, at levels too deep to be reflected, and in vital and formative ways, they, and most of us, all think alike. A mechanistic conception of human life and mind and of the human individual has permeated all their – and our – habits of thought, feeling and even perception.

We are constantly assured (says Koestler) that 'the crudely mechanistic nineteenth-century conceptions in biology, medicine, psychology, are dead, and yet one constantly comes up against them in the columns of textbooks, technical journals and in lecture rooms'.

Nineteenth-century mechanism can in large part be understood as the unreflected inheritance of the Humpty-Dumpty situation in which Descartes left the concept of mind. Imposing a neat apartheid on Mind and Body, Thought and Extension, the thinking individual entity and what it had to think about, he never managed to put them together again and could account for their interinfluence and cooperation only by an automatic timing-device of which the Almighty had remote control.*

The philosophy of mind has remained in this schismatic if not schizophrenic state ever since. It is not necessary to go into the Idealist-Materialist controversy which it helped to generate, except to say that in a sense the two sides are mirror-images of one another and that to say that 'everything' is Mind or Spirit, or that 'everything' is Matter, is really only another way of

* Actually the theory of the Two Clocks was invented by disciples of Descartes: mind and body are separately wound up by God so as to synchronize perfectly. This makes it look as if it were my will which moves my body.

registering the Cartesian split and our apparent inability to heal it, or to conceive of a naturally organic approach to living processes, particularly to the concepts of human existence, mind and individuality.

Now if it is true, as Koestler maintains and, I think, demonstrates, that the *whole* of modern psychology, both academic and psychiatric, suffers from this undiagnosed disease of mechanism, why pick on Behaviourism as the worst source of infection? A variety of psychological schools rejects and strongly opposes Behaviourism.

The answer, I think, is that the Behaviourist Horse, not dead, if somewhat wooden, is better described as a troop of Trojan horses, in many disguises, which pop up all over the place: as Koestler demonstrates, in much contemporary academic philosophy; in the science of linguistics (and, as an item of curiosity, in a freak branch of contemporary poetics – computer-poetry).

That the Watson–Hull–Skinner tradition is immensely powerful, exercising in particular 'an invisible stranglehold' on academic psychology, can, with Koestler, be maintained, but still needs explaining. The explanation lies partly no doubt in the great fascination that over-simplification holds for all of us: especially in fields where specialist learning bears on our lives and where we have almost inevitably a large acreage of ignorance. (That applies to specialists too, outside their specialization.) To be handed some concise and definite answers not only relieves us from the wearisome personal investigation of problems, it is also reassuring, as well as looking peculiarly *scientific*. In our post-Cartesian era we are inclined to identify 'science' with proof and prediction, rather than with inquiry or with understanding or explanation. Here I am referring more to laymen, or rather to that majority who are not professional scientists or technologists, but who after all respire the intellectual climate – they breathe it in *and* out.

What we can prove or predict with anything approaching certainty is limited to what we can measure or calculate or reduce to mathematical formulation – which in sociological literature is often prestigious (and perhaps illusory or even magical).

Behind this there is an epistemological or existential attitude that is also in consonance, and not in contradiction, with our profound human interest in assurance. Descartes began by doubting the existence of everything but quite obviously with the intention of ultimately establishing two very useful certainties – the existence of God and his own. The 'negative capability' – to Keats one of the most important characteristics of poetic mind – the capacity to be in doubts and hesitations, absolute openmindedness, all this is rare.

We cannot measure or calculate what we cannot observe and therefore cannot know to exist: and it has been the ruling of the dominant contemporary philosophy that we cannot even talk – or not talk – sense about any matters which lack these epistemological certificates. That excludes from meaning a large range of human feelings and intuitions (by which I mean not 'emotions' or emotive utterances, but forms of perception and awareness, which may be both spontaneous and universal but which often cannot be put into either verbal or mathematical language).

Both Behaviourism and Behaviour-therapy fulfil surpassingly these desiderata of assurance and prestige. They deal only with what can be observed, with animal and human behaviour; with what can therefore, theoretically at least, be quantified and in so far as it can be quantified, to that extent predicted. Above all, they have a formula – 'S–R' or 'Stimulus-Response' – which they use not only as the explanatory mechanism of every kind of living behaviour but as a magical expunction of all the other psychological complexities by which human organisms insist on believing at least that they are troubled.

Koestler, who is scrupulously fair to the Behaviourists, thinks that they have improved on their original rigid reflexology; but he may be over-generous. As is well known the original experiments from which they generalized their formula (S–R) were conducted on animals: notably, in Pavlov's case, dogs.

Later with Hull, Skinner and others, the commoner study was the rat. Both types were experiments in associational conditioning and in the theory of learning: but perhaps for the immediate purpose, the rats have more to teach us. From time to time, especially when he is alluding to the philosophy behind it, Koestler refs to Behaviourism as ratomorphism. Because the rat experiments have more to tell us about motivation or at least about the Behaviourists' conception or even about their precipitate interpretation of it, this appears justified. It was on these experiments that the Behaviourists built a whole theory of human behaviour and indeed of human 'nature' and 'mind' – if these expressions may be pardoned.

By a system of rewards and punishments (food-pellets in the case of the rats, obtained by pressing the right releasing-mechanism, and withheld as long as the right associations were lacking) rats learn everything that may be useful or significant to rats: and they learn it, anyway to begin with, in random fashion. The original rats were conceived as totally lacking in originality. Stimulated in their experimentally limited environment by the smell of the food, they ran artificial mazes till they hit the jackpot. After a sufficient number of tries, they would be more often – and eventually, in the case of the more successful rats, 100 per cent – rewarded. Those rats may be said to have passed their general certificate of education.

The human analogy here must be allowed because we cannot deny that a good deal of what we call learning does take place through a process of conditioning by rewards and punishments. And in some form the belief that conditioning is the sole or main agent of human psychological and moral education and development is present in or even shapes the other leading schools of psychology or psychotherapy. Freudianism, for example, holds that we are rigidly conditioned by our infantile past. But in ascribing all motivation, either of rats or human beings, to conditioning by reward or deprivation, the Behaviourists are surely begging a most important human question. I have no doubt that these leading contemporary spokesmen lack the scientific impartiality which they claim. Far from 'challenging refutation' – as Karl Popper describes the valid scientific attitude – they are out to prove their case, and their wish to intervene in social and moral engineering begins with grinding their axes.

This is illustrated by the contortions, forced for instance upon Skinner in his book *Verbal Behaviour* (New York 1959), to eject from his terminology any such inconvenient subjective concepts as 'meaning', 'idea', 'image' – this too in a discussion of poetic 'behaviour'.★

As Koestler grants, the extreme rigidity of the earlier Behaviourist position with its total rejection of any subjective concept has relaxed to the extent that later experimentalists have for some time been allowing a kind of 'insight', even to the rat which, in time, instead of repeating its dreary routine of actions conditioned by the successes of the past, forms a kind of 'map' in its perceptual apparatus by which it is guided to its goal. But the unprofessional amateur of human psychology may and does wonder if this is much of a contribution towards explaining the origin and development of human understanding.

Behaviourism is totally unable to tell us anything new about the actual processes of thinking and imagination. It does not matter whether we call these 'mental' phenomena or not. We know that they go on from the fact that results are produced – not only in what we are pleased to call the 'minds' of the great 'creative' artists and scientists, but even in our own doubtless more rudimentary ones – which are unexpected and unpredictable.

Sometimes in retrospection and in the hinterland of our awareness we can catch a glimpse of how at least some parts of these processes originate; and sometimes if we look back on the history of discovery we can see how they arose in the context of common or public patterns of existing or established experiences, habits, assumptions and concepts. The novelty, the new creation or discovery, appears to arise, spontaneously, by a sudden flash of intuition (what we used to call 'inspiration'). We all know about Newton's apple and James Watt's kettle-lid, and we are likely to assume that Newton and Watt were instantaneously 'imprinted', instead of having been lifelong preoccupied with problems of gravitation or energy. As Koestler puts it (THE ACT OF CREATION): 'The scientist . . . suddenly discovers the connection between a banal event and a general law of nature.' Here there is

★ Behaviourism identifies thought with speech. Skinner wants to get rid of the speaker too – and invents some extraordinary substitutes, e.g., 'controlling relations,' 'intraverbal statements'.

a proviso that the 'connection' may also appear as contradiction or antithesis to existing theory or practice. Koestler's theory of creative innovation or originality entails his basic concept of *bisociation,* which runs through all the trilogy: a structure which he finds at the root of processes as apparently diverse as humour, thinking, and artistic and scientific creation. The novelty or discovery arises as a result of perceiving a situation or idea 'in two self-consistent but habitually incompatible frames of reference' and overcomes the antithesis in a new synthesis, emerging as a new joke, a new hypothesis or theory, or an original work of art.

The generalization involved here is that any discovery or novelty, however suddenly it may appear, has the underlying form of a solution to a long existing problem: it is the abrupt end-term to a long gestated process of evalutation which is unconscious or subconscious. This experience of gestation is a commonplace for every mathematician and every poet, however minor, and naturally too for everyone who thinks at all. The two former classes differ chiefly from the rest in being more likely to think about their own thinking.

Creative novelty originality is in truth the great 'scandal' of Behaviouristic philosophy. In THE ACT OF CREATION and also in THE GHOST IN THE MACHINE, Koestler quotes the by now notorious passage from *Behaviourism* (1925) by J. B. Watson, a primitive Fundamentalist of Behaviourism:

... How do we get new verbal creations? ... We get them by manipulating words ... shifting them about until a new pattern is hit upon ... How do you suppose Patou builds a new gown? Has he any picture in his mind? ... He has not ... he manipulates the material until it takes on the semblance of a dress ... Not until the new creation aroused admiration and commendation ... would manipulation be complete – the equivalent of the rat's finding food ... The painter plies his trade in the same way.

Koestler explains that he uses the same quotation twice because it is in fact the only quotation in Watson's book which refers to (and tries to dismiss) the subject of creation. But in later Behaviouristic writings it has often appeared as an irresistible challenge – irresistible partly, perhaps, because logically unavoidable;

and in the popular Pelicans of Eysenck, that ultramountaineer, it appears almost as a difficult prize – like the edelweiss. Eysenck too does not recognize any creative *process* as characteristically pursued by individual human organisms. In his study of painting it seems to depend very much on how you do in your art-school examinations – it is an assessment of competitive *results*. This parallels his study of Intelligence (*The Inequality of Man,* 1973): IQ is what decides how near you get to the top. He appears well-satisfied and even self-congratulatory about what he calls his 'beginning' from which he feels he will be able to proceed to a scientific assessment of the 'great creative works' having established his claim that 'Beauty' can after all be measured although it may be a concept no less mysterious to others, including many artists, than 'Mind, 'Consciousness' and the rest are to Behaviourists. No doubt it can, by reducing it to certain simple elements in certain works of art plus certain simple elements of pleasurable association in appreciation.

There is a sense in which all Koestler's remarkable trilogy is a corrective rebuke to this particularly Behaviouristic Behaviour: that he reveals creative originality as omnipresent not only in artistic and scientific mind but in the whole of the objective evolutionary process; and is able to demonstrate convincingly the structure of order in complexity by which these processes alike develop; and further, how species and forms, including mental and physical skills, can mutate into viable or useful innovations.

Earlier it was said that Behaviourism has been able to flourish only in the 19th and 20th century Neo-Darwinian intellectual climate of reductionism and atomism which also fosters the current predominant schools in biology and ethology. We call them 'Darwinian' – however qualified – chiefly because they depend on two evolutionary assumptions which derive, though not without deviation, from Darwin: the first, that evolutionary changes take place through natural selection from purely random mutations; the second, the doctrine of the survival of the fittest. It should be easy to see that the second is a circular notion: having been selected and thus having survived is the only test of fitness to survive.

Before glancing at the first assumption, here chiefly relevant, we may mention that there are encouraging signs in the contemporary literature that Darwin may be turning in his grave, because of the base uses his own creative thinking has been put to.

Koestler points out that the Behaviourist's approach to human psychology exactly parallels the reductive atomism which we find in Neo-Darwinian biology and genetics: it has its 'unit of behaviour' in S–R – the basic atomic brick from which it structures its whole description of human complexity. Because this is likewise a concept of randomness one might be deluded into thinking that it allowed for unpredictability and in that sense for freedom and choice. On the contrary it is continuous with the pre-Heisenbergian physics of the old 'billiard-ball' (or shove-atom) kind; we can see what this means in the moral field, when Skinner adjures us to give up 'freedom' and 'dignity' – our lingering illusion of having some responsibility for ourselves and some (if limited) preference of values – and thus to succumb to his rather naive dogma about the 'inconspicuous contingencies' which ineluctably determine all our moves.

To all this Koestler opposes the view that we are, and have been from our evolutionary origins, throughout our phylogenetic history, organisms and beings which partly organize our environment, instead of being merely the passive recipients of its 'stimuli'. Thus to the 'unit of behaviour' he also opposes an organic and organizing structural and instrumental pattern which runs through the whole of life and living activities. In all its manifestations and in its evolutionary development, life is the hierarchic organization of components which are themselves organisms. To this concept he gives the name 'holon' because it is complete in itself, with a local freedom and flexibility, while it is also part of a whole at a higher level of organization to whose more complex order it is subordinate.

Koestler uses a mechanical analogy* to symbolize this hierar-

* 'The parable of the two watchmakers' (THE GHOST IN THE MACHINE, page 45), one of whom assembled his watches bit by bit and, whenever disturbed, had to start again from scratch, while the other began his work by constructing sub-assemblies of components and, if interrupted, had only to reassemble the particular one on which he was working.

chic structure. This is not only legitimate, it is helpful, because it enables him to give an equally organic and hence a meaningful and purposive account of the infinite variety of skills which combine to make us human and – in the whole creation of which we are still an evolutionary part – unique; and to rescue our 'behaviours' from the unitary mechanism of the biological and psychological reductionists.

His range of illustration is enormous – I must be content with one or two: as a description of perhaps our most important learned skill, his theory of the generation of language; on the genetic and evolutionary side, the marvellously concrete account of the bird's 'instinct' of nest-building; and on the theoretical side, the argument for the specific organism's capacity to reject harmful mutations – a decisive blow at Neo-Darwinian randomness.

No one could say that Koestler is an evolutionary optimist, certainly no one who has read the later apocalyptic pages of THE GHOST IN THE MACHINE, which diagnose our inbuilt evolutionary error, the aboriginal disharmony, indeed one might say antagonism, between the old irrational brain and the new (and rationalizing) cortex. On the other hand, he has restored a realistic, even a pragmatic and referential, meaning to concepts like 'freedom', 'choice' and 'purpose', and thus indicated to us the road that evolutionary hope, if there has even been any hope for us, would take because it has always been taking it.

As a kind of postscript I should like to add that, without perhaps deliberate intention, indeed *en passant,* he has solved the problem of the Two Cultures – if that elderly cliché stands for any real problem other than an unnatural (and Behaviouristic) schizophrenia. In art, as in science, as in all our skills and behaviours of thinking, learning, feeling, the creative vision and purpose is of one structure and pattern, following a major canon of rules of thinking and perceiving, which localizes and embodies itself in an infinite variety of interests and media.

Wrestling Jacob:
Koestler and the Paranormal

Renée Haynes

In tracing the development of Arthur Koestler's interest in the paranormal – telepathy, clairvoyance, precognition, psycho-kinesis – it has been fascinating to find that he always seems to be considering it not so much in itself as in relationship to other subjects. True, it appears first as a fact of elusive experience, later reinforced by evidence drawn from large-scale experimental work, and later still entangled with theories of coincidence. But having once accepted its existence his attempts to understand it are linked with his lifelong struggle to understand the total strange universe into which we are all born, willy-nilly; a uni-verse experienced sometimes as no more than 'one damn thing after another', sometimes as a temporary web of people and things perceived and known in interconnection, sometimes as an intellectual structure emergent from chaos, and sometimes as on fire with indefinable meaning. It is worth remembering that when Moses saw the burning bush by the wayside it was a scientific impulse that first moved him to go and look more closely. He could not understand why the flames did not destroy it.

ARROW IN THE BLUE (1952) and THE INVISIBLE WRITING (1954), the two volumes of Arthur Koestler's autobiography, record piecemeal encounters with the paranormal. The first happened very early in his life and – typically – there is a choice of interpretations. It occurred in a Viennese *pension,* where he and his parents were living. An only child, nine years old, isolated and full of inner turbulence, 'I was reading in my room one lonely afternoon when there was a loud report and a hard object hit me on the back of the head . . . A big can of baked beans that had been standing on the radiator cover had exploded, presumably from the effects of fermentation.' But do tinned beans ever ferment to such a pitch as to become tinned bombs? Solitude, powerlessness, high emotional tension produce optimum conditions for the release of psychokinesis. Other inhabitants of the *pension* must have interpreted the incident in paranormal terms, for thenceforward 'I was much sought-after for table-turning séances'. He does not mention what, if anything, happened. Perhaps they proved intolerably boring.

Nevertheless, his interest seems to have been aroused. It survived in lively interaction with two other currents of thought.

The first of these flowed from a conviction formed during his school days that 'geometry, algebra and physics . . . contained the clue to the mystery of existence', a secret whose solution 'seemed the only purpose worth living for'.[1]

The world of mathematics has of course been both the material and the means of contemplation to men as diverse as Pythagoras and Rainer Maria Rilke, Plato and Eddington, Paul Valéry and Charles Williams. It is something already present, already *there,* something to be discovered – not invented – by the human mind. Like the glorious world of the senses, seen, heard, touched, tasted, smelt, it is given from outside; but unlike that world its recognition does not depend on the physical aptitudes of the perceiver, long-sighted or colour-blind, sharp-eared or deaf. Its interpretation is not subjective but the same for everyone. There can be no argument about the structure and validity of the *pons asinorum,* which can bridge the gulf between the warm inconsequence of everyday living and the realization of an abstract truth.

The conviction with which Arthur Koestler had lived so long was suddenly and vividly illumined for him when, under sentence of almost immediate death in a Spanish prison in the 1930s, he worked out with a pencil on the whitewashed wall 'the Euclidean proof that the number of primes is infinite', and realized with 'utter lucidity and calm' that this was a case in which 'a meaningful statement about the infinite is arrived at by precise and finite means'. The knowledge brought about in him 'an absolute catharsis, the peace that passeth understanding'.

This given intellectual awareness recurred several times during his long stay in Cell No. 40, 'where every day was judgement day', and filled him with 'a certainty that a higher order of reality existed, and that it alone invested existence with meaning';[2] a higher order interpenetrating that order of abstract concepts which in turn gave significance to the everyday world of patchy experience.

Here even the clear, objective, eternal truth of mathematics is subordinated to something else; to the ultimate *Mysterium tremendum et fascinans.*

It was at this point that the second strong stream of Koestler's thought burst through into the first, with which it had so long run concurrently. This stream was impelled by an undefinable but certain sense of an 'invisible writing', an elusive 'hidden meaning' inherent in clusters of events whose causes seemed to be unrelated, but whose combined effects were of intense symbolic importance; signals, as it were, from some unknown source, signals whose message was vital but could not be deciphered by ordinary processes of reasoning. He wrote in this connection of 'the tugging at the sleeve by apparent coincidence . . . which André Malraux called "*le langage du destin*" '.[3]

Interest in this 'invisible writing' had led him to notice and collect odd, spontaneous and apparently inexplicable happenings. Already in 1931 he was advertising in four daily papers for 'authentic reports on occult experiences – telepathy, clairvoyance, levitation, etc.', reports to be 'verified beyond any reasonable doubt by independent, trustworthy witnesses'. He received only some thirty-five replies. None could be verified in the way he wanted.

But inexplicable happenings kept goading and teasing him. In one, he went with a newspaper colleague and the highly respectable head porter of a great firm to see the then famous 'thought-reader and psychometrist' Eric Hanussen, who had never met any of them before. Hanussen, holding the head porter's keys, spoke of an illness, of the birth of a child, of a long-expected inheritance and of a local burglary. The head porter remarked that he had had those keys for thirty years, and that during all that time none of the events described had happened to him. It turned out, however, that they *had* all occurred over the previous twelvemonth to the other journalist, who was prepared to prove the fact.

There were also, among other odd incidents, the events of an uncomfortable lunch with a very tense friend who had already proved to be telepathic, and who had said apprehensively, as the meal began, that 'something is going to happen'. It did. A large picture suddenly crashed down upon the sideboard over which it hung, breaking a row of glasses of yoghurt that had been put there to mature. The picture-wire and the picture-hooks in the wall were unbroken and in perfect condition.

They had been arguing for a while with strong feeling about the question of determinism and free will. Koestler felt unable to accept the latter because he would have to accept with it 'ultimate responsibility for one's actions . . . an unbearable load of guilt and shame without the comforts of an ethically neutral science . . . I was not ready for the burden of freedom'. In the same way he could not accept the implications of psychical phenomena, since to recognize 'the existence of another plane of reality inaccessible to the rational mind . . . meant a minor spiritual death and rebirth'.[4] Though he had a strong feeling that some invisible writing might be deciphered here he fled from it.

Both these currents of thought, then, gave energy to that illumination in the Spanish gaol.

The impact of such an experience is total, but its implications usually have to be worked out in detail through years of oscillation and uncertainty.

It was already becoming clear to Koestler – though the process was piecemeal and slow – that the glorious precision of mathematical logic could not be applied to individual lives without reducing spontaneous selves to zombies, programmed automata; or to political organization without producing an intolerable totalitarian tyranny. He finally left the Communist Party in 1938, and looked at other modes of thought. In THE YOGI AND THE COMMISSAR, which did not appear till 1945, he contrasted the general effect of attempts to withdraw from the world into a gaseous, numinous sphere occasionally lit by flares of paranormal cognition, with the general effect of attempts forcibly to dominate, process, and run that world in accordance with rigid political theory.

Both contemplation and reason were needed, it appeared, and with them a deep respect for living facts. The objective study of extra-sensory perception must be relevant. He took a lively interest in the industrious cumulative work of Dr J. B. Rhine and his colleagues, and in their methods of evaluating in statistical terms the results of large-scale experiments. Such methods were useful both as a way scientifically to establish the existence of paranormal cognition, and as a way of enabling minds formed in the discipline of experimental research to look at the facts, however disastrous the effect on their preconceived ideas might be; as happened when in 1952 he told the then Professor of Physics at Harvard that Dr Rhine's statistics had been checked by the great expert R. A. Fisher, and received the miserable reply, 'If that were true, I should have to scrap everything.'

As time went by he was increasingly irked by the continuing resistance to the concept of paranormal cognition shown in many quarters, and particularly by academic psychologists, notwithstanding the fact that 'the giants had always taken telepathy and allied phenomena for granted – from Charcot and Richet through William James to Freud and Jung';[5] notwithstanding all the evidence soberly accumulated and statistically evaluated by the Rhines; notwithstanding the discussions at symposia on the subject organized by the Royal Society of Medicine and at the Ciba, Fulbright and Rockefeller Foundations; and notwithstanding Professor Eysenck's trenchant remarks that 'unless there is a gigantic conspiracy involving some thirty University Departments all over the world and several hundred highly respected scientists in all fields . . . the only conclusion that the unbiased observer can reach is that a number of people have extra-sensory perception', though this does not give 'any support to survival after death, philosophical idealism or anything else'.

Another passage from this essay deals with a symposium held in San Francisco on the Control of the Mind; here he was again interested – and maddened – by the curious contrast between the academic philosophers, such as Ayer and Ryle, and the experts actively and directly concerned with the functioning of the brain, notably the neurophysiologist Wilder Penfield and the psychopharmacologist Jonathan Cole. The philosophers maintained a thorough-going materialist point of view, arguing that the mind was entirely dependent on the brain. Penfield and Cole differentiated sharply between the two, and believed that it was possible for the mind to stand away, in detachment, from the physiological effects of brainwashing, coercion and drugs. As to the oddly different experiences reported by those who have voluntarily taken hallucinogens he quotes Cole's remarks that they are affected by their own expectations, by the atmosphere of the environment, and by the attitude of the person in charge; and concludes that, however different the experiences may be, 'the reality is the individual, an elusive entity with a blur of unpredictability at its core'.

Awareness of the unpredictable, the elusive, was never very far away. In THE ACT OF CREATION (1964) Koestler discussed in depth the processes of living, perceiving, learning, thinking – and intuition. He pointed out that the mind can work not only by informed rational, disciplined, logical argument, but also by sudden flashes of illumination (whose results have to be verified and are often brilliantly accurate). He pointed out, also, that where two apparently valid interpretations of scientific data are incompatible, or where a newly established fact does not fit into an accepted structure of theory, the puzzle has to be recognized and endured in conscious painful ignorance if intellectual honesty is to be preserved. It will, of course, be tempting to accept one side of the contradiction and reject – or gloss over – the other; but work done after yielding to this temptation will have no roots in reality. The need is to remain uncommitted and in darkness as long as the problem cannot be solved. Such a solution may be brought about not through the grinding mills of thought but by some unexpected and dazzling illumination, showing how the apparent contradictions co-inhere in an underlying pattern, a synthesis never perceived before. Although this book does not explicitly discuss paranormal cognition, its argument can clearly be linked with the 'hunches', the veridical dreams, and the straight or symbolic visionary experiences through which the psi-function works in its 'wild' state.

THE GHOST IN THE MACHINE (1967) examines from the angle of evolutionary physiology the difference between the rational and the emotional modes of understanding, and the need to integrate them; arguing that 'there is insufficient co-ordination between . . . the phylogenetically old areas of our brain and the new, specifically human areas which grew up so fast in the Pleistocene Age'; suggesting that 'poetry could be said to achieve a synthesis between the reasoning of the new cortex and the primitive emotional ways of the old brain'; and speculating as to whether extra-sensory perception is 'an emergent level of supra-individual consciousness or . . . an earlier version of psycho-symbiotic awareness preceding self-awareness, which evolution has abandoned for the latter'.[6]

But there seemed to be more to it than either alternative would suggest. Already in THE LOTUS AND THE ROBOT (1960) Koestler was being nagged again by that sense of 'the tugging at the sleeve by apparent coincidence' of which he had so long been intermittently aware. 'I have always suspected,' he wrote this time, 'that certain meaningful coincidences follow a causal law of their own, whose equations are written in symbols other than those of physics.'[7]

Though the existence of extra-sensory perception might be tested and demonstrated by applying mathematical reasoning to the results of mass experiments, its meaning could not. Though the study of brain-functioning might show why it was so difficult – and so important – to integrate the processes of reason, of instinct and of intuition, it could not finally establish to which of the last two categories extra-sensory perception belonged, whence it came, or what its significance might be.

Any sheer accumulation of facts becomes a heavy, formless, slithering weight on the mind until one can rough out at least some tentative explanation, some working hypothesis as to why and how they come to happen, and what they imply. Koestler had long been looking for such a hypothesis, one which should not exclude the teasing element of the spontaneous, the incalculable.

Baffling, fascinating and sometimes self-contradictory contributions to the subject are to be found in C. E. Jung's *Synchronicity, an a-causal connecting principle,* which first appeared in a collection of essays in the early fifties. The subtitle, though it may be clearer in the original German, is very confusing to the English reader, until he ultimately discovers that 'a-causal' means no more than 'without *physical* cause', a phrase which could, of course, be applied to any event resulting from a personal choice, an act of will. If I decide to throw crumbs to the birds in the garden what happens stems from my personal decision; the movements of my arm, the trajectory of the crumbs, are secondary. The action is initiated by a mental cause, not a physical one. It cannot be described as a-causal, so far as the English language is concerned, without limiting and distorting the concept of causality.

An idea put forward by Sir Cyril Burt[8] about ten years afterwards has some kinship with Jung's suggestions, and is easier for those bred in an empirical tradition to follow. He outlined a theory of 'a system of psychical interactions, in addition to the system of physical interactions that constitutes the universe . . . the two systems intersecting at certain given points'. The strange 'meaningful coincidences' of which Jung wrote so vividly would, of course, occur at the common points of intersection; and it is to be noted that in everyday experience those points of intersection are as unpredictable as the whereabouts of the first drops in a shower of rain, which always seem to spot the pavement where you are not looking.

But Burt's ideas were not linked – as Jung's were, rather uneasily – with the strange notion, put forward in 1919 by the Austrian biologist Paul Kammerer, of a 'law of seriality'[9] at work in the universe to complement 'the causality of classical physics'. Kammerer labelled himself an atheist and a materialist, so that this law, as he envisaged it, was truly a-causal, involving no sort of mental or psychical interaction with physically determined sequences of events. It was part of the nature of things, and to be accepted as such.

The evidence from which this law was to be deduced was coincidence in the everyday sense of the word, the occurrence of similar events, all about the same time, for which no rhyme or reason can be found; no meaning, implicit or explicit and no logical explanation. They may be trivial, as when a bus ticket, a theatre ticket and a cloak-room ticket all taken on one day all bear the same number. They may be irritating, as when 'accidents go in threes' and, say, the handle is knocked off a cup, a wine glass snaps from its stem as it is being dried, and someone steps on the dog's plate all in a single evening. Or they may be part of 'runs of luck', good or bad, recognized in such proverbs as 'misfortunes never come singly' and 'it never rains but it pours'.

It is not completely clear how, and to what extent, the physicist Wolfgang Pauli, who discussed Jung's essay with him during the period when it was being written, shared Kammerer's views on seriality; but he was certainly committed to the belief that there is something in the nature of things quite different from mechanical deployment of 'the armies of unalterable law' which had brought a sense of sad but satisfying comprehension to nineteenth-century thinkers. Many of the observations, speculations and calculations of modern physics are incompatible, within their own sphere, with accepted ideas of time, space, motion, and the rule-of-thumb workings of cause and effect in ordinary life.

It is possible, though, to doubt whether the association of Jung and Pauli clarified or muddied the waters. It certainly led to verbal confusions. The fact of 'meaningful coincidence' – a falling star, a flaming signal – is surely different in kind from the theory of serial coincidence, which is, in the phrase of Sir Alister Hardy, 'something implicit in the nature of randomness'. They have of course one common feature: they can be recognized by the human mind.

Arthur Koestler has been deeply interested in both themes, though not always wholly happy about the attempt to merge them, despite his remark in THE ROOTS OF COINCIDENCE (1972) that Jung's essay was notable as 'the first time in the history of modern thought that the hypothesis of a-causal factors working in the universe was given a joint stamp of respectability by a psychologist and a physicist of renown'.

'Synchronicity and Seriality', he continued later, 'are as similar as a pair of gloves, each of which fits one hand alone.' Later still he suggested that both are 'derivatives of the archetypal belief in the fundamental unity of all things, transcending mechanical causality', and that the two different terms should be replaced by the phrase 'confluential events'.

It is towards the end of this book that he attempts to draw all the data of psychical research into the web of a remarkable theory set out in earlier studies; the theory of 'Janus-faced holons' existing at every stage of biological and psychological development, each simultaneously a self-reliant whole and a dependent part of something greater than itself. 'One face . . . says I am the centre of the world, the other I am a part in search of a whole.' There follows a definition:

We may regard the phenomena of parapsychology as the rewards of this search . . . ESP would then appear as the highest manifestation of the integrative potential of living matter – which, on the human level, is typically accompanied by a self-transcending type of emotion.[10]

This is probably the most significant general statement about the paranormal to be found in Koestler's work. That it is by no means final is plain from his most recent discussion of the subject, the last of the three essays which constitute THE CHALLENGE OF CHANCE (1973). The first two come from Alister Hardy and Robert Harvie, and the book was written to examine the possibility that the results of a series of large-scale experiments carried out by the former yielded evidence for the workings of 'seriality' rather than for the existence of the psi-function.

The third essay, then, begins with a collection of anecdotal cases of spontaneous coincidence 'which appear to resist classification . . . in terms of . . . classical ESP'. Some are instances of what used to be called sheer luck. Some, in other contexts of thought, might be considered precognitions, or even purposeful interventions from some unknown quarter. Some, like the episode of the Rosenheim office poltergeist, may one day be explicable in a scientific idiom; the investigators said no more than that what happened defied explanation in terms of current physical theories, and might open up fundamentally new problems (perhaps of the interaction between psyche and energy?). Some are grotesque or comic; as when Jacquetta Hawkes, having hung up a beautiful lithograph of a grasshopper, found that night, for the first and only time, a live grasshopper in her bed. This, Koestler remarks, cannot be providential, as Providence has never been thought to have a sense of humour. But what about those collisions of two matrices of thought, two frames of reference, of which he wrote in THE ACT OF CREATION, collisions which may spark off new light on old problems, occasionally by something as primordial as a pun?

He goes on to consider all manner of things which may be relevant to parapsychology. There is the extraordinary nature of probability theory, which works on a large scale and not on a small, can forecast pretty accurately how many people will be bitten annually by dogs in New York, but can give no indication of which dogs will bite which people or why. He reflects that 'the unthinkable phenomena of parapsychology appear somewhat less preposterous in the light of the unthinkable propositions of quantum physics'; whence, of course, one may rightly conclude that it is necessary to suspend belief in the incomprehensible, but not that two sets of incomprehensible data must at some level be identical with one another. The fact that each is unthinkable but *there* supports the other's credibility, but does not necessarily mean their natures are the same; though perhaps it has something to do with the proneness of physicists 'to infection by the ESP virus'.

Koestler's last word on the subject, for the moment, seems to run thus: 'Whether one believes that some highly improbable meaningful coincidences manifest some unknown principle operating beyond physical causality or are produced by that immortal monkey at the typewriter is ultimately a matter of inclination and temperament . . . *No amount of scientific knowledge can help a person to decide which of these alternative beliefs is more reasonable or nearer to the truth.*'[11]

Does the act of creation coincide with Pascal's leap? The argument goes on. The search continues – *Ad multos annos*.

REFERENCES

1. ARROW IN THE BLUE, Hutchinson, 1952.
2. THE INVISIBLE WRITING, Hutchinson, 1954.
3. ARROW IN THE BLUE.
4. THE INVISIBLE WRITING.
5. 'The Poverty of Psychology', 1961, an essay subsequently published in DRINKERS OF INFINITY, Hutchinson, 1968.
6. THE GHOST IN THE MACHINE, Hutchinson, 1967.
7. THE LOTUS AND THE ROBOT, Hutchinson, 1960.
8. Cyril Burt: *The Scientist Speculates*, Heinemann, 1952.
9. cf. Koestler: THE CASE OF THE MIDWIFE TOAD, Hutchinson 1971.
10. THE ROOTS OF COINCIDENCE, Hutchinson, 1972.
11. Hardy, Harvie, and Koestler: THE CHALLENGE OF CHANCE, Hutchinson, 1973.

The Imitative-Creative Interplay of Our Three Mentalities

Paul D. MacLean

I have coined the term 'bisociation' in order to make a distinction between the routine skills of thinking on a single 'plane', as it were, and the creative act, which, as I shall try to show, always operates on more than one plane (pp. 35–6).

The creative act, by connecting previously unrelated dimensions of experience, enables . . . [one] to attain to a higher level of mental evolution. It is an act of liberation – the defeat of habit by originality (p. 96).

. . . the creative process involves levels of the mind separated by a much wider span than in any other mental activity . . . (p. 659).

Arthur Koestler, THE ACT OF CREATION

When I think of Koestler, I think especially of his abiding interest in the creative process. It is a recurring theme not only in a number of his books, but also in his conversation. In THE ACT OF CREA-TION (1964) he uses the joke as a paradigm of the creative process: 'The pattern underlying all varieties of humour', he writes, 'is "bisociative" – perceiving a situation or event in two habitually incompatible associative contexts.' In my image of him as he thumbs through the present volume honouring him on his seventieth birthday, I picture him as being as imperturbable as the British lion. I am therefore going to risk a play on his formulation of the creative process and hope that I will come off without too hard a cuff! The meaning that Koestler assigns to the word 'bisociation' in the creative process is evident from the above quotations. In discussing the imitative-creative interplay of 'our three mentalities', I am going to add to his formulation a word that rhymes with 'bisociation'. The word is dissociation, and it will turn out to have a *double entendre*. It applies to a factor that under some circumstances may be a necessary adjunct to the creative process. In THE ACT OF CREATION, Koestler deals with various topics related to dissociation as I shall define it, but he does not consider a particular subtractive function that I have in mind. It is one of the fascinations of words, as opposed to numbers, that by 'adding a subtraction' one can sometimes come out with more than by simple addition. As Koestler himself has observed (1964), ' . . . personally I found that with most people the click [the eureka moment] occurs through the reversal of the direction of thought from addition to subtraction. . . .'

As background for the discussion of 'dissociation', I am going to describe some of my recent research that is relevant to the evolutionary and neural roots of imitation and then consider in behavioural and neurological terms how it may be possible for some individuals to insulate themselves from the powerful, attractive forces of imitation and to achieve creativity. In no way depreciating other forms of creativity, I shall allude principally to scientific creativity.

René Dubos (1967) has commented that fashions in science (which could also be called imitation in science) determine 'professional appointments and allocation of research facilities' and starve out 'investigators whose interests differ from those of the majority'. Regrettable as this may be, it is hardly surprising that imitation which infects the whole world also infects scientists.

Imitation works in myriad ways to maintain group indentity and to promote group survival. Case histories of autistic children provide illustrations of the devastating consequences of an inability to imitate. As opposed to this situation, excessive imitation may lead to undesirable consequences by closing the door to innovation. This matter is a concern to all of us, living as we do in a world in which the mass media seem to operate according to the cynical dictum that 'imitation rules the world'. What may be the consequences to the human race if through frivolous imitation, or even through the seemingly desirable adoption of a universal language, we follow one another into a meaningless cul-de-sac?

Because of the mass media, the matter of imitation looms more important than ever in human affairs not only as it applies to fads, fashions, and drug cultures, but more significantly to mass hysteria and violence in a world being crowded by an exponential increase in population. The behavioural studies of Calhoun (1962), Myers (1971) and others provide evidence that the conditions of crowding are conducive to aggression and combative behaviour. In addition to promoting aggressiveness, crowding also increases the opportunities for imitation. Consequently, there is the possibility that violent behaviour can lead to a vicious circle through the positive feedback of imitation (cf. MacLean, 1973c). It is one of the perversities of television that it brings crowding, violence, and imitation right into the living room. Someone has calculated that by the age of fourteen the average child will have seen 18 000 murders on television.

As Koestler (1968) reminds us, however, ' . . . the damages wrought by individual violence . . . are insignificant compared to the holocausts resulting from self-transcending devotion to collectively shared belief-systems'. He lays the blame on the human paranoid streak. But would the paranoid streak get anywhere without the primitive forces of imitation? It has been argued that the Dupreel Theorem, which holds that in conflict the 'aggressor' and 'defender' soon tend to imitate one another in the nature of their actions, also applies to world politics (cf. Maynes, 1973). In the past, primitive imitative forces have afforded survival on the grand scale under the banner of militant nationalism. Today this brand of imitation is potentially more deadly than imitation is to science. To quote Koestler (1968) again, 'Before the thermonuclear bomb, man had to live with the idea of his death as an individual; from now onward mankind has to live with the idea of its death as a species.'

WHAT IS IMITATION?

As a beginning, working definition, we may think of imitation as a reciprocative form of behaviour in which two or more individuals engage in similar activities. This statement serves to make a distinction between imitation and the term 'mimicry', used by zoologists to refer to superficial resemblances between animals or between animals and their environment, or indeed to parts of the same animal, a condition known as automimicry. Mimicry, of course, exists everywhere in the botanical world, but would there have been any need for it without the presence of animals? In mechanical terms, mimicry would be regarded as static, whereas imitation would be dynamic. Both may be involved in attractive or repulsive processes, serving variously to provide concealment or protection of the individual or to promote group identity and reproduction of the species.

Curiously enough, except for echolalia and echopraxia which are often associated with damage of the frontal or parietal cortex, one will find hardly any discussion of the question of imitation in neurological textbooks. Recently, I thumbed through twenty current neurological texts without finding the word imitation or one of its equivalents listed in the index. As opposed to neurology, the psychological literature is replete with articles and books on imitation, but always without any reference to the question of underlying mechanisms. In psychology, the question of imitation is of basic interest because of its important role in acculturation, education, and so many other kinds of human activity.

In their book, *Social Learning and Imitation,* published in 1941, Miller and Dollard begin by saying, 'All human behaviour is learned.' At the same time, they emphasize the well-recognized difficulty of teaching animals to imitate one another. Both assertions appear to be overstatements. In the case of animals, it seems that they are not interested in learning what the experimenter wants them to imitate. Left to themselves and their own natural tendency to imitation, they may show a remarkable capacity for learning to imitate. We have, for example, three squirrel monkeys born in our colony that do backward somersaults, something never seen in animals coming from the wild. This behaviour originated with two squirrel monkeys, Cain and Abel, which imitated the backward somersaults of a capuchin monkey living in the same soom. And now a young female squirrel monkey called Naamah has since learned it from them. There is a colony of rhesus monkeys in Japan that has become famous for having adopted the custom of one of its females of dunking sweet potatoes in sea water before eating them (Miyadi, 1964). Recently, I learned of a group of chimpanzees in Louisiana that have taken to imitating one of their members by urinating in their hands and drinking the urine (Gajdusek, personal communication).

In this article I shall focus not on learned imitation, but rather on natural species-typical forms of imitation, which seem to provide the foundation for learned forms of imitation. A natural form of imitation is illustrated by Dian Fossey's (1971) observations on gorillas in the wild. The gesture of scratching, apparently, is reassuring to gorillas. Miss Fossey, in her final and successful effort to establish contact with a young adult gorilla, utilized the social signal of scratching in her overtures. Shortly afterwards, the seemingly impossible happened: she was able to reach out and touch the hand of the gorilla.

Because 'imitation' is such a 'loaded' word in the social and behavioural sciences, commonly implying 'conscious' learning or mimicking, I shall avoid it in the context of the experimental work, referring instead to isopraxis, or isopraxic behaviour, meaning the performance of the same kind of behaviour. (I shall also avoid the psychological expression 'social facilitation' since it suggests a functional explanation of how animals engage in like behaviour.)

NON-VERBAL FACTORS

Before turning to the brain and behavioural studies, there is one more topic to consider. In THE GHOST IN THE MACHINE, Koestler states, ' . . . creativity often starts where language ends, that is, by regressing to pre-verbal levels of mental activity.' Human communicative behaviour can be broadly categorized as

verbal and non-verbal. Like P. W. Bridgman (1959), the physi-
cist-philosopher, the great majority of people would probably
conclude that 'most communication is verbal'. Contrary to the
popular view, many behavioural scientists would give greater
importance to non-verbal behaviour in day-to-day human activities. It must be admitted, however, that like the submerged part of
an iceberg, we are so ignorant of the hidden aspects of non-verbal
behaviour that it would be impossible to make any quantitative
assessment of its influence.

Non-verbal behaviour mirrors in part what Freud (1900)
called 'primary processes'. In drawing a distinction between verbal
and non-verbal behaviour, it is easier to see differences than
similarities. But in a very real sense, non-verbal behaviour, like
verbal behaviour, has its semantics and syntax – in other words its
meaning and orderly arrangement of specific acts.

It is non-verbal behaviour that we possess in common with
animals. Since it is hardly appropriate to refer as some do (cf.
Hinde, 1972), to non-verbal behaviour of animals, it is desirable
to use some other term for this kind of behaviour. The Greek
word 'σημα' pertains to a sign, mark, or token. By adding the
prefix 'προ' in the particular sense of 'rudimentary' one obtains
the word 'prosematic' which would be appropriate for referring
to any kind of non-verbal signal – vocal, bodily, or chemical
(MacLean, 1974b, c).

It has been the special contribution of ethology to provide the
first scientific insights into the semantics and syntax of animal
behaviour (e.g., Lorenz, 1937; Tinbergen, 1951). Ethology has,
so to speak, begun to give us a translation of the Rosetta stone of
animal behaviour. This translation promises in turn to give
needed insights into the semantics and syntax of human 'prosematic' behaviour.

An analysis of prosematic behaviour of animals reveals that
somewhat parallel to words, sentences, and paragraphs, it becomes
meaningful in terms of its components, constructs, and sequences
of constructs. Since the patterns of behaviour involved in self-
survival and survival of the species are generally similar in most
terrestrial vertebrates, it is rather meaningless to speak, as in the

past, of species-specific behaviour. But since various species perform these behaviours in their own typical way, it is both correct and useful to refer to species-typical behaviour.

FOREBRAIN MECHANISMS OF PROSEMATIC BEHAVIOUR

For the past twenty-five years, my research has been concerned with identifying and analysing forebrain mechanisms underlying prosematic forms of behaviour which on phylogenetic and clinical grounds might be inferred to represent expressions of 'paleopsychic' processes. In this work I have taken a comparative evolutionary approach which has the advantage that it allows one to telescope millions of years into a span that can be seen all at once, and as in plotting a curve makes it possible to see trends that would not otherwise be apparent. It also shows the justification of using animals for obtaining insights into mechanisms underlying human prosematic behaviour.

In its evolution, the human forebrain expands along the lines of three basic patterns which can be characterized both anatomically and biochemically as reptilian, paleomammalian, and neomammalian (Fig. 1). Radically different in their chemistry and

Fig. 1. In its evolution, the human forebrain expands in hierarchic fashion along the lines of three basic patterns that may be characterized as reptilian, paleomammalian, and neomammalian (from MacLean, P. D., The brain in relation to empathy and medical education, *J. Nerv. Ment. Dis.*, 1967, *144*: 374–82).

structure and in an evolutionary sense countless generations apart, the three basic formations constitute, so to speak, three-brains-in-one or, more succinctly, a triune brain (MacLean, 1970, 1973b). What this immediately implies is that we are obliged to look at ourselves and the world through the eyes of three quite different mentalities. Each mentality may be inferred to have its own special kind of intelligence, its own special form of subjectivity, its own sense of time and space, its own type of memory, etc.

My scheme for subdividing the brain may be criticized for being simplistic, but thanks to improved neuroanatomical, histochemical, and physiological techniques, the three basic formations of the forebrain stand out in clearer detail than ever before. Moreover, it should be emphasized that despite their extensive interconnections, each brain type is capable of operating somewhat independently. Most important in regard to the 'verbal–non-verbal' question, there are clinical indications that the reptilian type and paleomammalian formations lack the neural machinery for verbal communication with the human neocortex. To say that they lack the power of speech, however, does not belittle their intelligence, nor does it place them subjectively in the realm of 'the unconscious'.

The basic neural machinery required for self-preservation and the preservation of the species is built into the neural chassis comprising the lower brain stem and spinal cord. By itself, the neural chassis is as useless as the chassis of a car without a driver. Otherwise this is a poor analogy because with the evolution of the forebrain, the neural chassis acquires three drivers, all sitting in the front seat and all vying for a turn at the wheel.

THE REPTILIAN TYPE BRAIN

Let us first look at the reptilian driver. One of the fascinations of the reptilian type brain in regard to imitation is that it requires us to think not only in terms of individual and species isopraxis, but also of phyletic isopraxis. In mammals, the major counterpart of the reptilian forebrain is represented by a group of massive ganglia including the corpus striatum, globus pallidus, and satellite grey matter. Since there is no name that applies to all of these structures, I shall hereafter refer to them informally as the R-complex. The stain for cholinesterase reveals a remarkable chemical contrast between the R-complex and the two other cerebrotypes. The shaded areas in Fig 2. show how this stain sharply demarcates the R-complex in animals ranging from reptiles to man. In applying the fluorescent technique of Falck and Hillarp, it is striking to see how the bulk of these structures glow a

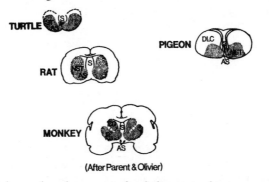

(After Parent & Olivier)

Fig. 2. Shaded areas show how a stain for cholinesterase demarcates part of the R-complex in animals ranging from reptiles to primates. With the fluorescent technique of Falck and Hillarp, the same areas shown above would glow a bright green because of the high content of dopamine. The pallidal part of the striatal complex does not fluoresce. No existing reptiles represent the forerunners of mammals. Birds are an offshoot from the *Archosauria* ('ruling reptiles') (adapted from Parent, A. and Olivier, A. Comparative histochemical study of the corpus striatum, *J. Hirnforsch.*, 1970, *12*: 75–81).

bright green because of large amounts of dopamine (Juorio and Vogt, 1967).

Curiously enough, ethologists have paid little attention to reptiles, focusing instead on fishes and birds. Some authorities believe that in regard to existing reptiles the behaviour of lizards would come closest to resembling that of mammal-like reptiles which were the forerunners of mammals. At all events, lizards and other reptiles provide illustrations of complex prototypical *patterns* of behaviour commonly seen in mammals, including man. One can quickly list more than twenty such behaviours that may primarily involve self-preservation or the survival of the species

(MacLean, 1974a): (1) selection and preparation of homesite; (2) establishment of domain or territory; (3) trail-making; (4) 'marking' of domain or territory; (5) showing place-preferences; (6) ritualistic display in defence of territory, commonly involving the use of coloration and adornments; (7) formalized intraspecific fighting in defense of territory; (8) triumphal display in successful defence; (9) assumption of distinctive postures and coloration in signalling surrender; (10) routinization of daily activities; (11) foraging; (12) hunting; (13) homing; (14) hoarding; (15) use of defecation posts; (16) formation of social groups; (17) establishment of social hierarchy by ritualistic display and other means; (18) greeting; (19) 'grooming'; (20) courtship, with displays using coloration and adornments; (21) mating; (22) breeding, and, in isolated instances, attending offspring; (23) flocking; and (24) migration.

There is a pentad of prototypical forms of behaviour of a general nature that may be operative in the above activities and have varying degrees of survival value or special prosematic significance. These five propense forms of behaviour may be denoted as (1) perseverative; (2) 're-enactment'; (3) tropistic (both positive and negative); (4) deceptive; and (5) isopraxic behaviour (MacLean, 1974c).

Before proceeding to consider forebrain mechanisms of isopraxic behaviour, I should say parenthetically that I am mindful that fish and amphibia, which have a counterpart of the R-complex, provide many examples of how a particular behaviour of one individual may trigger similar behaviour in another. The schooling of fish is an example of how whole groups may behave in a like manner (so-called allelomimetic behaviour). Years ago, Noble (1936) showed that the destruction of the forebrain in fishes eliminates schooling behaviour. But for our purposes the fish is a poor prototype because it has a so-called 'everted 'brain, and there are other reasons for skipping over amphibians.

There are four existing orders of reptiles, none being directly antecedent to mammals. What are some of the behaviours of reptiles which involve isopraxic factors? To begin with, it should be noted that isopraxic behaviour enters into the aggressive and courtship display of such forms as lizards and snakes. Isopraxic factors come into play in the reptile's choice of homesite and in places and times chosen to feed, drink, and mate. Marine iguanas go *en masse* to graze on the ocean bottom and all return at the same time to bask in the sun. The mass choruses of geckos and the bull-like vocalizations of large numbers of crocodiles begin and end at scheduled times. Evans and Quaranta (1951) described a group of turtles at the Bronx Zoo that observed the follow-the-leader ritual in going out in the yard at certain times in the morning and returning to the den at the same time at night. Isopraxic factors are involved in the mass migrations seen in turtles and snakes, and in their collective reproductive behaviour. After coming out of their hibernation dens in spring, large numbers of snakes will be found rolled up in so-called snake-balls, all copulating.

As yet, hardly any investigations have been conducted on reptiles in an attempt to identify specific structures of the forebrain involved in isopraxis or other prototypical forms of behaviour. All that is known thus far is that the neural guiding systems for species-typical, complex forms of behaviour lie forward of the neural chassis.

In contrast to reptiles, the R-complex of mammals has been subjected to extensive investigation. Curiously enough, however, 150 years of experimentation have revealed remarkably little about its functions. The finding that large destructions of the mammalian R-complex may result in no obvious impairment of movement speaks against the traditional clinical view that it subserves purely motor functions. At our Laboratory of Brain Evolution and Behaviour, we are conducting comparative studies of reptiles, birds, and mammals in which we are testing the hypothesis that the R-complex plays a basic role in species-typical, prosematic behaviour.

CURRENT STUDIES

In the work thus far, crucial findings have developed out of observations on the effects of various brain lesions on the species-typical display behaviour of squirrel monkeys (Saimiri sciureus). It is a remarkable parallel that like some reptiles and lower forms, monkeys of this species perform the same kind of display in courtship as in the show of aggression. In the aggressive display shown in Fig. 3, a male will vocalize, spread one thigh, and direct

Fig. 3. Drawing depicts aggressive genital display of squirrel monkey to a lower-ranking male. A similar display is seen prior to attempts at copulation with females (from Ploog, D., and MacLean, P. D. Display of penile erection in squirrel monkey (Saimiri sciureus), *Anim. Behav.*, 1963, *11*, 32–9).

the erect phallus towards the other animal. The display is seen in its most dramatic form when a new male is introduced into an established colony of squirrel monkeys. Within seconds all the males follow suit in displaying to the strange monkey, and if it does not remain quiet with its head bowed it will be viciously attacked. We found that the incidence of the display among males in a colony is a better measure of dominance than the outcome of rivalry for food (Ploog and MacLean, 1963).

The display is also used as a form of greeting, and I have described one variety of squirrel monkey that will regularly display to its reflection in a mirror (MacLean, 1964). We refer to the mirror displaying animal as the gothic type because it has an ocular patch which comes to a peak over the eye like a gothic arch, thus distinguishing it from the 'roman' type in which the arch is round like a roman arch. The display of both varieties is quite similar in the communal situation, but only the gothic type will regularly display to its reflection in a mirror.

Ploog and his colleagues (1967) have since observed that without exposure to any other animal than its own mother, an infant squirrel monkey will display as early as the second day of life to another monkey, clearly indicating that the display is an innate form of behaviour.

Having found that the gothic type monkey will consistently display day after day to its reflection in a mirror, I have used the mirror test as a means of learning what parts of the brain may be involved in display rituals and (because of the reciprocative type of behaviour involved) in isopraxis. I should remark at this point that it is relevant to mechanisms of isopraxis that partial representations or phantoms have the capacity to trigger reciprocative behaviour. It is well known that in reptiles and lower forms, part of a dummy may trigger complicated sequences of reciprocative behaviour in territorial defence and mating. In the case of the squirrel monkey, the reflection of a single eye is enough to elicit a full display (MacLean, 1964).

All of our display testing is done in the monkey's home cage with a mechanical contrivance for exposing a full-length mirror for thirty seconds. The monkeys are tested twice a day, and on the protocol we record the latency and magnitude of the erection and the other main components of the display – namely, vocalization, spreading of the thigh, scratching, and urination. After a monkey shows near-perfect performance in thirty or more trials it is subjected to bilateral removal of target structures and then retested for several weeks or months.

Thus far, I have made observations on more than 100 monkeys. I have found that large removals of parts of the paleo- or neo-mammalian formations of the brain may have either no effect or only a transitory effect on the display. In another series of experiments on the R-complex, however, the analysis of findings on twenty monkeys has revealed that bilateral coagulation of the pallidal part of the R-complex or its projections may eliminate the display (see MacLean, 1972 and 1973a for preliminary reports). Figure 4 illustrates the outcome in one such case. Significantly enough, without a test of the innate display behaviour, one might have concluded that these animals were practically unaffected by the loss of nervous tissue.

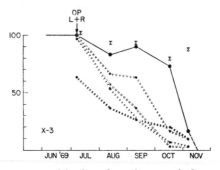

Fig. 4. Performance curve of display of Monkey X–3 before and after bilateral lesions of globus pallidus. Each large black dot represents an accumulation of thirty trials. The curves shown by letters give percentage incidence of various elements of the display: V, vocalization; T, thigh-spread; U, urination; S, scratch. Σ refers to penile index, a value of the average magnitude of erection whenever it was observed during the course of thirty trials.

The experiments just mentioned are of special interest because they show for the first time in a mammal that the R-complex plays a basic role in species-typical, prosematic forms of behaviour such as ritualistic displays in aggression, courtship, and greeting. Since the display also involves isopraxic factors, the experiments also indicate that the R-complex is implicated in natural forms of imitation.

EVOLUTIONARY ASPECTS OF ISOPRAXIS

In circular language, a species might be defined as a group of animals that has genetically acquired the perfect ability to imitate itself. The findings that have been presented are not only relevant to individual and species isopraxis, but also to what one might call phyletic isopraxis, referring to prototypical patterns of behaviour that are found among animals over a wide range of the phylogenetic scale. It is traditional to belittle the role of instincts in human behaviour, but how should we characterize those proclivities that seem to result in such activities as a struggle for position and domain, obsessive-compulsive behaviour, super-stitious obeisance to precedent, devotion to ritual, resort to treachery and deceit, and imitation? If, as many claim, all human behaviour is learned, how does it happen that human beings with all their intelligence and culturally determined behaviour con-tinue to engage in the basic, ordinary things that animals do? In order to engage in some reptilian rhetoric and at the same time make sure that no one will accuse me of making an actual comparison of reptiles and human beings, I shall use the additional signaling device of creeping into small print for asking the following questions:

Gay Talese in *The Kingdom and the Power* (1969), pointed out that where one sits in *The New York Times* newsroom is never a casual matter. There was one bright reporter who moved himself up from the back of the room to an empty desk five rows further forward. When an assistant editor discovered this self-advancement a few days later, the young reporter was back at his old desk and within a year was out of a job altogether. At a higher level, an editor made the mistake of sitting in the Managing Editor's chair when the latter was sick. After learning of this the Managing Editor was furious, and the culprit who was considered in line for his job got no further. Now did these highly educated people learn to behave this way from reading Llewellyn Evans' (1951) description of a hierarchical struggle of black lizards living on a cemetery wall?

A few pages later Talese describes the late journalist Freedman, mentioning that one could set a watch by his comings and goings. At precisely the same time each evening the office car was waiting to take Freedman to dinner; exactly one hour later it brought him back. Did Freedman learn to do this by reading about the punctilious dining habits of Angermeyer's marine lizards in the Galapagos? (see Eibl-Eibesfeldt, 1961).

A well-known American neurologist was accustomed throughout his long career to arrive at an exact time and to take a particular seat at the weekly staff conference (see Walsh, 1971). Did he learn to do this from having observed the 'place-preference' behaviour of lizards?

In the attempted assassination of George Wallace, Arthur Bremer stalked his victim for days at a time, and if he was not around, went for bigger game. Did he learn to do this by reading Auffenberg's account (1972) of the predatory and deceptive behaviour of the giant Komodo lizards? These animals weighing up to 200 pounds will relentlessly stalk a deer for days or wait in ambush for hours, activities requiring a detailed knowledge of the terrain and a good sense of time. Waiting for just the right moment, the huge lizard will lunge at the deer, cripple it with a slash of the Achilles tendon, and bring it to an agonizing death by ripping out its bowels.

Bullying and hazing have a long history. Did schoolboys and collegians learn to bully by reading Llewellyn Evans' accounts (1938, 1951) of the ganging up of lizards on a newcomer?

The mention of deceptive behaviour of lizards is a reminder that white collar criminality has never been so much in the news as during the past few years. If we have learned through our culture that 'honesty is the best policy', why is it that so many people are willing to take such enormous risks to practice deception? Why do the games that we teach our children put such a premium on deceptive tactics and terminology of deception?

Did people learn the restlessness attending migrations by watching the preliminaries of migrating reptiles? For many years there was a unidirectional migration from the northeastern part of the United States towards the south and west. Now with the population pressures on each coast, migrations have become bidirectional and more frequent. Do analysts pause to consider that the feelings of restlessness and alienation so commonly experienced today may be a reflection of migrational fever? The collections of thousands of young people at the Woodstock and Watkins Glen music festivals are not so unlike aborted migrations.

Enough of reptilian rhetoric! Let us look next at the driver represented by the paleomammalian brain.

PALEOMAMMALIAN FORMATION

There are behavioural indications that the reptilian brain is poorly equipped for learning to cope with new situations. The reptilian brain has only a rudimentary cortex. In the lost transitional forms between reptiles and mammals – the so-called mammal-like reptiles – it is presumed that the primitive cortex underwent great elaboration and differentiation. The primitive cortex might be imagined as comparable to a crude television screen, providing the animal a better means of viewing the environment and learning to survive. In all existing mammals, the old cortex is found in a large convolution which the nineteenth-century anatomist, Broca (1878), called the great limbic lobe because it surrounds the brain stem. As illustrated in Fig. 5,

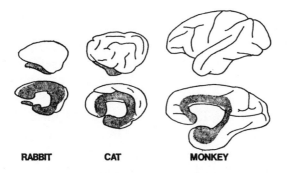

RABBIT   CAT   MONKEY

Fig. 5. The limbic lobe of Broca (shaded) is found as a common denominator in the brains of all mammals. It contains the greater part of the cortex representative of the paleomammalian brain. The cortex of the new mammalian brain (shown in white) mushrooms late in evolution (after MacLean, P. D., Studies on limbic system ('visceral brain') and their bearing on psychosomatic problems. In: *Recent Developments in Psychosomatic Medicine*, Wittkower, E., and Cleghorn, R. (Eds.), London, Pitman & Sons, 1954, pp. 101–25.

the limbic lobe forms a common denominator in the brains of all mammals. In 1952, I suggested the term limbic system as a designation for the limbic cortex and structures of the brain stem with which it has primary connections. This system, it should be emphasized, represents an inheritance from lower mammals. In the past forty years, clinical and experimental investigations have provided evidence that the limbic system derives information in terms of emotional feelings that guide behaviour required for self-preservation and the preservation of the species.

Clinical observations provide the best evidence of the role of the limbic system in emotional behaviour. Epileptic discharges in or near the limbic cortex result in a broad spectrum of vivid emotional feelings. Particularly pertinent to the topic of the present paper are eureka-type feelings experienced during the aura by a small percentage of patients with limbic epilepsy. Their eureka feeling may be expressed by such words as 'I have it, this is it – the absolute truth'; 'This is the answer to the secret of the universe'; 'This is what the world is all about' (cf. MacLean, 1970). Characteristically, these intense feelings are free-floating, being attached to no specific solution or idea.

In THE SLEEPWALKERS Koestler (1963) has given one of the best illustrations of the eureka experience in connection with scientific discovery. It is found in the passage describing Kepler's experience on 9 July, 1595, when he hit upon the idea of five perfect solids as the basis for the six planets. I quote it without implying in any way that Kepler suffered from limbic seizures. In Koestler's words, Kepler was 'drawing a figure on the blackboard for his class when an idea suddenly struck him with such force that he felt that he was holding the key to the secret of creation in his hand'. Although the inspiration was false, and as Koestler emphasizes, persisted as an *idée fixe* for the rest of Kepler's life, it led to the formulation of his three famous laws. It is hard to imagine anything of greater epistemological interest than that the ancient limbic system seems to have the capacity to generate strong affective feelings of conviction that we attach to our beliefs and 'discoveries', regardless of whether they are true or false.

THREE SUBDIVISIONS OF THE LIMBIC SYSTEM

As illustrated in Fig. 6, the limbic system comprises three subdivisions, the two older of which are closely related to the olfactory apparatus. Our experimental work has provided evidence that the two older divisions are respectively involved in oral and genital functions. The findings are relevant to oral-sexual manifestations in feeding situations, in mating, and in aggressive behaviour and violence. Parenthetically, in regard to

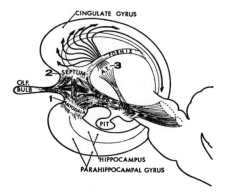

Fig. 6. Diagram of three main subdivisions of the limbic system and their major pathways. See text for summary of their respective functions. Abbreviations: AT, anterior thalamic nuclei; HYP, hypothalamus; MFB, medial forebrain bundle; PIT, pituitary; OLF, olfactory (after MacLean, P. D.) Contrasting functions of limbic and neocortical systems of the brain and their relevance to psychophysiological aspects of medicine, *Amer. J. Med.,* 1958, *25,* 611–26.

discovery, it is of interest that Kekulé's dream of a snake swallowing its tail suggested to him the configuration of the benzene ring.

The close relationship between oral and genital functions seems to be due to the olfactory sense which, dating far back in evolution, is involved in both feeding and mating. The main pathway to the third subdivision bypasses the olfactory apparatus. In evolution, this subdivision outgrows the other two divisions and reaches its greatest size in man. An assortment of evidence (MacLean, 1962; 1973b) suggests that this remarkable expansion reflects, in part, a shift in emphasis from olfactory to visual influences in socio-sexual behaviour. Elsewhere I have discussed how the third subdivision may be implicated in the evolution of empathy (1973b) and in what I have referred to as 'social creativity' (MacLean, to be published).

AVENUES TO THE PERSONALITY

In mammals, the major pathways to and from the reptilian type and paleomammalian type brains pass through the hypothalamus and subthalamic region. If the majority of these pathways are destroyed in monkeys, they are incapacitated, but with careful nursing may recover their ability to eat and move around. They retain, of course, the great motor pathways from the neo-mammalian-type brain to the neural chassis. The most striking characteristic of these animals is that although they look like monkeys, they no longer behave like monkeys. Almost everything that one would characterize as species-typical, simian behaviour has disappeared. If one were to interpret these experimental findings in the light of certain clinical case material, one might say that these large connecting pathways between the reptilian-type and paleomammalian-type brains provide the avenues to the basic personality. Here, certainly, would seem to be the pathways for the expression of prosematic behaviour.

THE NEOMAMMALIAN BRAIN

Compared with the limbic cortex, the neocortex (shown in white in Fig. 5) is like an expanding numerator. As C. Judson Herrick has commented, 'its explosive growth late in phylogeny is one of the most dramatic cases of evolutionary transformations known to comparative anatomy' (1933). The massive proportions achieved by the neocortex in higher mammals explains the designation of 'neomammalian brain' applied to it and structures of the brain stem with which it is primarily connected. The neocortex culminates in the human brain, affording a vast neural screen for the portrayal of symbolic language and the associated functions of reading, writing, and arithmetic. Mother of invention and father of abstract thought, it promotes the preservation and procreation of ideas (MacLean, 1973c). There are clinical and other indications that a feeling of personal identity and reality depends on information received from the internal and external environment (cf. MacLean, 1970). As opposed to the limbic cortex, the sensory systems projecting to the neocortex are primarily those giving information about the external environment – namely, the visual, auditory, and somatic systems. In other words, the neocortex seems to be primarily oriented towards the external environment.

I suggested earlier that the reptilian brain is a neural repository for species-typical, prosematic forms of behaviour. Other bits of evidence suggest that with the evolution of the old and new mammalian brains, nature economically uses the reptilian brain as a storage mechanism for parroting learned forms of emotional and intellective behaviour acquired through limbic and neo-cortical systems (MacLean, 1972). We are all aware, for example, that once having acquired a verbal or other skill we can later repeat it, so to speak, almost instinctively. Indeed, if we stop to think how we do it, as, for example, playing a musical piece learned by heart, it may interrupt the continuity of performance. As Plutarch taught us to say, 'Habit is almost a second nature.'

Discussion

The triune concept of the brain and behaviour that has been outlined could be used as a springboard for discussing several aspects of the creative process. For example, in regard to protoreptilian propensities, how might such propensities pertain in the field of science, say, to the establishment of intellectual domain or 'territory', the *idée fixe* of such a scientist as Kepler, obeisance to precedent, adherence to doctrine, and intolerance of new ideas? It is unnecessary to linger in this area, however, because a discussion of a number of these topics, including the *idée fixe,* reached a high-water mark in Koestler's book THE SLEEPWALKERS. Here, I shall limit myself to a brief discussion of the role of *dissociation* in creativity that was mentioned in the introductory remarks. As already mentioned, in focusing on the field of science, I in no way intend a slight of creativity in other areas.

In a world abounding with imitation, how are we able to explain that some individuals are able to achieve true, innovative creativity? In this connection, I need not dwell on the condition which psychologists refer to as contra-imitation, which possibly results from rivalry between individuals, with each attracting his or her own group of imitators. Imitation of this kind possibly has territorial origins, and we see it best expressed in the numerous religious cults and the many political ideologies. In both the imitative and contra-imitative process, the person's territorial and imitative propensities may be presumed to be abetted by limbic affective and neocortical intellective functions. In science, as in politics, the emotions are capable of standing on any platform, and wherever there are fashions in science, there is commonly a strong, affective aroma among supporters of a particular school.

The easiest way, of course, for one to resist the forces of group imitation is to be dissociated from the group. Such isolation may come about as a result of a number of factors, the most notable being (1) voluntary dissociation, (2) accidental dissociation, and (3) dissociation occurring because of a variety of constitutional factors.

Since Einstein stands out so conspicuously among the creators of modern times, it is natural to cite him as an example. A kind of isolation characterized his whole life. In a recent biographical sketch, Bernstein (1973) described Einstein's childhood as solitary and introspective: 'He was a dreamy child who disliked sports and games, talked with some difficulty (he began to talk only at the age of three), and, because he preferred to keep to himself, was dubbed *Pater Langweil* . . . by his nurse.' As a young adult, his relative isolation continued while working in the patent office: 'He once remarked that he did not meet a real physicist until he was thirty years old', four years after the publication of The Special Theory. The loneliness followed him the rest of his life: 'Einstein never fully belonged to any institution, any country, or any one person or group of people. . . . Those who knew him always had a sense that his thoughts were elsewhere. He needed absolute solitude for his work, but this need produced an inevitable loneliness. . . . In September 1952 he wrote to a friend: "For my part, I have always tended to solitude. . . . It is strange to be known so universally and yet to be so lonely.' " (Bernstein, 1973)

Just as Einstein seemed unable to reciprocate speech until the age of three, there is some indication that he may have had difficulty in simulating laughter. As a friend commented, 'On one occasion, I told Einstein a joke to which he responded with one of the most extraordinary kinds of laughter I have ever heard, then or since. It was rather like the barking of a seal.' (See Bernstein, 1973.) It is also worth noting that Einstein had a reputation for eccentricities such as not wearing socks.

What I wish to emphasize in this discussion is the creative role of dissociation occurring as the result of constitutional factors. Let me lead up to it by a play on Romer's rule. Romer's rule is the name given by Hockett and Ascher (1964) to a principle that is partly based on Romer's explanation of how man branched off from the tree-swinging apes. Whether or not the explanation is correct is immaterial here because it serves as a parable. Presumably, with a climatic change in Miocene times, the tropical forests shrivelled up into little islands. The strongest of the hominoids held on to these lush little islands, whereas the weaker ones were, so to speak, driven out of Eden and forced to eke out an existence on the fringes of the forest by the work of their hands and the sweat of their brows. As Hockett and Ascher comment, our ancestors were failures; they did not abandon the trees because they wanted to, but because they were pushed out. In Calhoun's words (1971), 'Romer's rule proposes that there is a survival of the weak.' If so, the biblical beatitude that the meek 'shall inherit the earth' is true!

In a variation of Romer's rule, I would suggest that some individuals may become creative because of a constitutional incapacity for successful imitation. In other words, I am suggesting that what is a deficit may add up to a benefit. An everyday illustration would be the poor athlete who because of his incoordination is forced to retire from group sports and do his 'own thing'. But closer to what I have in mind are those eccentrics who seem to find it impossible to do things in the prescribed way. In some cases, it is conceivable that an anomalous condition or defect of the nervous system might interfere with the intercommunicative isopraxic process. In view of the work reported here the finger of suspicion would point to the R-complex. Of several conditions that might affect its neural circuitry, I will mention only one. It has been long recognized that because of peculiarities of its vascularization selective damage may occur to parts of the R-complex either because of interference with its arterial supply or venous drainage (see, e.g., MacLean, 1972). It is possible that in cases of congestive disturbances at the time of birth there might result a diffuse loss of cells and that there would be no clear indication of the reparative process or cell loss upon examination of the adult brain. Current developments in computer technology promise to make it possible to obtain actual cell counts in various cerebral structures.

Finally, one more comment that will lead us back to Koestler's use of the term bisociation. In the promotion of research during the past twenty-five years much emphasis has been given to the training of research scientists. Training is obviously necessary for the professional who is flying a plane or taking care of a patient, because his or her performance may be a matter of life or death. But when it comes to the researcher, training after a certain point should perhaps be regarded as an anathema. Placing a major emphasis on the *training* of researchers amounts to expressing the desire to develop imitators. As for the experienced scientist, many would claim that there is still the need for a retreat into the ivory tower, as well as the need to resist perseverative attendance at workshops, symposia, and meetings of the kind lampooned by Koestler (1973) in his recent book THE CALL GIRLS. As used here, 'retreat' and 'resistance' would be forms of *dissociation,* and would also fit into the meaning of the expression *reculer pour mieux sauter* used by Koestler again and again for emphasizing a condition that may be essential for bisociation and 'sudden leaps of the creative imagination' (Koestler, 1964). To conclude with a quotation from THE ACT OF CREATION: 'I have mentioned', Koestler writes,

. . . the perennial myth of the prophet's and hero's temporary isolation and retreat from human society – followed by his triumphant return endowed with new powers. Buddha and Mohammed go out into the desert; Joseph is thrown into the well; Jesus is resurrected from the tomb. Jung's 'death and rebirth' motif, Toynbee's 'withdrawal and return' reflect the same archetypal motif. It seems that *reculer pour mieux sauter* is a principle of universal validity in the evolution of species, cultures, and invididuals, guiding their progression by feedback from the past.

Parts of this article have been adapted from a paper entitled 'Evolutionary Trends of the Triune Brain: From Imitation to Creativity' presented at the

Sesquicentennial Celebration of the Institute of Living, Hartford, Connecticut, 23 May 1972, and from a discussion published in: Morin, E., and Piattelli-Palmarini, M. (Eds.), *L'Unité de L'homme: Invariants Biologigues et Universaux Culturels*, Paris, Editions du Seuil, 1974, pp. 186–212.

REFERENCES

Auffenberg, W., Komodo dragons, *Nat. Hist.*, 1972, *81*, 52–9.

Bernstein, J., The secrets of the old one, *The New Yorker*, 10 March 1973, pp. 44–101; 17 March 1973, pp. 44–91.

Bridgman, P. W., *The Way Things Are*, Cambridge, Mass., Harvard University Press, 1959, 333 pp.

Broca, P., Anatomie comparee des circonvolutions cérébrales. Le grand lobe limbique et la scissure limbique dans la série des mammifères. *Rev. Anthrop.*, 1878, *1*, 385–498.

Calhoun, J. B., Population density and social pathology. *Sci. Amer.*, 1962, *206*, 139–46.

Calhoun, J. B., Space and the strategy of life. In: Esser, A. H. (Ed.), *Behavior and Environment*, New York, Plenum Press, 1971, pp. 329–87.

Dubos, R., We are slaves to fashion in research. *Scientific Research*, 1967, *2*: 36–7 and 54.

Eibl-Eibesfeldt, I., *Galapagos; The Noah's Ark of the Pacific*, Garden City, N.Y., Doubleday and Co., 1961, 192 pp.

Evans, L. T., Field study of the social behavior of the black lizard, Ctenosaura pectinata. *Am. Museum Novitates*, 1951, No. *1493*, 1–26.

Evans, L. T., Cuban field studies on territoriality of the lizard, Anolis sagrei, *J. Comp. Psychol.*, 1938, *25*, 97–125.

Evans, L. T., and Quaranta, J. U., A study of the social behavior of a captive herd of giant tortoises, *Zoologica*, 1951, *36*, 171–81.

Fossey, D., More years with mountain gorillas, *National Geographic*, 1971, *140*, 574–84.

Freud, S., *Beyond the Pleasure Principle*. Trans. by C. J. M. Hubback, London and Vienna, The International Psycho-Analytical Press, 1922, 90 pp.

Freud, S., *The Interpretation of Dreams*. (1900) Standard Edition, London, Hogarth Press, 1953.

Herrick, C. J., The functions of the olfactory parts of the cerebral cortex, *Proc. Nat. Acad. Sci. USA*, 1933, *19*, 7–14.

Hinde, R. A., *Non-Verbal Communication*, Cambridge, Mass., The University Press, 1972, 433 pp.

Hockett, C. F., and Ascher, R., The human revolution, *Curr. Anthrop.*, 1964, *5*, 135–68.

Juorio, A. V., and Vogt, M., Monoamines and their metabolites in the avian brain, *J. Physiol.*, 1967, *189*, 489–518.

Koestler, A., *The Sleepwalkers*, New York, The Universal Library, Grosset & Dunlap, 1963, 624 pp.

Koestler, A., *The Act of Creation*, New York, The Macmillan Company, 1964, 751 pp.

Koestler, A., *The Ghost in the Machine*, London, Hutchinson and Co., 1967, and New York, The Macmillan Company, 1968.

Koestler, A., *The Call Girls*, A Tragi-Comedy, Hutchinson, and Random House, New York, 1973.

Lorenz, K. Z., The companion in the bird's world, *Auk*, 1937, *54*, 245–73.

MacLean, P. D., Some psychiatric implications of physiological studies on frontotemporal portion of limbic system (visceral brain), *Electroenceph. Clin. Neurophysiol.*, 1952, *4*, 407–18.

MacLean, P. D., New findings relevant to the evolution of psychosexual functions of the brain, *J. Nerv. Ment. Dis.*, 1962, *135*, 289–301.

MacLean, P. D., Mirror display in the squirrel monkey, Saimiri sciureus, *Science*, 1964, *146*, 950–2.

MacLean, P. D., The triune brain, emotion, and scientific bias. In: Schmitt, F. O. (Ed.), *The Neurosciences Second Study Program*, New York, The Rockefeller University Press, 1970, p. 366.

MacLean, P. D., Cerebral evolution and emotional processes: New findings on the striatal complex, *Ann. N.Y. Acad. Sci.*, 1972, *193*, 137–49.

MacLean, P. D., Effects of pallidal lesions on species-typical display behavior of squirrel monkey, *Fed. Proc.*, 1973a, *32*, 384.

MacLean, P. D., A triune concept of the brain and behaviour, Lecture I. Man's reptilian and limbic inheritance; Lecture II. Man's limbic brain and the psychoses; Lecture III. New trends in man's evolution. In: Boag, T., and Campbell, D. (Eds.), *The Hincks Memorial Lectures*, Toronto, University of Toronto Press, 1973b.

MacLean, P. D., The brain's generation gap: Some human implications, *Zygon J. Relig. Sci.*, 1973c, *8*: 113–27.

MacLean, P. D., Bases neurologiques du comportement d'imitation chez le singe-écureuil. In: Morin, E., and Piattelli-Palmarini, M. (eds.), *L'Unité de l'Homme: Invariants Biologiques et Universaux Culturels*, Paris, Editions du Seuil, 1974a, pp. 186–212.

MacLean, P. D., The triune brain. In: *Medical World News*, Special Supplement on 'Psychiatry', New York, October, 1974b, Vol. 1, pp. 55–60.

MacLean, P. D., An evolutionary approach to brain research on 'prosematic' (non-verbal) behavior. In: The Daniel S. Lehrman Memorial Symposium on Reproductive Behavior and Evolution, Institute of Animal Behavior, Rutgers University, 1974c (to be published).

Maynes, C. W., Op:Ed, *New York Times*, 25 July 1973.

Miller, N., and Dollard, J., *Social Learning and Imitation*. New Haven, Yale University Press, 1941.

Miyadi, D., Social life of Japanese monkeys. *Science,* 1964, *143*: 783–6.

Myers, K., Hale, C. S., Mykytowycz, R., and Hughes, R. L., The effects of varying density and space on sociality and health in animals. In: Esser, A. H. (Ed.), *Behavior and Environment,* New York, Plenum Press, 1971, pp. 148–87.

Noble, G. K., Function of the corpus striatum in the social behavior of fishes, *Anat. Rec.,* 1936, *64,* 34.

Ploog, D., Hopf, S. and Winter, P., Ontogenese des Verhaltens von Toten-kopf-Affen (Saimiri sciureus), *Psychol. Forsch.,* 1967, *31,* 1–41.

Ploog, D., and MacLean, P. D., Display of penile erection in squirrel monkey (Saimiri sciureus), *Anim. Behav.,* 1963, *11,* 32–9.

Talese, G., *The Kingdom and the Power,* New York, Bantam Books Inc., 1970.

Tinbergen, N., *The Study of Instinct,* Oxford, The Clarendon Press, 1951,

Walsh, F. B., On the Neurologist Dr Frank Ford, *Johns Hopkins Med. J.,* 1971, *128,* 105–7.

The Contributors

FRANK BARRON, Ph.D.

Professor of Psychology at the University of California, Santa Cruz, and Research Psychologist, the Institute of Personality Assessment and Research, University of California, Berkeley. He received his Ph.D. at Berkeley in 1950, after earlier graduate work, both before and after World War II, at the University of Minnesota and Cambridge University. In 1964–5 he held a Faculty Research Fellowship from the Social Sciences Research Council and during that time initiated cross-cultural research on creativity in Ireland and in Italy. He has also held a Guggenheim fellowship (1962–68) and in 1969 he received the Richardson creativity award of the American Psychological Association.

Dr Barron is author of *Creativity and Psychological Health* (1963), and co-editor (with C. W. Taylor) of *Scientific Creativity* (1963). Among his other works are *Creative Person and Creative Process* (1969), and *Artists in the Making* (1972).

JOHN BELOFF, Ph.D.

Senior Lecturer in the Department of Psychology of the University of Edinburgh. He is the author of *The Existence of Mind* (1962) which was a contribution to the philosophy of mind, and of *Psychological Sciences* (1973) which bears the sub-title 'A Review of Modern Psychology'. He has also edited a volume of invited articles by leading researchers in the field of experimental parapsychology entitled *New Directions in Parapsychology* (1973) to which Koestler contributed a postscript. John Beloff is currently president of the Society for Psychical Research.

T. R. FYVEL

Lives in London and has been active for many years as a writer, journalist and broadcaster. In 1940 he was joint editor with George Orwell of the Searchlight Books and later in the war was employed in psychological warfare in North Africa and Italy. In 1945 he succeeded Orwell as literary editor of *Tribune,* and after that he worked for a number of years for the External Services of the BBC. Among his best-known works are *The Malady and the Vision,* an analysis of the causes of the Second World War, and *The Insecure Offenders,* a study of juvenile delinquency in the consumer society.

MARK GRAUBARD, Ph.D.

Professor Emeritus of Natural Science and the History of Science at the University of Minnesota where he taught from 1947 to 1972. Educated in New York City (B.S. College of the City of New York, Logic Medal, 1926; M.A. and Ph.D. in Zoology at Columbia University, 1931) he spent a few years in biochemical research (enzymes and hormones), but soon devoted full time to research in the history of science, specializing in the psychology of belief and reason in sciences now outlived and rejected, such as magic, primitive and Galenic medicine, astrology, alchemy and witchcraft. He published papers and books on these topics and was guest lecturer in Japan, India, West Indies, Mexico etc. on his special contributions.

JOHN GRIGG

Political journalist. Born 1924. Educated Eton and New College, Oxford. Associate editor, then editor, *National and English Review* (until 1960), columnist for the *Guardian* 1960–7. Succeeded father as Lord Altrincham 1955; disclaimed title, 1963. Author of *Two Anglican Essays* and *The Young Lloyd George*. A trustee of the Arthur Koestler Awards scheme, and honorary treasurer of the National Campaign for the Abolition of Capital Punishment. Married with two sons.

IAIN HAMILTON

Author, journalist, literary critic, poet. Former editorial director of Hutchinson Publishing Group and former editor-in-chief of the *Spectator*. Author of the forthcoming biography of Arhur Koestler.

HAROLD HARRIS

1957–62, literary editor of the London *Evening Standard*, 1962–75, editorial director of the Hutchinson Publishing Group, now deputy managing director. He has been the editor responsible for all Arthur Koestler's books since THE ACT OF CREATION.

RENÉE HAYNES

The daughter of E. S. P. Haynes and Oriana Huxley Haynes and the widow of Jerrard Tickell, the novelist. She has herself written three novels and several other books; her best known work is *The Hidden Springs,* whose sub-title is *An Enquiry into Extra Sensory Perception.* She has been a member of the Council of the Society for Psychical Research since 1959 and became editor of its Journal and Proceedings in 1970.

CYNTHIA KOESTLER

Born in 1927 in Pretoria, daughter of the late James Finbarr Jefferies, F.R.C.S., she spent her childhood in South Africa, except for two years at Lady Walsingham's school in England from 1938 to 1940. Among a variety of jobs (including working for a Russian-born Pavlovian psychologist), she also worked in New York, 1953–5, for the bridge champion and political scientist, Ely Culbertson. She married Arthur Koestler in January 1965.

PAUL D. MACLEAN, M.D.

Chief of the Laboratory of Brain Evolution and Behavior at the National Institute of Mental Health, Bethesda, Maryland. He is the recipient of several awards for his comparative, zoologic research on the brain, the two latest being the Mider Lectureship Award of the National Institutes of Health and the Lashley Award of the American Philosophical Society. In his interdisciplinary lectures and writings, Dr MacLean has repeatedly emphasized that evolutionary insights into the brain's anatomy, chemistry, and functions may help to illuminate human psychology in both health and disease.

KATHLEEN NOTT

Educated at London and Oxford, she was an Open Exhibitioner at Somerville where she read PPE, specializing in philosophy. She has written four novels, three volumes of poetry, three of criticism and philosophy, and several others of a more general kind, including a book on Sweden where she lived for some years. She is now finishing a book on the possibilities of liberalism, and is a contributor to the *Observer, Encounter,* the *Times Literary Supplement,* the BBC and various American publications. She became President of English PEN in 1974.

GORONWY REES

Educated in Wales and at New College, Oxford. After taking a first in Philosophy, Politics and Economics, he was elected to a fellowship at All Souls. Before the war, he worked on the *Manchester Guardian* and *The Times,* and was assistant-editor of the *Spectator.* During the war, he served with the Royal Welch Fusiliers and on the planning staff of Field Marshal Montgomery's 21 Army Group. From 1953–57 he was Principal of the University College of Wales, Aberwystwyth. His published works include *Where No Wounds Were, A Bundle of Sensations, The Great Slump, A Chapter of Accidents* and *Conversations with Kafka* (translation). He is a member of the editorial board of *Encounter,* to which he contributes a regular monthly column.

W. H. THORPE, F.R.S.

Professor Thorpe is one of the pioneers of the comparative study of animal and human behaviour, more commonly known as ethology, and is one of the world's leading authorities on bird song. His publications comprise numerous scientific papers in various biological journals as well as his books which include *Learning and Instinct in Animals, Bird Song, Science, Man and Morals* and *Animal Nature and Human Nature*. He has been a Fellow of Jesus College, Cambridge, since 1932 and served as tutor, senior tutor and President. He has held visiting professorships or lectureships at Harvard University, University of California, St Andrew's University, Durham University and Balliol College, Oxford. He is Emeritus Professor of Animal Ethology in the University of Cambridge.

ROY WEBBERLEY, Ph.D.

Senior Counsellor at the Open University, which he joined in 1971 as an Educational Studies Tutor and Counsellor. Currently preparing material on the teaching of creativity for an Educational Studies Course on Personality and Learning. Graduated in English and French from University of Leicester, 1960, and after teaching in a variety of institutions in the UK and Ireland, became involved in research into creativity at Trinity College, Dublin. His doctoral dissertation investigated Koestler's relevance to education.